TO Katie WITH Love

ERICA LUCKE DEAN

THE BIRTHDAY PARTY

"Look around, Katie. Somewhere out there is the perfect man for you. You just need to take your nose out of a book long enough to find him." Vicky's crimson lips spread in a wide smile, and I resisted the urge to stick my tongue out at her.

"Oh, leave her alone," Silvia said, peering at Vicky over her leopard-print reading glasses. "It might do *you* some good to read once in a while. I assume you know how."

"Very funny." Vicky rolled her eyes, tossing her flaming hair with a flourish. "You clearly didn't notice the leaning tower of paperbacks on her nightstand. I don't think I've ever seen so many books in one place. They practically block the light coming in her bedroom window. And that—" She poked my arm with a lacquered fingernail. "—is bordering on pathetic. You're just a few cats away from being a cliché."

I opened my mouth to speak, but she cut me off.

"*Come on*, Katie, wouldn't you rather have a flesh and blood man in your bed instead of a dusty old book? There are dozens of guys in here. Don't you think at least one of them could drag you away from your stupid romance novels for a change? I'll bet you've got a book stashed in your purse right now." Vicky pointed at the bag I clutched in my lap. "Go ahead, Silvia. Prove me wrong."

Silvia shook her head and chuckled. "I'm not going to dig through her purse."

"There's nothing wrong with reading romance novels," I

whispered, releasing the strangle hold on my bag to shove it behind my back against the booth.

"Oh, sweetie..." Silvia patted my hand. "Vicky isn't saying there's something wrong with reading romance novels."

"No, that's *exactly* what I'm saying," Vicky said, then took a long slurp of her frozen margarita. "And for the record, you don't just *read* them. You read them again, and again, and *again*. Most of the books I saw were held together with tape. Do you ever get anything new, or do you keep reading the same ones over and over?"

"I get new ones... sometimes."

Vicky had one thing right. I did have a book stashed in my bag, and I should have been home, tucked into bed with it. So what if I had a thing for romance novels? Okay, maybe *thing* wasn't a strong enough word. It didn't quite define the entire scope of my relationship with the paperback romance. *Involved* would be more accurate.

But despite what my coworkers might think, I wasn't some un-dateable old maid, spending her nights curled up with six cats while crocheting gaudy afghans in retro-seventies colors and sipping warm milk. I didn't even own an *actual* cat.

"If you ask me, you're wasting the perfect opportunity to find Mr. Right," Vicky chirped.

What did *she* know about *my* Mr. Right? A quick scan of the smoke-filled bar proved my point. Not a single guy in the place even remotely resembled the lead in my nightly fantasy. Okay, so it wasn't a very big room, but like Vicky said, the place was packed with a wide assortment of men—like the guy with cheese dip down his front and his buddy, laughing hyena-man. As far as I was concerned, not a single one warranted a second glance, certainly not an invitation into my bedroom. Definitely no one worthy of butterflies in my stomach.

Vicky raised an eyebrow. "Well?"

"Well, he isn't here now," Silvia answered, and I could

have kissed her. "Which reminds me, what happened to June and Phil?"

Vicky shrugged, slurping down another mouthful of her drink.

"Maybe they aren't coming." I was ready to slide out of the booth and make my escape. "We should probably just go."

Silvia glared at me. "You're not going anywhere. I'm sure they're on their way. They wouldn't dare skip your birthday party."

Perfect. I was trapped.

"You know," Vicky said, "you're way too old to be single."

My mother was fond of saying that very thing, far too often. But they were both wrong. *I'm still in my prime. As a matter of fact, I don't think I've even reached my prime yet. I'm only twenty-eight years old.*

"Happy birthday, Katie!"

Oh, wait.

Twenty-nine.

The rest of my coworkers had finally arrived, honking plastic party horns and waving a heaping shot of Grand Marnier in my face. Just what every girl needs on her birthday—liquor. Twisting my lips to the side, I contemplated the drink placed in front of me.

Vicky picked up the shot and shoved it into my hand. "You *do* know you actually have to swallow to get drunk, right?"

I examined the glass filled with orange-colored liquid and shuddered. "You guys. You know I don't drink." A rush of heat spread across my face and down my throat as I remembered the last, disastrous time they'd talked me into drinking.

June smiled, her rich brown skin crinkling around her eyes. "Drink it." As the permanent designated driver of our group, she lived vicariously through the rest of us.

"Oh, come on. You're such a novice, James." Phil, my

branch manager—or BM as we liked to call him behind his back—made a point of never using my first name. He shook his bald head. "Just drink the damn thing."

Holding my breath, I put the glass to my lips and, with another shudder, took a sip, the first of what I feared would be many.

By nine thirty, Silvia, June, and Vicky were flitting around the room, trying to convince Phil to sing karaoke. I sat alone at the table, wishing I was home with my imaginary cat and my fictional boyfriend.

"Aren't you going to come watch Phil make a fool out of himself?" Silvia's sudden reappearance startled me back to reality. Her highlighted, teased hair reminded me of one of her Yorkies.

"Uh..." I wasn't about to stand elbow deep in strangers by the stage just to listen to our boss sing karaoke, especially not dressed in the *Hookers R Us* outfit Silvia had given me for my birthday, no matter how amusing that might be. I also didn't want to be anywhere near there after the morbid dedication they just played. Who would dedicate a song to a murdered politician? And did they have to mention a dead guy on my birthday? That might very well be a jinx. *Well, at least I'm wearing black.*

"Come on, Katie. It'll be fun."

Tugging at the tight leather skirt barely covering my thighs, I glanced down at my knee-high stiletto boots, remembering the way my legs wobbled dangerously when I walked in them. "No, I'm fine." I flashed Silvia the best fake smile I could manage.

She frowned. "You aren't going to find anyone worth checking out over here, sweetie. Trust me, Vicky already looked."

Vicky leaned over the booth, her red hair only inches from my face. "There's nobody worth bending over for, that's for sure," she said with a wink.

Silvia snorted. "We'll be back in a few minutes." Then she turned to Vicky, grabbing her by the elbow. "Come on. Let's go watch Phil sing."

I watched Silvia's spiky caramel hair bob as she dragged Vicky away from the table and made her way through the crowd—shoving bodies out of her path with a perfectly manicured hand—and it occurred to me how much she reminded me of my mother. They were both a little bit scary. And like my mother, Silvia was forever trying to drum into my head how I would never find a real man as long as I kept pining for a character in a book.

Ironically, Silvia was the one who gave me the first three volumes in a series of vampire romance novels, introducing me to my fictional boyfriend... and my new favorite author—*Elizabeth Jayne*. Like we were kindred spirits, the woman spoke to me, as if she'd poked through my fantasies and written them down. I'd already read every book of her *Immortal Blood* series cover to cover and back again so many times the pages were pulling loose.

What I wouldn't give to jump back into volume five, *Blood of the First*, the one I'd tucked into my bag. Bright orange sticky notes peeked out from between the pages to mark my favorite sections, and I'd seriously considered pulling out my trusty highlighter from the desk drawer and highlighting a few really juicy parts. But at midnight, the time I was typically immersed in the story, I hardly felt like climbing out of bed to dig for a marker. And besides, that would be pathetic.

So instead, I'd memorized the page numbers.

I reread my favorite passages each night before slipping off to sleep, hoping Mr. Tall, Dark, and Handsome would visit my dreams. Sometimes, I imagined I was falling asleep in his arms.

My fantasy man was simply better than any real man I'd ever met. Romantic, mysterious, and did I mention hot? Sure, hot in print, but I had a really good imagination.

Besides, real men all seemed to be interested in the same type: the cocaine-chic supermodel. But that definitely wasn't me.

So what if my dream guy had a few drawbacks? Besides being completely one-dimensional, which was not much different than a lot of the real men I've dated, and a seven-hundred-year-old vampire with fangs—he was and always would be trapped inside the pages of a book.

But all men had their flaws. *Didn't they?*

"Oh my God! Did you hear Phil?" Vicky landed in the booth across from me, and I nearly jumped out of my skirt. "I laughed so hard I almost peed myself."

"Oh, I'm pretty sure she *wet* herself." Silvia flashed a wicked grin as she slid in beside me.

Vicky pursed her lips and glowered at Silvia as she waved for the waitress. "How long does it take to get a drink in this place?"

June squeezed her plus-sized bottom into the booth beside Vicky. "He wasn't so bad. I thought he was almost good. I believed he found paradise by the dashboard light. That was a Meatball song, right?"

"Meatloaf, June. Meat. Loaf," Vicky said.

Meatball or Meatloaf, it didn't really matter. I'd heard Phil sing. In fact, I was pretty sure all of Atlanta had heard Phil wailing up on stage. June was being too nice. But June was always too nice.

"James, did you drink my beer?" Phil shouted as he got closer to the table.

"Don't be ridiculous. Katie would never drink beer, let alone *your* beer," Silvia said. "You drank it before you went up there."

"Did you find any hot guys in the five or so minutes we were gone?" Vicky asked me.

"Do you mean besides Phil and his Day-Glo golf pants?" I bit back a grin. "It's not like I could've missed him coming from a mile away."

"What's wrong with my pants?" Phil laughed, and I practically got a contact high from his beer breath. "You don't like green?"

"Don't you listen to them, sweetie." Silvia patted my hand. "I have a feeling you're going to find a nice man very soon, someone with infinitely better taste than Phil, and a lot more hair."

"Hey now, don't hate. I have hair. I just choose to shave it off."

"Because you're essentially bald," Silvia said, laughing.

I didn't have to say anything. Silvia already knew the only *real* man I'd ever be interested in. And he was completely off limits.

So where did that leave me?

Right here. Smashed into a booth, three hundred sixty-five days away from the big three-oh, breathing in secondhand smoke and sucking down shots with the people who were nearest and dearest to me in the whole wide world... the people from work.

I had just one word for that. Pathetic.

The waitress came by with another round and handed me a shot I didn't order. Perfect. Like I said, what more could a girl ask for on her birthday?

I pressed up against the wall of the booth and sipped from my second drink. The amber liquid warmed me all the way down, and I felt my inhibitions drifting away. Silvia gave me a thumbs-up, and I threw back the last swallow, eyeing the room once again. The place had gotten crowded, but I still didn't see anyone worthy of a good stomach flip. I was, however, vaguely aware of my name being called over the speaker system.

I cringed as I heard, "... birthday girl, Katie James. Where are you, Katie?"

My friends started to cheer, and a beaming Silvia shook my arm. "That's you! Get up. Go sing!"

Crap. As my clapping and shouting coworkers nudged

me out of the booth, I felt the color drain from my face and thought I might faint.

The simple fact was I loved to sing... when I was alone. I'd never sung in front of a crowd, certainly not at a karaoke bar. Yet, there I was, being propelled toward the stage by Silvia, the real manager in my office, title or no title.

I dragged myself forward, feeling more like I was headed to the guillotine than the stage, looking back to my table for moral support the entire way. They waved me on, cheering like a bunch of high school girls at a pep rally. Even Phil.

I spun around to watch where I was going, and a guy shoved a microphone in my hand. Next thing I knew, I was facing a crowd filled with semi-drunken college students and business bankers. Dozens of eyes stared at me, and I really wished I hadn't worn the short skirt and form-fitting blouse Silvia had promised would make me look hot.

I was a banker, not a prostitute. I didn't dress *hot*. I dressed professionally—not *that* kind of professionally. Well, not usually, anyway. But on the night of my big birthday soiree, I was Silvia's science project.

I stood in the wash of the spotlight, my heart slamming in my chest beneath the sheer black blouse. My insides did a mini flip as I started to sing the first line of the Etta James song.

At last...

Then I saw *him* step through the door—the most beautiful man I'd ever seen in all my twenty-nine years. He was the epitome of *tall*—at least six-two if I was any judge—*dark*—thick wavy hair, just long enough to run my fingers through—and *handsome*—with that sexy just-rolled-out-of-bed look that always made my heart race.

A serious ripple began to build in the pit of my stomach. I could only see him in profile, but he obviously hadn't shaved that morning, maybe not the day before either. He could have stepped right out of one of my romance novels. I couldn't have written him better myself.

My mystery guy appeared to be searching the crowd for something or someone. And when he ran a hand through his hair, the way I'd just imagined doing, it was all I could do to breathe.

Sing, Katie, I reminded myself. It was a wonder I could sing at all. From his dark jeans and gray Henley shirt, to his battered brown leather bomber jacket, I quickly memorized every inch of him to recall later. He didn't notice me, but I was barely aware of a single other person in the room. I was trying to send a telepathic message for him to turn my way, and either my message got through or he felt my eyes burning a hole through him because he spun around to look directly at me.

Even from up on the tiny stage, half-blinded by the lights, I saw a flicker of heat radiating from his dark eyes. Then he flashed his perfect white teeth in the most dazzling smile, threatening the last shred of my composure, not to mention setting loose a swarm of butterflies.

But I knew that smile... didn't I?

The little fantasy I'd created cracked along the edges and reality spilled out. How could I not have realized it was him right away? I tried to chalk it up to the two shots I'd polished off before stepping onto the stage and the sheer terror coursing through me as I belted out the song.

It couldn't be.

He was too unbuttoned. Too disheveled. Too... perfect?

Mr. Off Limits himself.

Cooper Maxwell.

I THINK I'LL HAVE JUST ONE MORE

OH. MY. GOD.

The bottom completely dropped out on me with a big whoosh. I reached the top of a rollercoaster and tumbled over the crest, screaming all the way to the bottom. I wondered how, in all the time I'd known him, I had never noticed how off-the-charts sexy he was.

Oh sure, I knew he was sexy, drop-dead gorgeous even, but seven-hundred-year-old vampire sexy? No way. Maybe because I was his banker, or maybe because he was way out of my league, I honestly had no clue.

How long have I been staring?

More than a minute? Less than two? Somehow I managed to keep my breathing steady enough to make it through the whole song, but even as I handed the microphone to the outstretched hand of the DJ, I couldn't drag my eyes away from Cooper. Locked in his hypnotic gaze, I struggled to flash an innocent smile.

Oh, I was in deep trouble, and I knew it. It was too late to pretend I wasn't just lusting after him like a school girl... while dressed like a hooker. I needed to get back to the safety of my secluded booth in the corner and my rowdy little bunch of coworkers.

"Very nice job, James!" Phil slid out of the booth to let me in and slapped me between my shoulders, nearly capsizing me out of my scary four-inch heels. "We barely heard the tremor in your voice."

"You were great," Silvia chimed in with a wink. "I thought you said you couldn't sing."

"I can't. You're just drunk," I teased. Despite my terminal case of nerves, I was proud I'd managed to find my way around the song, considering my entire office was watching.

Not to mention Mr. Off Limits... who happened to be still staring.

"Hey." Silvia nudged me. She tried to whisper discreetly but instead shouted to be heard over the music. "Isn't that Cooper Maxwell staring at you from the bar? He looks good without the suit. A little more rugged, don't you think?"

"Oh." June craned her neck to see. "He looks taller in that jacket."

"I'll be damned. Is that *really* Cooper Maxwell?" Vicky asked, waving at him.

He flashed an awkward grin and waved back.

Yes. It certainly is. "I didn't notice." I quickly sipped from the fresh shot that had been waiting for me when I got back to the table—my third so far—and desperately tried to avert my eyes from the bar area. I didn't have to look in his direction to know he was watching us.

Watching me.

I had to peek around Silvia to see him. He leaned against the bar, drinking a beer straight from the bottle, looking all tousled and yummy. I would have never been able to concentrate on work if the new Cooper had been in my office. The Cooper Maxwell I knew was all business. He was always clean shaven, with his hair neatly combed, and dressed in designer suits that fit him nicely but didn't draw attention to his body.

And he never paid personal attention to me. He was impeccably polite, but most days he seemed so completely indifferent it was almost enough to set my self-esteem back to my high school days. I had no idea why he would be staring so intently at me.

Silvia squinted toward the bar and fanned her face with her hand. "He looks hot. As a matter of fact, I don't think I've ever seen him look so hot. And June's right, he does look exceptionally tall tonight. I can't believe you didn't notice."

"Nope, sure didn't." I didn't notice how his dark hair was wildly and uncharacteristically messed up. I didn't notice his lips turned up in the most kissable smile, or how he looked as though he was thinking about something delicious. And I certainly didn't notice how well he filled out a pair of jeans.

Nope. Not. At. All.

"I would totally do him," Vicky blurted. "My husband and I have this 'fantasy threesome list.' You know, like fantasy football? And I'll tell you what—" She hooked her thumb in Cooper's direction. "—he's my first-round draft pick. I don't care what people say about how he makes his money." She picked up her frozen margarita and took a long gulp from the straw. "My husband picked you."

"Me?" Silvia gasped.

Vicky snorted out a laugh. "No, Sil. Katie."

"Oh my God." I choked on my drink, and Vicky rolled her eyes.

"That's why it's called the 'fantasy threesome' list." She made quotation marks in the air with her fingers and shook her head as if *I* was the crazy one. "We don't actually have threesomes. We just talk about it and get turned on." Vicky sucked down the last of her drink with a loud slurp and refilled her glass from the pitcher. "Although, I have to tell you, I wouldn't mind it a bit if he suddenly wanted to do it for real. I absolutely love sex. If there was a way to somehow hide my face so my father wouldn't know it was me, I'd do porn."

We all gaped at her. Vicky had an uncanny knack for making people blush. For a pretty girl, she had a tendency to try too hard to get noticed.

"Oh, roll your tongues back up. I wasn't going to get up on the table and demonstrate. Geez." Vicky laughed. "Not unless Cooper is willing, that is." She stared off into space as if she were imagining that very thing. "He would be a lucky guy. I give a great blow—"

Silvia cut her off. "Oh, I think that's enough out of you." She casually moved Vicky's drink away from her, eliciting a scowl.

I may have thrown up in my mouth a little. I sort of couldn't feel my tongue anymore and quickly waved over the waitress to get another drink.

"Maybe we should invite him over," Silvia said. "He seems to be all alone, and he keeps looking over here. I feel like we're being very rude pretending we don't see him." She wasn't talking to anyone in particular, but more running the idea past herself for approval.

June automatically jumped up from the booth to let her out.

"Oh, don't," I pleaded. "He's probably waiting for some tall, leggy blonde." *Certainly not a shy banker with too many hours on her hourglass figure.*

"Don't be ridiculous, Katie. You're not fat," Silvia tossed out as she slid out of the booth.

Did I say that out loud? I didn't think so.

"Oh, God, no," June added with an encouraging smile. She took Silvia's place against the wall. "You're not fat at all. You're curvy. Men like curvy women. Don't they, Phil?"

Phil had the good sense to pretend he was listening to the bad Johnny Cash impersonation on stage and didn't respond.

Who said anything about fat? What was the line from *Macbeth*? The lady doth protest too much? My bottom lip pushed out all on its own. "I never said I was fat!" *I just thought it a little too loudly.*

"Of course you didn't *say* it." Silvia waved a dismissive hand. "You don't have to say it. I know how you think."

"Besides," June droned on, "I think blondes are highly overrated. Your hair is such a lovely chocolate color.

Although, if you added a few caramel highlights, it would make the green in your eyes really pop."

Oh, good. My drink had arrived. Perfect timing. I took the glass directly from the waitress rather than waiting for her to set it on the table.

"You should see yourself in that outfit," Silvia said.

I'd definitely seen myself. And it would take me until my next birthday to figure out how she'd managed to convince me to wear it.

Silvia gave me one last smile, and then she walked toward Cooper. Even from our table way in the back, I could see his dark eyebrows rise as Silvia approached. The slight turn of his lips blew up into a full-blown smile, and he turned to offer his hand. I watched their animated conversation, wishing I could read lips. I didn't need to wish for long because Cooper pushed away from the bar and escorted Silvia back to our booth.

"Scoot in, Katie. Make room for Cooper." Silvia orchestrated the seating arrangement to include Cooper, while Phil hopped up to take another turn at the microphone.

Cooper took my hand as if he was going to shake it, but instead, he bent down and brushed his lips across my knuckles. "I didn't know you sang, Kate." He beamed.

Cooper always called me Kate, never Katie. It took me almost six months to get him to stop calling me Ms. James or, God forbid, "ma'am." We were the same age, for Pete's sake!

"It was my idea," Silvia chimed in. "She didn't want to. You have no idea how hard it was to pry her out of this booth to get her up on stage." She giggled like a teenager and leaned in, doing the whisper-shout thing to be heard over the music. "She doesn't know it yet, but I put another song in for her." She turned her eyes to me, and I saw the mischief lurking in them.

Vicky snickered. "It's too bad Dean didn't come tonight. Katie could have done a duet with him. He would have *loved* that outfit."

Cooper raised an eyebrow. "Dean?"

"Dean Maynard. He's one of Katie's clients," Silvia said.

"Dean's an actor. He's been on Broadway." Vicky leaned toward Cooper and lowered her voice. "He likes to come in and serenade Katie in her office."

Cooper stared at me. "He serenades you?"

My face flushed, and I shrugged.

Silvia shook her head and chuckled. "Vicky's making it sound like much more than it is. He sings to everybody."

"Oh, come on! You know I'm not exaggerating. He's got his eye on her, if you know what I mean." Vicky winked at Cooper. "I wanted to invite him, but Silvia—" She glowered in Silvia's direction. "—said absolutely not. Hey, why did you just kick me?"

Silvia glared at Vicky across the table.

"Cooper, did you know today is Katie's birthday?" June asked.

He pulled his eyes from Silvia and Vicky and turned to June. "Yes, Silvia told me." Then he tipped his head slightly to the side and smiled. "Happy birthday."

"Thank you." The heat crept up my throat, and my lips twitched with the threat of a smile, but I couldn't quite bring it out. I was too busy feeling sick to my stomach. The flip-flopping had reached a fevered pitch. I told myself it was because there was another slip of paper with my name on it up there somewhere, but deep down, I knew it was because Cooper's thigh was pressing against mine. I could feel his warmth through the denim.

I tossed back the remaining liquid in my glass and quickly waved for the waitress to come back. "Who wants another round? Cooper? What are you drinking tonight?"

He held up his bottle. "I'll have another one of these, thanks. And put everyone's drinks on my tab."

Cooper smiled at the waitress, and I realized how much I liked his smile.

I bet he's a good kisser. I must have been crazy or

drunk to even entertain such thoughts. I wasn't supposed to be thinking about his mouth or about kissing it. I had worked very hard to convince myself I shouldn't want him. I managed a full smile and actually met his eyes for the first time since I was on stage. At first, I thought they were just plain stormy gray, but up close, I realized they were more of a blue-green.

"I'd like another one of these, please." I tipped my empty shot glass in a little salute. The alcohol had made me brave. "So, Cooper, what brings you here tonight?"

He looked at me for a long moment with an amused expression, and I suddenly felt as if I had an imaginary wart on my nose.

"Are you drunk, Kate?"

"Don't be silly," Silvia said. "She's hardly had anything, as usual."

Cooper locked his eyes with mine and leaned in closer—as if that were even possible—until I could taste his warm breath, all peppermint and Heineken. "Are you sure you're not drunk?"

I bobbed my head a few times.

Cooper grinned. "How many candles did you put on your cake today?"

I tried to speak, but no sound came out. Not that I would have had a chance.

"She's twenty-nine," June blurted.

Cooper didn't take his eyes from mine. "I wouldn't have guessed," he said in a low voice. Then he gave me the same high-voltage smile as before, the one that sucked the air from my lungs and stopped my heart from beating for almost a whole second. "In honor of your twenty-ninth birthday—" He turned to the waitress. "—I'd like to order a bottle of your best champagne."

I started to protest, but everyone erupted in laughter at something Vicky had said. I pushed my hair away from my face with both hands, desperate for something to distract me from the riot of butterflies in my gut. I hadn't heard her remark, but I hoped it didn't involve threesomes and blowjobs. I sort of feared it might.

Vicky zeroed in on Cooper. "You know, we come here once a week, and this is the first time I've seen you."

Cooper shifted his weight slightly, causing his leg to press harder into mine from hip to knee. I wondered if he could hear the sizzle over the music and chatter.

"Once a week, huh?" His eyes caught mine again. "I guess I've been missing out then."

"I don't come every time," I quickly added and immediately regretted it, not wanting him to think I had no life, which of course, I didn't.

"That's because she always has to chase down her stupid cat. I swear, you need to get a collar for that thing, Katie," Vicky said. "With a bell."

Cooper raised his eyebrows, amusement dancing in his eyes. "Sounds like a crafty cat. Does he have a name?"

My lips fell open as I floundered for something to say. I'd never given my imaginary cat a name.

"So, Cooper," Vicky purred, leaning across the table toward him. "Were you ever going to tell us what you do for a living? I'm not the only one who thinks it's more than just a little suspi—ouch! Again with the kicking?" she sputtered, glowering in Silvia's direction.

"Oh, sweetie, did I kick you?" Silvia smiled sweetly.

The waitress returned with the champagne. She placed a fluted glass in front of me and said she would be back with the rest of the drinks right away. I picked up the flute and gulped a mouthful of the fizzy drink, catching a shocked look from Silvia. I wondered if she'd been keeping count. I figured one of us should. I was on the verge of completely losing track of how much I'd had to drink. I did a mental tally, adding the swallow of champagne to the total. It was definitely a personal high. *Are my fingertips supposed to be so tingly?*

June put her elbows on the table and rested her chin on her folded hands. "Do you sing, Cooper?"

Cooper burst into nervous laughter. "The only serenading *I* do is in the shower." He cleared his throat. "Of course, a shampoo bottle is hardly an enthusiastic audience."

Not fair. I was imagining Cooper in the shower, water running down his back and chest, soaking into his hair. Big gulp of champagne. I needed to add that to the drink tally.

"You really look different tonight. It suits you," June said.

It must have been the alcohol talking, because I kept hearing the little voice telling me to lean in and kiss him. I sucked in a ragged breath at the mental image of my mouth pressed against his. I must have groaned out loud because everyone turned to stare at me.

"See? Even Katie thinks you look good tonight." Vicky smirked, and I felt the heat flowing up from my neck to my hair.

Cooper's lips quirked up. "Is that so?" Then he leaned in close again—too close—catching my eyes before I could find somewhere else to look.

I wasn't certain, but it was almost as if it wasn't the imaginary wart on my nose he so intently noticed, but my bottom lip as I caught it between my teeth. I took a long last gulp of my champagne for something to do that would draw his attention away from my mouth.

The song Phil was singing had ended—the image of my boss riding a steel horse would haunt my nightmares for months to come—and I heard my name called from the stage again. I was never more thrilled to take my turn singing karaoke.

"That's me," I said with just a little too much enthusiasm.

Cooper finally took his eyes from mine so he could slide out of the booth. The waitress came by, and I snatched the shot before she could even place it on the table. I threw the drink back in one swallow, blinking back tears as the liquid burned its way down my throat.

In the dark recesses of my mind, I knew I'd crossed the imaginary line that would leave me deeply, deeply sorry.

THOSE WERE MAGNIFICENT SHEETS

WHERE THE HELL AM I?

I sat bolt upright in a pitch black room and knew instantly that *one*, I should not have moved so quickly—I was still very drunk—and *two*, I was not in my own bed. I would know my pillows anywhere, and as luxurious as those were, they were definitely not mine.

This is not good. This is worse than not good. This is downright bad.

I fell back against the exquisite pillows, tugging the soft sheet up to my chin. The warm linen caressed my bare skin. They were the nicest sheets I'd ever nestled into. My brain did a slow double take as my thoughts rolled back to linen on skin. Every muscle in my body tightened.

Oh. My. God. *I think I might be naked.*

Wait. I dared to peek under the sheet, barely able to see my body in the dark. Okay, not completely... only mostly naked. I was wearing my bra and—thank goodness— panties. But that didn't answer the nagging question of where I was. I put my head back down and stayed perfectly still, listening. No breathing. Nothing.

I was alone... at least at the moment.

I wracked my brain for the slightest shred of a clue as to how I'd gotten there. I remembered singing the last song, and I'd been pretty good if I did say so myself. I remembered a drunk with awful breath, I remembered tripping and falling into some guy's lap, and I remembered being rescued by Cooper.

Oh. My. God!

I was in Cooper's house... which meant I was in Cooper's bed. *This is bad. Really bad. Even colossally bad.* There had to be some policy I was violating by being semi-naked in a client's bed. I had no idea what policy it was, but I was certain I would spend the first part of Monday morning looking for it so I would have a complete understanding as to why I was being fired. I would most definitely be fired. Unless no one found out...

I suddenly thought of Silvia. And worse... Vicky.

Everyone would know.

I needed to find my clothes, but other than the slice of moon peeking through the window, the room was completely dark. I could barely see my hand in front of my face. What time had we left the bar? Ten? Eleven? Midnight?

Phil was right.

I'd always been a total novice when it came to drinking. I was a novice when it came to most everything. I certainly wasn't used to finding myself half-naked in a strange man's bed in the middle of the night.

Then again, he was hardly a stranger. He was Cooper Maxwell. I knew him fairly well, didn't I? I'd seen him twice a week for the past year. I liked him... a lot. Though I had no idea how much until he'd walked into the bar, channeling James Dean. I'd always placed him in the out-of-reach category: rich, handsome, mysterious, and as it turns out, amazingly sexy. But last night, when he looked into my eyes, I felt it. Need. Desire. He suddenly didn't feel quite so out of reach.

So if I was in his house, where the hell was Cooper?

Again, I sat up a little too quickly and immediately regretted it. The room spun, and even my hair hurt. I should have skipped that last drink. Who was I kidding? I should have skipped the last three. I was definitely still drunk. It couldn't have been very long since leaving the bar if I still felt the effects of the liquor.

I slipped a leg over the side of the bed and pulled the blanket with me as I eased myself up. My bare feet sank into the plush carpet, and I let my eyes adjust to the little bit of light coming from the moon before I carefully made my way to the bedroom door.

Cautiously, I ran my hands across the door and discovered it wasn't one door, but two. French doors. They led to a sitting room with a fireplace. The orange glow from a recent fire gave off just enough light for me to make out the layout of the cozy little room. The stone fireplace was flanked on each side by matching leather sofas.

Lying across one, looking unbearably sexy, was Cooper. He slept on his back, still wearing his jeans and the long-sleeved gray shirt from the previous night. His bare feet hung off the side, and one arm was draped across his face as if to block out the light.

While I stared down at him, the alcohol started talking to me again, telling me to drop the blanket and jump the guy.

I am not that kind of girl. I didn't jump men on the first date. And we weren't even on a date. I wasn't sure what to call it.

I decided I needed to hightail it out of the sitting room before he woke up. I didn't want to try to explain the blanket. Of course, I might have asked him to explain the underwear and how I'd ended up wearing nothing else. I made a mental note to thank Silvia for the matching bra and panties to go with the new outfit.

I figured the smartest thing to do was go back into the other room, find my clothes, and go to sleep. I wasn't going anywhere until morning. I certainly wasn't going to walk home, and if I had to wake him, it wouldn't be to drive me anywhere other than crazy.

There it was, the little voice putting ideas into my head again—very bad paperback romance ideas. I seriously needed to do something about that. Not listening would be the first thing. Not drinking ever again would be next. I let out a ragged breath—okay, a moan—and knew instantly I should have held it—my breath, my thoughts, the whole shebang. Because the moment I made the sound, Cooper stirred on the sofa. When I turned to slowly wobble my way back toward the French doors, I heard the sofa groan under his weight.

"Do you always stare at people while they sleep?"

I didn't have to look to know he was sitting up. "I... um... I was..." *Oh, great, Katie. Think of something good.* "I wasn't sure if it was you?" *Brilliant. Now he'll not only think you're a drunk, but an idiot too.*

I practically heard the corners of his mouth tip up in a smile. "Oh, really? How many choices were there?"

I pulled the blanket tighter around me. "It was so dark, and I was a little disoriented." And naked. And drunk. And totally crazy, apparently.

Behind me, the floorboards creaked slightly, and I shivered. I didn't dare face him, but I was frozen in my spot.

"Do you wake up in strange places often?" He was having way too much fun at my expense.

"Of course not. I never wake up in strange places."

He moved to stand directly behind me, so close I could feel the heat coming off his body. "Good. I'd hate to think of you waking up in a different bedroom every weekend."

His mouth was just inches away from my ear, and his breath against my neck sent shivers down my spine and goose bumps up my arms. "Are you cold? You're shivering."

I finally found my nerve and turned to face him. "I am a little cold. I think I'll go bury myself under the covers in that nice warm bed you left me in. Thank you for driving me... um... here. I hope I wasn't much trouble." *There.* That was much more professional and composed. Maybe he wouldn't notice I was wearing a blanket.

He gripped me with both hands and slid them up and down my arms, lighting little fires everywhere he touched. "No trouble at all. It was my pleasure."

His eyes skimmed down my blanket-cocooned body and I knew he was remembering undressing me. He smiled, and my knees nearly buckled. I tried to look at him but only got as far as his mouth. I instinctively sucked in my lower lip and bit down to hold it in place.

He made a sound as if he was in agony but didn't want it to stop. And the little voice, the one that had been talking to me all night—telling me to kiss him and jump him and do other very naughty things—screamed for me to grab a fistful of his hair and drag him down to kiss me.

"Okay!"

"Okay, what?" He cocked his head slightly to the side, and even in the dark I could see the little smile threatening to come out.

I let go of my death grip on the blanket, letting it fall to the floor, and slid my hands up his chest and shoulders, then hauled him against me with all of my might, drawing him in until our lips almost touched. "Okay, this."

If I thought I was going to be making the moves on him, I was wrong. The second my lips brushed against his, he took over. It was plenty dark, so I didn't need to close my eyes, but I did. I guessed I was trying to hide a little, but I didn't need to worry about embarrassment because that out-of-reach, mysterious, deliciously sexy client of mine was kissing me back. He used his tongue to part my lips, and my tongue tangled with his. He slid his hands into my hair and grabbed the back of my head, tipping it to an angle he seemed to prefer. He pressed the length of his body against mine, and I moaned into his mouth. I felt him against my stomach, the same stomach swarming with fluttering wings, and I knew I would not be satisfied with just a kiss.

My hands roamed over his chest and under his shirt, raising it up to be as close to him as possible. His skin brushed against mine, making me all kinds of hot in the cool air. I reluctantly pulled away to ease the shirt over his head and dropped it to the floor. He cupped my cheek, caressing the side of my face with his thumb as his lips skillfully drove me mad with desire.

His free hand slid up between us and found its way to the rounded underside of one of my breasts. I shuddered as he slipped his hand under the silk to skim my sensitive flesh with his fingers. I grabbed his arms to hold myself upright. I was afraid if I let go, I'd become nothing but a puddle at his feet.

Cooper pulled his mouth from mine and trailed his lips down my throat, over my chest, and to my now-exposed breast. He flicked his tongue over my hardened peak, and I let out a whimper as the shock waves of pleasure pulsed directly to my core.

In all my twenty-eight—*sigh*—twenty-nine years, I'd never felt such a deep, aching need. Electricity shot straight through my body and down between my legs. I desperately wanted him to touch me there, but I knew I would die of embarrassment when he discovered how wet I was.

I gasped. "Oh, God." My head was spinning, and I wasn't sure if I was drunk on liquor or pleasure. I tipped my face to the ceiling and heard the rush of my own breathing and my heart pounding in my ears. I was certain if he didn't carry me off to his bed right that second, I would die.

Cooper pulled his mouth from my breast and kissed his way back to my neck, drawing me back from the brink. I raised my head to meet him in another passionate lip-lock.

And then I woke up for real.

Holy crap!

My head rested on the same luxurious pillows I vaguely remembered snuggling into earlier in the night. The same linen sheets were wrapped around my fully dressed body. Fully dressed, as in I was wearing the same ridiculous leather skirt and sheer blouse. No boots, but definitely *not* even close to naked.

Oh, I was in Cooper's bed all right, but my wonderfully delicious dream slowly faded into the dark.

Damn!

The room was still pitch-black, yet clearly some of the memories from the dream came from my own vivid subconscious. I must have had some recollection of Cooper guiding me, half passed-out drunk, to his bedroom.

How excruciatingly embarrassing. Well, at least I didn't have to go on an expedition to find my clothes in order to sneak out. If I didn't run across my boots on the way, I would simply hike out in bare feet.

And Monday? Well, I had yet to use a single sick day. I could surely invent some horrible illness to keep me from work for at least one day.

But I didn't need to get too far ahead of myself. I still needed to find my phone. I flipped back the sheets, wrenching myself from the decadence of the bed. If I got lucky, I could escape before Cooper had a chance to miss me.

"Kate, you're awake. I was beginning to worry about you."

The glow from the fire in the sitting room outlined Cooper's silhouette in the doorway.

I was midway into my escape, one foot barely touching the carpet, one hand still gripping the linen sheet. *Caught.* "I was... um... looking for the bathroom?" It wasn't meant to be a question, but it ended up as one. I was not the best liar.

He chuckled as he padded across the room. "You don't sound convinced. Are you sure it's the bathroom you're looking for?"

"Of course. I need to use the bathroom. I drank a lot." My attempt at feigning irritation was a complete failure. Even to my own ears, I sounded confused.

He reached into the darkness and flipped a switch,

lighting a room I hadn't noticed. It was gorgeous, as if it sprang straight out of a magazine... or a French hotel suite.

"Wow. Nice."

"Yeah, thanks." He sounded almost embarrassed. I decided to tuck his reaction away for later, when I wasn't still under the influence.

"Do you need me to show—" he started.

"No! I can find my way." The last thing I wanted was for Cooper Maxwell to stand outside the door while I was peeing.

I reluctantly let go of the sheet and walked toward the light. I heard the bed creak behind me as I wandered into the enormous room. The crystal chandelier alone screamed money, and the marble floor was warm against my bare feet. *Radiant heat. Figures. Definitely nothing like my icy bathroom floor.*

I caught my awestruck reflection in the mirrors—all of them—as I took in the scrumptious party shower with four heads and assorted other spouts that would undoubtedly shoot water from every angle all at once. After a glance at the shampoo bottle in the corner—*that shampoo bottle has seen him naked*—I quickly shifted my attention to the huge claw-foot tub. Simple but elegant, right down to the ornate silver feet.

His bathroom had everything. Except for maybe... "Hey, Cooper? Where's the—"

"Around the corner, first door on—"

"Got it. Thanks." I closed the door behind me and fought the urge to hyperventilate. I wasn't sure if I could pee in his bathroom. Once my heart settled down to its normal rhythm, I managed to do what I had come to do, but I cringed when the sound of the toilet flushing echoed in the quiet room.

I waited until the water stopped running before I opened the door. I almost ran to the sink to wash my hands, careful not to break the spout on the silver-plated soap dispenser, and debated as to whether I should use the impossibly perfect hand towel or simply wipe my wet hands on my blouse. I finally decided on the towel and spent almost a minute trying to shape it back into the same careful folds I'd found it in.

When I stepped back into the darkness of the room, he jumped up from the bed. "Better?"

I bit my lip, thankful he couldn't see me blush in the dark. "Much. Thanks."

"You must be tired. It's after one. Can I get you anything? Some water maybe? You should probably hydrate yourself. It will help with the hangover later." He moved to lean against the wall next to the bathroom doorway and fidgeted with the buttons on his shirt.

He fidgeted. Cooper Maxwell fidgeted? It didn't seem possible. I was the nervous one. I didn't think I'd ever seen him so anxious. "You're being very nice, but I should just call a cab so you can get some sleep. You shouldn't have to babysit me."

"I don't mind," he answered too quickly, flashing that high-voltage smile for just a half a second before reining it back in. "Besides, it's late. Why don't you just stay the night." He said it more like a statement than a question. "You looked like you were rather enjoying the bed."

"You have the nicest sheets. I'll bet they feel amazing on bare skin." The line had sounded innocent enough when I tested it out in my head, but as the words sputtered out of my mouth, I knew they hadn't come out that way.

His eyebrows shot up, and he grinned. "Be my guest. I'd love to get your opinion on that."

My mouth fell open. I stood there, gaping like some sort of fish, for an impossibly long minute while I pulled myself together. "Um... could I get that drink of water now?"

"Sure." He laughed. "Be right back."

He left me standing in the dark beside his bed while he disappeared into the adjacent sitting room. He came back in less than a minute with a cold bottle of water. He took off the cap and held out the bottle.

"Thank you," I managed to whisper, infinitely aware of the fact that even in the dark, he could probably see the bright red blush burning my face. I could feel it. I practically glowed. I took a swig from the water, and then another, catching a drop with the back of my hand as it ran down my chin.

"The sheets really are magnificent against bare skin." His smile wasn't mocking but sweet.

"So... um... could you tell me how I ended up in your bed?"

A distinct flush colored Cooper's cheeks. "I didn't know where you lived, so I brought you home."

"As drunk as I was, I'm surprised I was able to walk."

He hesitated. "I had to carry you."

"Oh."

"May I?" He waited until I nodded before he reached out to touch the sheer fabric at my shoulder. "This can't be very comfortable to sleep in. I'll get you something of mine. Wait here." He disappeared into what I had deemed the Chandelier Room with Adjoining Toilet—CRWAT for short.

I shifted my weight, leaning against the massive bed, unsure if I should sit or stand. "I don't want to cause you any trouble. I'm fine, really," I lied. I was extremely uncomfortable in the claustrophobic outfit Silvia had gotten me. I wanted to say how I had been dying to get out of it all evening, but I knew how that would sound, so I kept quiet and took a big sip of water.

He stepped back into the room and handed me a long-sleeved, white cotton T-shirt and a pair of gray sweat pants. "It's no trouble at all. And while I certainly enjoyed seeing you in this—" He touched the sleeve of my blouse again. "—it doesn't really suit you very well, does it?"

I laughed. "No, it certainly doesn't. This was all Silvia. I can promise you that." I took the clothes into the CRWAT and locked myself in to change. His shirt was too big, and the sweats were way too long. The sleeves fell past my hands, so I pushed them up my arms a little and tugged on the sweats to pull them up as far as possible. I had to roll the waist band over three times to keep from tripping on the bottoms. When I came out, he watched me with a look I couldn't quite interpret, but it didn't make me uncomfortable. The entire situation was awkward, but at the same time, I felt safe with Cooper.

"Silvia will be glad her outfit was a hit." I flashed my most innocent smile and set my folded clothes on his nightstand.

"Remind me to thank her the next time I see her." He grinned.

My legs turned to Jell-O. I took a step back to put a little distance between us and tripped over the leg of the sweatpants, shattering my fragile grasp on stability.

He stepped forward and grabbed me before I hit the carpet. "How do you manage to get through the day when you fall so much?" he whispered against my hair as he hauled me back to my feet.

I was instantly aware he hadn't let go of me, despite the fact that I appeared to be standing again. He held me against his chest with his hand splayed lightly across my back, heat radiating through the thin cotton of my shirt. My heart hammered in my chest so loudly there was no question he could hear it and probably feel it too, given his close proximity.

"I-I'm just a little clumsy, I guess. Do you think I'm still drunk?" I could barely hear my own voice over the rushing in my ears.

But his grin told me he had no trouble hearing me. "Well, if you are, then I'm going to have to abandon my next thought. I would never take advantage of you that way."

When did he get that grin? I'd seen it more times in one night than I had in the whole year I'd known him, and each time he flashed it, I was liquid mush. I couldn't manage more than a raised eyebrow in response.

"I was going to kiss you. But if you're still drunk, that would be ungentlemanly of me."

Okay, that did it. I groaned.

He leaned in, lips not even an inch from mine. "Well?"

I held my breath and waited to see if I would wake up again, but I didn't. "I don't feel drunk, really." I let out a breath.

"I've wanted to do this for a year," he murmured, then closed the narrow gap between our lips.

He kissed me tenderly, holding himself against me but not so close as to be ungentlemanly. Even in my earlier sex dream, the butterflies had been tame compared to the fluttering going on with *this* passionate kiss.

His breath tasted faintly of the peppermint I had smelled earlier, as if he had brushed his teeth recently, and I decided I would always remember Cooper that way, with wonderful, minty-fresh breath. The incredible restraint in the way he kissed was just enough to send my heart flying but not so much as to stop it completely.

I wanted more of him. I reached around and tangled my fingers in his hair, and he stepped up the kiss another notch. His arms wrapped around me, smashing me harder against him, until I could feel every inch of him against every inch of me, and still it wasn't enough. He whispered my name between breathless kisses, and I could have sworn he called me Katie.

The instant the kiss broke off, I was extremely aware of my situation.

Oh. My. God.

I'd just made out with Cooper Maxwell. While I was *awake!*

"Okay, well, that was... wow. So, I really should be getting back to bed now."

Cooper's eyebrows shot up, and my cheeks burned.

"Alone."

"But it's my bed," he argued, leaning in and placing kisses on each corner of my mouth then trailing down my neck. "Shouldn't I get to go, too?"

I had no idea if he was serious or trying to completely unhinge me, but God, that sounded really good. My stomach did flips again. But not the good kind. In fact, my stomach was starting to do crazy dives, like seagulls do at the beach.

Oh, no.

"I think I'm going to be sick." My hand shot up to cover my mouth as the first wave started from the deep recesses of my stomach and ended up all over his bare feet and expensive carpet.

IS IT POSSIBLE TO DIE OF A HANGOVER?

OMEHOW, I MANAGED TO DRAG myself out of bed Monday morning and get dressed for work without throwing up again. Oh, I was completely recovered from the hangover. I'd spent a miserable Saturday afternoon sprawled out across my bed, stopping just short of slapping a rubber nipple on the Pepto-Bismol bottle as I nursed from it like a baby.

No, my ailment on Monday morning had very little to do with that kind of hangover. I was suffering from a love hangover. Well, lust hangover, maybe. And my sense of dread at going back to work where I might have to answer questions about Friday night was getting to me.

I'd ignored Silvia's calls all weekend. Instead, I sent her a text to say I wasn't feeling well. That was actually pretty easy. No one could possibly question my not feeling well all weekend. I'd been rather intoxicated when they last saw me.

And speaking of the last time they saw me...

If I wasn't completely terrified to bring up the topic, I would rail at them all for having run out of the bar, leaving Cooper to deal with my drunken ass. I wasn't afraid of the ribbing I would get. I would gladly take it with a smile if I could avoid the obvious, "So... Cooper drove you home?" I could hear them already, each of them taking turns, asking me questions, and then compiling the data until they had the whole picture.

That was one picture I was not interested in seeing plastered all over the walls of the bank. The entire weekend was already spent replaying it in my head until I could see and smell and taste every tactile moment of the time I spent with Cooper. Oh, the humiliation of it all. I had made out with him like the high school girl Silvia was apparently trying to turn me into, then barfed all over his floor.

He'd insisted on taking care of me while I vomited first onto his feet and then into his toilet. Then he made me a cup of tea and tucked me into his bed where I slept most of it off. Late Saturday afternoon, Cooper finally drove me back to my car while I sat in abject silence. I sensed that he wanted to say something, but I played sick to avoid conversation.

Talk about your great first dates... if I could even call it a date. I could pretty much forget about a second one. Worse than that, I didn't know if I could ever face him again.

I wasn't at work for more than forty minutes when I looked up and caught Silvia doing her third sweep past my office. She hadn't lost a bit of that smug look on her face. She was waiting me out until I couldn't resist telling her about Friday night.

I could resist. It was too much of a horror story. And just like every horror story, it had started out pretty good—a secluded cabin in the woods, or moving into the perfect house that had been priced to sell after the "accident," or spending time with your dream guy—but disintegrated into madness and mayhem. I pulled out my calendar and stared at my list of appointments for the day. Of course, Cooper was right there, sandwiched between Mrs. Gilroy and lunch. But his name wasn't written in my handwriting. No, Silvia's swirly script taunted me from the page. She obviously found great pleasure in torturing me.

This is a recipe for disaster. And with the way things had gone since my birthday, I didn't have much hope for the *rest* of the year, unless he'd just changed his appointment. I flipped through my datebook to Tuesday. There he was, just like every other Tuesday. Nope, it hadn't changed, just Cooper, two days in a row.

I considered faking a migraine and passing off my appointments to Vicky or June, but June wouldn't put up enough of a fight when Vicky called "dibs" on Cooper, and I didn't think I could stand it if he were sitting across a desk from Vicky. Not when I knew about her Fantasy Threesome list. He was her number one draft pick, after all.

I shuddered. No way was Vicky getting anywhere *near* Cooper if I had anything to do with it. I would simply have to endure the embarrassment of seeing him. I could manage professionalism; I was sure of it. What I wasn't sure of was how he would react to seeing me again. Would he laugh at me for having been so wretchedly drunk? Would he be disgusted by the memory of me puking on his floor?

My face grew hot at the memory. Could anything be more hideously mortifying? I only hoped he'd been able to get the stain out of the carpet.

Vicky took her turn pausing outside my office with a smug look of her own. She wore her cut-low-in-front and slit-high-up-the-side work suit. I recognized an emerging pattern. She always seemed to wear something inappropriate when Cooper had an appointment with me. Or was that just my imagination? Either way, I felt a jolt of protective fury. I stamped it down, shaking my head a little.

"You'll never guess what I did on Saturday," Vicky blurted as she tossed her jacket onto a hook and spun around to face me.

I didn't even want to guess. It was too scary. It could be anything.

"I got a piercing!" she squealed.

I'd heard her talking about it often enough to know exactly what she'd gotten pierced, and my barely recovered stomach rolled at the thought.

"Feeling better?" Vicky asked, flipping her fiery hair over her shoulder. "I hear Cooper's coming in today." She flashed a wide grin that reminded me instantly of why I preferred Silvia as a friend.

I couldn't care less about the professional ramifications of Vicky wanting to steal my client because there were none. Her zeal had nothing to do with Cooper's portfolio and everything to do with Cooper himself, and I didn't want her dragging him further into her fantasies.

I knew I couldn't have him for myself. Not really. I had to maintain our professional relationship. I definitely wouldn't be able to kiss him again. That was the hardest truth to accept. And I was seriously waffling on that part. I wanted more, but more wasn't possible. In fact, I wanted more so badly I hadn't read a single page from any of my books since *the kiss*.

That was a big deal. I never went to bed without reading at least two chapters. And it wasn't as if I didn't try. I just couldn't concentrate. I would start to read, but my mind would wander back to Cooper... and his amazing peppermint breath.

The first thing I did when I got home Saturday morning was scatter my stack of books across the floor and plant myself in the middle of the pile, newest book in hand. Desperate to disappear like always, I flipped through to the sticky notes tucked between the pages. I'd only read that one a few times so far, but the desire to lose myself in the book had vanished. Even my favorite vampire had no draw for me.

One stupid kiss and I was abruptly thrust back into the real world where real men could break your heart, a place I'd purposely steered clear of by living in my safe little bubble of fictional romances. And no matter what I wanted, I couldn't begin a relationship with a client.

So if I could only have him professionally, then I was going to fight tooth and nail to keep that little bit of him, even if that meant going up against Vicky to keep him.

I managed to extract myself from her and her insanity and closed myself in my office for the rest of the morning, only surfacing for my first appointment, the blue-haired Hitler herself, Mrs. Philomena Gilroy.

From the moment Mrs. Gilroy—lamenting her poorly producing retirement portfolio— stormed out the door an hour later and I'd settled myself in my chair, my desk phone had been ringing nonstop. I recognized the name on the caller ID and ignored the calls for as long as I could. Each ring drove me closer to the Cliffs of Insanity, so I finally had no choice but to answer. She wouldn't have stopped calling, and no one else would be able to get through if she kept the line tied up. I was merely delaying the inevitable anyway. I hadn't returned her phone calls all weekend long. I knew what she wanted—the same thing she always wanted.

I hit the speaker button. "Hi, Mom."

"Well, did you meet anyone nice this weekend?"

Yep, same question as always. She didn't even bother with the usual pleasantries, just cut right to the chase. Worse, she knew I'd gone out for my birthday. My only hope to get off the phone before lunch was to keep my responses short and sweet. "Nope."

"Do you mean to tell me with all the people you were out with, you didn't meet anyone at all? No nice men? Not even a maybe?" She sighed. "Have you ever wondered if perhaps your standards are too high?"

"Maybe." No doubt about it. My standards had just been raised into the stratosphere.

"Well, did you at least dress nicely? If you don't dress up, you won't attract anyone, you know. You didn't wear one of your boring work suits, did you?" Her questions almost made me think she might be psychic. Almost.

Then again, if I didn't know better, I'd worry about Silvia talking to my mother, feeding her information and conspiring against me. But I knew that wasn't possible.

Mom didn't have the self-control to keep something like that a secret from me. Besides, she hated Silvia. She thought of her as competition.

Pathetic.

Why couldn't I have two gorgeous men vying for my affection? Instead, I had my mother competing with my coworker for my attention. I rolled my eyes at the absurdity of it all and launched into my best lie-but-don't-lie defense. "Oh, I dressed up all right. You wouldn't have recognized me." Technically, not a lie.

"Well, if you didn't meet anyone, why didn't you call me?"

Now, I was going to have to lie. I couldn't possibly tell my mother I had passed out drunk, woken up in the bed of the most beautiful man I'd ever seen, and after kissing him senseless, puked on his ridiculously sexy feet.

I took a deep breath. "My phone is broken." Big lie, but it always worked. For all she knew, I had broken six cell phones in less than a year's time. I reminded myself to come up with a new excuse next time. And I was sure there would be a next time. I checked the clock again. "Mom, I have to get back to work. I have a really busy schedule today. I'll call you later."

"Do you promise?"

Damn! I wasn't really planning on calling her later. Maybe I'd get hit by a bus on the way home. I laughed. *Yep. Pathetic.* "Okay. I promise. I'll talk to you later. Bye."

Crossing my mother off my reluctant to-do list, I decided to go check my hair and makeup. Cooper was due in my office in T-minus twenty minutes.

I mentally slapped myself for even thinking that way. Why should I care what my hair or makeup looked like just because Cooper Maxwell was on his way? I didn't check my hair or makeup for any of my other clients.

I sat in my chair for a minute, twirling my pen between my fingers before getting up to check my hair and makeup anyway. I still wasn't used to the new cut Silvia had talked me into getting. I liked it, but I had no idea how to style it yet.

I dampened my hands and smoothed down the places that poked up. I checked my makeup and clothes in the mirror. I was as ready as I would ever be. I'd dressed a little extra special. I told myself it was because the billowy blouse and wool pencil skirt were the most comfortable things I owned. Even though the fabric was scratchy, the outfit looked really nice, managing to make the most of my curves without making me look fat and without sacrificing my reputation.

Unlike Vicky.

I walked into the lobby to catch Vicky laughing at something Phil had said. I rolled my eyes. Even at my most desperate, I didn't think I would ever stoop that low.

I sat at my desk, trying to compose an email. I had to erase and start over three times. I finally gave up. I couldn't concentrate. I looked at the time again. Cooper was probably parking his shiny black BMW at that very second. I wondered if I would have that same thrill whip through me when he walked in wearing the usual designer suit and perfectly combed hair. Was the intense attraction I'd felt Friday night simply a product of too much liquor and an overactive imagination?

My stomach rolled at the memory. If he was wearing jeans and the gray Henley, I was doomed.

Silvia floated past my glass office door again and paused to wink at me. A surge of adrenaline rushed through my veins, and I jumped out of my chair, tipping it to the floor. Not an easy thing to do with a rolling chair. Quickly, I righted it then wrenched my door open and practically ran through it, slamming directly into the wall of someone's chest, just as I saw Cooper step around the corner.

"Kiss me, Kate!" Dean Maynard's sing-song voice carried throughout the lobby, vibrating against the walls.

The wind was knocked out of me, and I would have

fallen flat on the floor if Dean hadn't reached around to steady me.

I tried to wriggle free discreetly with no luck. "Cole Porter does *The Taming of the Shrew*?" I asked with a nervous laugh.

"Ah, she knows the show. But will she oblige me with a kiss?" He tilted his head in my direction.

I tried to laugh, but it came out strangled. "I didn't know you were coming in today."

"I always come in on Mondays. Usually the afternoons, I know. But I couldn't bear another minute away from my best girl Katie." Dean grinned. "Besides, I need help with my money."

Cooper stood quietly off to the side, his jaw clenching and unclenching. The contrast was immediately apparent as I stood gaping, first at Dean, then Cooper. I'd always thought Dean was good looking with his light brown hair and dark eyes, cute in a nerdy sort of way. But Dean was no Cooper Maxwell... not even close.

"I have an appointment right now." I smiled over Dean's shoulder at Cooper.

Dean wrinkled his brow and then turned to look. "You don't mind if I steal her away, do you?"

Cooper stepped forward. "Actually, I do."

Dean ignored him and linked his arm with mine. I flashed a panicked look in Cooper's direction as Dean dragged me toward my office.

"I've recently come into a rather large sum of money..."

I heard Dean speaking, but I wasn't paying attention. I was too focused on Cooper across the room. I glanced around Dean to see Silvia rushing out of her office. She patted Cooper's arm as she spoke to him, and he nodded, looking in my direction. Thank goodness Silvia got to him before Vicky.

"Katie, are you listening to me?" Dean gripped my chin and turned my face until we were eye to eye.

"I'm sorry. I was distracted."

He tapped the tip of my nose with his finger. "No more distractions."

"I really need to..."

Cooper paced across the lobby, his hands knotted in his hair. Silvia was still talking to him, but he shook his head and looked in my direction one more time.

Dean turned my face again. "Listen to me. That's what you need to do."

I sighed. "Very quickly, Dean. I really do have an appointment waiting."

Out of the corner of my eye, I watched Cooper follow Silvia into her office, and I relaxed for a moment. I even went all out and blew out the breath I'd been holding.

"I need to open a new account," Dean continued.

I nodded, glancing at Silvia's doorway every few seconds until Cooper paced back out again, Silvia close behind him. They looked to be arguing, but she was nodding and patting his arm. Finally, he smiled, and Silvia set out in my direction.

I took a step backward, bumping into the wall as Silvia came up behind Dean. She put her hands on his shoulders and got on tip-toes to get her lips to his ear. "How dare you come in here without stopping to say hi to me?"

Dean spun around. "Silvia," he sang.

"Dean, I'm afraid I need to take you away from poor Katie here. Her appointment is getting a little restless, so I'm going to personally take care of your banking needs today." Silvia linked her arm with Dean's, steering him to the door of my office.

"Not to worry, Katie. I'll wait for you," Dean called over his shoulder. "I'll come back when you're not so busy." He stopped in the doorway and turned to bow dramatically before taking his exit.

Cooper crossed the lobby in a few long strides and came into my office.

"Happy to see me?" he whispered, pulling me into an awkward hug. He didn't say a single word about Dean, for which I was infinitely grateful.

"Of course." I breathed him in before forcing myself to end our embrace. "I'm always happy to see you." *He has no idea.* A wide smile broke out on his gorgeous face.

I struggled not to hyperventilate—it was becoming a habit. I had hoped he'd walk in and be the same old Cooper. There was something reserved about him before, something that allowed me to keep a safe distance.

There would be no safe distance any longer. He was just as unbearably hot and sexy as he'd been Friday night. Instead of jeans and the gray Henley, he wore loose-fitting khakis and a dark blue pullover—a color that made the little flecks of blue in his green eyes more noticeable—under a long black leather car coat. His clothing was strictly designer but completely disheveled. He'd probably shaved the day before, but not that morning, and his hair was in that ridiculously unruly tangle that I had no idea appealed to me until he caught me staring at it. I made a mental note to find out what cologne he wore so I could dab some of the spicy citrus scent on my pillows at home.

"Come on in." I waited for him to clear the door so I could close it on the little crowd beginning to form outside my office.

Vicky and Silvia were positively oozing with excitement. I wasn't sure if Silvia was happy for me or just drooling over Cooper. Either way, I owed her one for getting Dean out of there.

I wished I had blinds that would close so I wouldn't be distracted by their ogling. I wanted to be completely alone with Cooper. I shook my head lightly to dispel the ridiculous notion.

With the inclusion of June, the mob outside my office grew. Silvia hadn't wasted any time sending out the alarm that Cooper had finally arrived. I knew what they were up to. They were watching for little signs and signals to figure out what was going on between us. They had not accepted my weak explanation from Friday night. They wouldn't be satisfied until they could see for themselves.

I didn't know what they expected. Probably that Cooper would take me right there on my desk for all the world to see. Something inside me—most likely my ovaries—exploded, and I sucked in a sharp intake of breath at the mental image. I needed to stay away from that dangerous train of thought.

Cooper noticed my reaction and raised one eyebrow. "How are you feeling this morning?" He leaned in and whispered as if he somehow knew that outside my door, a flock of hungry vultures had assembled to listen for any crumbs that might fall through the cracks.

"I'm much better today. Thank you again for taking such good care of me Friday and Saturday. That was really very sweet of you." The memory of Cooper holding my hair while I vomited into his pristine toilet was horrifying. My face got hot, and I pulled my lower lip through my teeth.

"It was my pleasure. Really." His lips quirked up at the corners. "So... did your *cat* survive the weekend without you?"

I choked out a laugh. "Shh... you're the only one who knows about my cat."

He turned to wave at the peanut gallery behind him. "So they all think you have a real cat?"

"Shush, he *is* real. He's also imaginary and runs away or gets a serious case of furballs whenever I don't want to go somewhere. It's not like I can tell them the truth. They'd all make horrible fun of me for making him up. Or worse... steal my idea. "

He shook his head with a chuckle. "I'm glad you trusted *me* with the truth." He leaned almost all the way across my desk, and I had to force myself to stay where I was. "Can I tell *you* a secret?"

I leaned in until our noses were just inches apart. My mouth opened to say yes, but I couldn't speak. I just nodded.

"I've never invited anyone to my home before." His fingers brushed the back of my hand. "I liked having you there."

I swallowed hard. "You have a lovely home." Though true, the admission didn't even begin to cover what I wanted to say.

He flashed his megawatt smile. "Have you had lunch yet?"

Good thing I was sitting down because my knees went weak. I just shook my head, reminding myself to breathe.

"Let me take you. I'm unbelievably hungry right now."

The ravenous look on his face made me replay his words in my mind. I sat up straight, trying to look professional. "I hate to take advantage of you any more than I already have. I still feel awful about your carpet." I cringed. "I don't normally drink so much. I have no idea what came over me. I'm sure you must think I'm a horrible lush."

"Horrible? Not a chance." He grinned. "I think you did a great job at being a lush. I was pretty impressed, honestly."

"I'm serious, Cooper. I don't drink. I mean, clearly I did, but that was unusual for me. I'm actually very boring most nights." I reached for a stack of papers and focused on arranging them so I wouldn't have to look into his eyes.

"That's just a shame." Cooper tipped my chin up with his fingers. "We should fix that, don't you think?"

I shook off his hand. "*We* can't do anything. I'm your banker. We shouldn't be doing what we're doing. I never should have..." The taste of his peppermint breath on my lips was suddenly the only thing I could think of.

He fell back in his chair. "Is that really all we are, after all this time?" A long silent moment passed, then he flashed his lopsided grin again. "Well, you could make it up to me. The carpet and all, I mean."

"What can I do to make it up to you?"

RIGHT... JUST LUNCH

OW DO I GET MYSELF into these things?

My briefcase bounced off the backseat of my Toyota and landed on the floor just as I slammed the door. It was only supposed to be lunch. Lunch! It should have been no big deal.

It was a big deal. A very big deal.

Half a day later, I could still smell his cologne all over me. How many times did he manage to hug me? The first awkward hug was almost expected, especially after the *Dean Situation*. The second time was when I agreed to have lunch with him. It wasn't really a hug, but more like he was laying claim to me. We stepped out of my office, and he wrapped his arm around my waist and held me against him as we walked to the main door. He was so close I could feel his breath in my hair.

It was... it was really wonderful and really awful at the same time. The whole crew was still standing there watching. Silvia looked smug, as though she was getting her way somehow. Anger rippled off of Vicky in waves. She acted as if I were playing with her toys, and she didn't like it.

I pretended not to notice them practically pressing their noses against the glass as Cooper opened the passenger door for me and closed it as I sank into his leather seat. It would be easy to get used to riding in his BMW. Too easy.

We didn't speak much on the way to the restaurant. I fiddled with the radio and asked him stupid questions like, "Do you have any CDs?" and "Does the BMW get good gas mileage?"

Cooper didn't answer. He just reached across my lap with a smile and pulled an iPod from the glove box. I pretended to shuffle through the songs as I watched him in my peripheral vision. Every few seconds, he glanced over at me.

I already knew his taste in music. We'd had countless conversations across my desk about our favorite artists, first concerts, and who we'd like to come back from the dead for just one last concert tour. I was hesitant to tell him my pick—a circa-1962 Rat Pack reunion—but when I finally voiced it, he wholeheartedly agreed. No, I didn't need to snoop through his iPod, but I wouldn't mind being able to read his mind for the next... oh... hour or so.

When we got to the restaurant, he opened the car door for me. I liked it. I liked it more because I knew he wasn't doing it just to impress me. I had seen him open doors for people all the time at the bank. He was very sweet. He possessed the kind of chivalry lost on most men his age. I knew about these things; I'd read a lot of books.

The restaurant was a quiet place about five miles from the bank. Even during the lunch hour, the small dining room was dim, with brick walls and dark wood trim, and candles flickered on every table. The hostess seated us at a booth way in the back, and I wondered if Cooper had arranged that in advance. I didn't think he could have when I had only just agreed to have lunch with him.

I stared at the menu for several minutes, unable to comprehend the choices. I knew I should be hungry, but my stomach was on another rollercoaster ride, and I was far too jittery. I swept my eyes down the menu and back up again without really seeing anything.

"Such a serious face. You don't know what you want?"

I looked up from the menu. He flashed his crooked grin, and I couldn't help but smile back.

He gestured at the menu. "Everything here is good."

I nodded absently. "That's good to know." I was in uncharted territory. I had sat across from him countless times and never had so much trouble knowing what to say. "I don't know why this is so awkward."

"Hey," he said, his eyes softening, "it's just me. We talk across a wooden surface at least twice a week."

"So... did you thank Silvia?"

He gave me a strange look. "Should I?"

"Well," I glanced back down at the menu, "you did say to remind you to thank her." I forced myself to look at him. I could do the flirting thing.

He grinned. "Yes, I did, didn't I? That was a great blouse. No, I haven't thanked her yet. I should really send her flowers."

I flashed my own crooked grin. "Flowers? She'd like that. Girls always like getting flowers."

He laughed. "I think I've heard that about girls. I don't suppose you know what sort of flowers Silvia likes, do you? I guess roses are always a good choice."

"Hmmm..." I tapped my lower lip with my index finger as I pretended to be deep in thought. "Roses are nice. *Silvia* would probably like roses."

His eyebrows came together. "You disapprove of roses?"

"Oh, not really." I shrugged. "They aren't my favorite, but we *are* talking about what Silvia likes. I'm sure *she* likes roses."

Cooper rested both elbows on the table. "You have definitely piqued my curiosity. What exactly are *your* favorite flowers?"

I fidgeted with my napkin. "There are so many to choose from."

"Just suppose someone wanted to get you flowers. What would you like?"

I laughed. "Why would anyone get me flowers?"

"Haven't any of your clients sent you flowers?"

"Many of my clients have sent me flowers."

The waiter approached the table to take our orders, rescuing me from Cooper's line of questioning.

"You go first." I peered at my menu. "I'm still deciding."

"I'd like the fettuccini Alfredo with extra Alfredo sauce," Cooper said.

"And for you, ma'am?"

"I guess I'll have the Caesar salad, light on the croutons and the parmesan. Dressing on the side, please?" I handed my menu to the waiter before he turned and walked away.

Cooper's eyebrows furrowed. "I thought you liked Italian?"

"Oh, I do. I love it. But I can't eat it, too many carbs. I'll probably gain five pounds just from the proximity to *your* plate." I tried to laugh it off, but Cooper's scowl deepened.

"You really don't have to worry about your weight. You have an amazing body."

My face got hot. "Well, with my luck, I'd end up with pasta sauce all over the front of me. It's safer if I stick with salad."

Cooper shook his head and chuckled. "So, was Dean Maynard one of those clients who sent you flowers?"

Twice. "Honestly, I haven't kept track."

He let it go, but I could see a flash of something in his eyes even while we moved on to small talk; he was still thinking about it. Every once in a while, he would look at me funny, as if trying to figure me out.

When the waiter brought our meals, I picked up a breadstick and brushed it against my lips. Cooper stared at me, open-mouthed. With my eyes locked on his, I darted my tongue out, tasting the buttery topping before taking a slow bite. He dropped his fork, and it clattered against his plate. I didn't know what had possessed me to be playful with a real guy. When was the last time that happened?

"Orchids," I blurted.

Cooper paused, then picked up his fork to take a bite of his pasta. That megawatt smile of his returned.

"White," I clarified.

"White orchids," he repeated, nodding.

I was sure he was going to catalog that somewhere to use against me later. Although having orchids used against me might be kind of nice.

Our lunch conversation steered clear of Friday night, as I hoped it would. He never once mentioned our kiss or my getting sick. We mostly talked about work. Mine.

"So in all this time I've been your banker, I don't think I've ever figured out what *you* do for a living."

Cooper chuckled. "I'm an international man of mystery."

I rolled my eyes. "No, really, Austin Powers, try me."

"I'm a contracted employee of a large organization," he rattled off quickly.

"What exactly does that mean?"

"It means I really can't talk about it."

I raised an eyebrow and leaned in to whisper, "It's a secret?"

I saw a sparkle in his blue-green eyes, and then the grin slowly fell from his face.

"Yes, it's a secret. In fact, if I told you..." He closed the narrow gap between us until our noses were all but touching. "I'd have to kill you."

My heart jumped to life. I was certain, given our close proximity, he had to have noticed.

He held a straight face for an impossibly long moment, and then smiled. "Kate, I'm kidding. Now eat. Your food's getting cold."

I took that to mean the discussion was closed. I found it strange how long I'd known him but never heard him mention work. It would have bothered me more if I wasn't so preoccupied with wanting him. I wasn't ready to go when the waiter brought him the check.

"Let me take that." I reached for the check. "I can expense it as a business lunch. My treat... for the carpet."

"I've got it," Cooper said and immediately slipped some

cash into the folder and handed it back to the waiter. "This is your punishment for the carpet, remember?" He grinned.

"You have a funny way of punishing someone."

"I'm sure I could come up with more intriguing ways, but I'd need some time to plan."

I could think of more intriguing ways too, but I pushed that thought out of my head and promised myself I would pay next time. I laughed. I was already planning a next time.

"What's so funny?" he asked, tilting his head to one side.

I wiped the stupid grin from my lips. "Nothing. I was just thinking."

"That's hardly fair. You tell me you're thinking, but you won't tell me what you're thinking about?"

"Silvia. That's who I was thinking about." I told myself I wasn't lying because I actually had thought of Silvia several times during lunch.

"What about Silvia?" His eyebrows drew together, but he was still smiling.

"I can't wait to see her face when she gets her flowers. She's likely to become quite smitten with you." I laughed.

Cooper took my hand as we walked back to the car. He held the door open for me again and waited until I was settled in before closing it.

"That's all it takes?" His unexpected question caught me off guard, and when I didn't answer, he angled his body toward me and leaned in closer. "*Is* that all it takes?" he asked again.

I could taste his peppermint breath as it washed over me. "Hmm?" I wondered how his breath could smell of peppermint when he'd just eaten pasta.

"Flowers... to make someone smitten with me? Because if that's all it takes, well..."

He was unbelievably close, and I was having a hard time reminding myself I needed to breathe. I managed to answer with a weak shake of my head, but I couldn't tear my eyes away from his upturned lips.

He tilted his head at the same time he put a warm hand against my cheek, and I couldn't have stopped the kiss if I'd wanted to. I didn't want to. His lips were every bit as exquisite as I remembered. His kiss was tender. I could tell he was holding back, which was a good thing because my resolve was dangling by a thread.

He broke from our kiss and wound his arms around me, pulling me against him in a hug. The third hug in less than two hours.

"Thank you for letting me punish you," he murmured.

"Any time." I breathed the words out before I could stop them.

I dropped into the driver's seat of my Toyota Prius, shaking my head clear of the memories. The engine didn't make much sound, and I needed a little noise to block the thoughts floating around in my head. I pushed a CD in and dialed up the volume to a ridiculous level. Beethoven's "Ode to Joy" blasted out of the speakers. Nothing like a good symphony to settle the nerves. Right. Bad choice. But it was all I had.

Why hadn't I just stayed home Friday night and read a book? Things would have been much less complicated. I'd be his banker and wouldn't be swathed in his unforgettable scent or still tasting the peppermint on my lips.

I was a creature of habit... most of the time. Or maybe I was developing new habits? Like kissing Cooper Maxwell. Was that really such a bad habit to get into?

Yes. It was. I had to put a stop to... whatever we were doing. He had his usual appointment at ten thirty the next morning. It was silly to think he would cancel just because he'd seen me today. At least I hoped he wouldn't.

I drove straight home and immediately took a shower to wash off any traces of Cooper. I didn't want to think about how much of him had worked its way under my skin.

Trying to wash that away was futile.

JUST ANOTHER TUESDAY

I WOKE UP EARLIER THAN USUAL on Tuesday, well rested but restless just the same. I'd dreamt about being locked in the vault with Cooper, and the things we did there would have made Vicky blush.

I forced myself to focus on the day ahead. I even forced myself to not think *his* name. I tried to dress casually, but I found myself tossing outfit after outfit onto my bed, completely dissatisfied with every article of clothing I owned. I settled on a long black cashmere sweater dress—something I'd bought quite a while ago but never worn—so I could wear my new boots with it. I knew wearing the scary heels again was dangerous, but I was living dangerously lately.

Even after taking the time to dry and style my impossible hair, I got to work early and closed myself in my office again. Silvia was back to normal. She didn't hover outside my door, as though she was satisfied I'd gone to lunch with *him* yesterday. She also seemed to approve of my outfit, which was somewhat unsettling given her propensity toward the unconventional. After all, she was the one who thought I looked hot dressed like Julia Roberts in the opening scenes of *Pretty Woman*.

I wandered out of my office at nine to send a fax. I caught the tail end of a conversation between June and Phil that managed to perk my mood right up.

"Phil, you're only one step away from being a full-blown asshole." She shook her finger inches from his nose.

I had never heard June so angry. I'd always thought she let people push her around too much. She'd obviously been holding back.

"Are you sure it's a whole step?" Silvia piped up as she rounded the corner. "I would have said he's closer to a half-step away."

I didn't think Silvia knew what he'd done either, but it didn't matter. It was apparently Pick-on-Phil day. That was perfectly fine with me, since yesterday's tension had apparently been lifted. As soon as June turned her back, Phil put his finger to his temple like a gun and squeezed his thumb like the trigger, jerking his head back and rolling his eyes dramatically.

"Katie, you look extra nice today. Is that a new dress?" June asked. "Are those the boots you got for your birthday?"

I laughed. "Yes to both. New dress, same boots. I don't know if I should have been so brave. I may need a ride to the emergency room if I wear these all day."

"Hey, Katie," Vicky purred as she joined the congregation surrounding the fax machine. "Your hair looks good. You must have gotten up really early today. I wonder why?" She winked and flipped her hair over her shoulder. "Wanna see my new piercing? I showed everyone else yesterday while you were at lunch."

"You showed everyone?" I darted a glance at Phil, who shook his head vigorously. I smirked at her. "I was certain it was someplace a little too private for public viewing."

"It is. Trust me. You don't want to see," Silvia assured me as she jumped up from her chair and went back out to the lobby.

Vicky didn't even have the decency to blush. "It's okay, Katie. You don't have to look. We all know you're a little on the shy side. It's not a crime." She flashed a friendly smile in my direction, and I was instantly suspicious.

I had no idea when we had become frenemies. We'd never been close or anything, but we'd never been adversaries, either. "It's just a little too much information for me, Vic." I flashed my teeth in a wicked grin. "There's not much uncharted territory left for you now, is there?"

"As a matter of fact..." she started.

I rolled my eyes. "There's nothing left that you could do or say that could gross me out any more than what I've already heard."

"I'm having my anus bleached," she deadpanned.

"That's my cue," Phil said and nearly ran out of the back.

"You're kidding, right?" I almost laughed, but her expression was so serious. "Anal bleaching? Where do you come up with this stuff?"

"I'm not joking. My husband found something on the internet about it, and I thought he might like that, so I'm having it done to surprise him. What man wouldn't want their wife's anus to be fresh and new?"

"Fresh and new?" I was completely flabbergasted. I didn't know whether to laugh or shudder with revulsion. I wondered what kind of internet search her husband had been doing when he ran across that bit of information.

Silvia walked back into the room and looked between my face and Vicky's. "Let me guess. She told you about having her asshole bleached? Why anyone would spend good money on something like that, I'll never know. If I'm going to fork out that much money to make something look new and fresh, it's going to be something people get to see a little more often. And the vaginal rejuvenation brochures she *anonymously* left on my desk is not an option either." Silvia grabbed an incoming fax and zipped back to her office.

I didn't waste any more time. I sent my fax and went to my desk to prepare for my morning appointments. I was pulling up the daily rate sheets when Vicky slipped into my office and dropped into the chair across from me.

I raised an eyebrow and smiled. "Still trying to shock me?"

"No. I just wondered if you were sleeping with Cooper yet." She rocked back in the chair and put her feet up on my desk.

My mouth fell open. "Excuse me?"

"Oh, don't play coy. You heard me. Are you sleeping with Cooper?"

"First of all—and this is really the most important thing—that is absolutely none of your business. I'm offended you would even ask."

Vicky opened her mouth to speak, and I held up one finger. "That being said," I continued, "I don't think you're capable of leaving it at that, so I will tell you no, I haven't slept with Cooper."

"You forgot the 'yet.' You haven't slept with Cooper *yet*."

"There is no *yet*. I'm his banker; he's my client. I don't think the bank would appreciate me crossing that line."

"Well, if you aren't going to cross it, I might. I just thought it would be fair to warn you first." Vicky stood and wrapped her hand around the door handle.

"You're married!"

She laughed. "I didn't say I want to marry him. I want to do the horizontal mambo with him." She swiveled her hips.

"Vicky, people don't actually say 'horizontal mambo' anymore. That's ridiculous." I was getting hysterical.

"They may not say it anymore, but believe me, Katie, they still *do* it."

"What... what about your husband?"

"My husband likes to watch." She tossed that out with a shrug and left, only to poke her head back in two seconds later.

"Oh, and one more thing..." she whispered just loud enough for me to hear. "I would ask him where he gets all that money you're investing for him, because the way I see it, it's not by conventional means... if you know what I mean."

"What are you talking about?" I snapped.

"Seriously, have you ever once heard him talk about a job?" She stared at me for a second, waiting for whatever weak comeback I might have attempted.

I had nothing.

"I didn't think so. At least Dean has a verifiable income." She left quite satisfied with herself, if her expression was any indication.

I spent the next couple of hours in a state of worry and panic. Worried about Vicky. Worried about Cooper. That was no way to live. I'd made it all the way to my birthday without a drop of anxiety. I could have been blissfully unaware of Cooper's skill at kissing if I'd just stayed home with a glass of wine and a book.

Knowing Cooper had an upcoming appointment, I was too nervous to function. By the time he finally showed up, I was utterly and completely uncomfortable in his presence—a predicament that in and of itself was new. I couldn't keep my mind from drifting back to our last kiss while he sat in front of me.

Cooper leaned back in the chair with his fingers entwined behind his head, making his white pullover tight across his hard chest. "You're staring at my lips again. Should I just come over there and kiss you or—" He turned and took a quick peek at the group of people outside my office pretending not to watch us. "—do you think it might cause a stir?"

I laughed, but it sounded sort of panicky. "I think it might cause more than *just* a stir. You seem to attract attention like a rock star."

Cooper rolled his shoulders back, angling his body to the opposite side of his chair. "That's ridiculous."

"What?" I asked, still trying to recover from his threat of coming over here and kissing me.

"The whole 'rock star' thing? I don't remember causing this much commotion in all the time I've been coming here."

"You haven't been paying close enough attention." I

glanced at the faces outside my office. "And now they see the potential for some action worthy of watching."

He unlaced his hands from behind his head. "What exactly do they think is going to happen in your office?" He tried to hold his lips in a straight line, but his lopsided grin threatened to shatter his serious face.

I leaned in to mirror his stance. "I think they're waiting for us to do it right here on my desk." My stomach fluttered at the mere mention of such a thing, and my boldness in saying it. I held my breath.

That undid his resolve and the grin was back—bigger than ever. "I'm game if you are."

After he left, I felt a little empty. I'd made a point of keeping the rest of the meeting professional, sitting up straight in my chair with my eyes glued to the computer screen. I spent the rest of the day retracing my steps over the past year. I tried to recall all the times I had been asked out. It was a short list—only two names. Not counting Cooper.

The first one didn't really count, or rather I didn't want it to count because it was so embarrassing. He was the bagger at the grocery store I shopped at. We flirted back and forth. He was cute; what could I say?

After several months of pushing my cart to the car, he leaned against my trunk and asked for my number. For some crazy reason, I gave it to him, probably either out of boredom or hormones. Whatever the cause, I was glad it hadn't gotten out to anyone at the bank. They would have absolutely loved hearing about how I almost ended up at the local high school prom.

High school boys looked older all the time. I had to switch grocery stores and change my cell phone number. Once, I dreamed I ended up on an online list of neighborhood predators and got pelted with tomatoes every time I left my townhouse. The saddest part was I really liked that grocery store.

The second date wasn't even worth mentioning. He was just a guy in my neighborhood. The only real importance my dating history had was that it was nonexistent. I toyed with changing my computer password to PaTh3T1c.

June popped her head into my office at two o'clock. She had the funniest expression on her face.

I laughed. "What?"

"He's back!" she exclaimed in a whisper.

I didn't need to ask who. I jumped out of my chair, caught the back before it tipped over, and ran to my office door just as Cooper came in through the main entrance. He had a very determined look on his face. Serious, yet smoldering. I darted back to my chair and fell into it. I put my hands on my desk, then changed my mind and pulled a sheaf of papers in front of me just as he walked through my door carrying the most wonderful scent of peppermint and spicy citrus with him.

DINNER?

"**S**ILVIA," I WHISPERED FROM THE doorway of my office the minute I was sure Cooper was gone. When she turned to look at me over her leopard-print reading glasses, I frantically waved her over.

She stood and came to my door. "What?"

"Cooper asked me to dinner," I choked out, gripping my long pearl necklace in one hand for support.

"Well, it's about damn time." She gave me that wicked little smile, making me think she knew something I didn't, and perched her perfectly manicured hands on her hips in triumph.

I looked down at my own hands as I mangled the long strand of pearls between my fingers, twisting and untwisting until the necklace creaked under the pressure. "I'm not going. I told him, as his banker, I really should maintain some level of professionalism." I was seriously getting tired of that word.

"Katherine Grace James! You did *not* say *no* to his dinner invitation?"

A chill cut through me at the way she said my full name. I'd never heard Silvia quite so upended. I was almost afraid to answer. "I didn't actually say *no*, but I didn't give him much to hope for, either. I just said it wouldn't be a good idea for us to get any further involved."

"Oh, Katie... you didn't. What did he say when you turned him down?"

"It was awful... the look on his face. He just nodded and walked out. I feel horrible."

Silvia glared at me. "You know damn well you've been pining for him for almost as long as he's been pining for you. It's been *ridiculously* difficult to watch without interfering."

Her revelation shocked me. I had no idea Cooper was pining for me. In fact, I found it pretty much impossible given the other choices he had.

"How could I possibly say yes? He's my client! You know the bank frowns on things like that. We're not just their bankers; we're accountants, priests... *babysitters*." I tried to sound firm, but my voice came off weak. "And I seriously doubt Cooper has been pining for me. He's just like Dean or Mrs. Gilroy or your Mr. Hannigan. They *all* come in once a week for us to hold their hands through the process."

Silvia clicked her tongue. "Oh, for heaven's sake, do *not* compare Cooper with other clients. He doesn't come see you twice a week because he's worried about his money. And don't you dare blame the bank for your fear of relationships."

That was precisely why I had refused his invitation to dinner. Fear.

"I'm serious, Katie. I'm going to kick your butt if you don't go." She took me by the elbow, steered me back to my desk, and gave me a little shove into my chair. "Dial." She pointed at the phone. "Get him on the phone and tell him to pick you up at five."

Yes, Mom. "What if he's already made other plans?"

"I seriously doubt he's made other plans in the less than ten minutes since he left here. Now dial." She tapped a pointed-toe pump against the low pile carpet.

I dialed Cooper's number from memory—a fact Silvia seemed to relish, given her smirk. I looked away from her to stare at the digital display on my phone, counting the seconds as I waited for him to answer.

"Hello?"

My breath caught in my throat. "Um... hi... Cooper?"

I felt like a complete idiot. Again. How often would he witness my graphic attempts to humiliate myself? "Yeah, hi... it's Katie James? From the bank?"

Silvia threw up her hands and shook her head.

"I don't know if the offer is still good, but I would very much like to have dinner with you tonight. That is... um... if you'd still like to... you know, have dinner with me." There. I did it. I managed to get all of the words out without dying of embarrassment. Of course, it could be a slow death.

"I'm glad you changed your mind."

"Me too." And amazingly I *was* glad. More than glad, I was relieved. I really hated that I'd upset him so badly. I wouldn't tell Silvia how happy I was. She would be impossible to live with if she knew how ecstatic her little matchmaking project had made me. "Can you pick me up at five? At the bank?"

So I'd swallowed my pride and pushed back my fears, and for the first time in I didn't even know how long, I had a real date. I wasn't counting the fact that I'd already slept in his bed, or that I had already tasted his lips and his peppermint breath... to the point I would always remember it with a stomach flip worthy of a rollercoaster.

Three hours stood between me and five o'clock. I managed to stay busy, which usually made the day go faster, but the time still dragged. By ten minutes to five, I was thankful for two things. One, I was wearing the cashmere dress. And two, everyone else had gone home early. Phil and I were the only ones left by five before five. And even though Phil was "just one step away from being an asshole"—or a half-step away if I were to believe Silvia—he was a welcome break from the watchful eyes of the others.

"Where is this joker?" Phil teased, but I knew he liked Cooper, and in a more rational way than the females in the office, myself included.

I looked at my watch: one minute past five. "Oh!" He was late. "I don't know. Should I call him?"

Phil rolled his eyes. "Even *I* don't count one minute as late. Wait until he's at least five minutes late to call."

I know Phil would hate it if I told him so, but I often thought of him as just one of the girls. He had his moments, but most of the time, he fit right in with the other women in the office.

"Ah... see?" He nodded toward the parking lot. "Here comes your knight in shining BMW as we speak."

I bolted for the door, elated and terrified at the same time. Cooper was already climbing out of the car as I reached the sidewalk.

He walked around to open the passenger door but then stopped. "You look nervous. Are you sure about changing your mind?"

You have no idea. "Of course I'm sure," I squeaked, a frisson of fear sinking in again.

He nodded then opened the car door. He stood there while I got in, then closed the door for me. After sliding into his seat, he pulled his seat-belt across his chest and clicked it into place.

A strange expression crossed his face, and I angled myself toward him so I could look into his eyes. "Is something wrong?"

He pursed his lips and pushed his hand into his hair. "Are you intentionally trying to keep me from knowing where you live?"

My mouth fell open. "Why would you think that?"

"You wanted me to pick you up from the bank. I've only ever picked you up from here, and when I drove you back on Saturday, you would only let me drive you back to the bar to get your car. I've never been to your house."

I caught my lip between my teeth. "My house is nothing special."

"Anywhere you sleep is some place special," he murmured.

The man was making a habit out of melting my insides. I leaned over and kissed him. I couldn't help myself. He was clearly caught by surprise, but he didn't stop me—more than that, he kissed me back. His seatbelt held him trapped in his seat, and it was all I could do to keep from climbing into his lap.

I ran my tongue over his lips and tasted the peppermint. "You always taste so good, like you've just brushed your teeth or something."

He laughed but didn't explain. "Will you *please* show me where you live?"

"Right *now*?" My heart began to race at the thought of him seeing my townhouse and the messy state it was in.

As if sensing my discomfort, he kissed the tip of my nose. "We don't have to go in. I just want to know where you live. And—" He paused to kiss my lips. "—you can drive your own car there so I can take you home tonight. Like a real date."

A real date. Was that all he wanted? It was kind of romantic in a way. I nodded and melted into his arms as he kissed me again. We sat in the bank parking lot kissing for a few more minutes before I remembered Phil was probably watching from the lobby. I was too happy to be embarrassed, but I broke off the kiss and slid back into my own seat. It had gotten dark while we sat, oblivious to anything but each other.

"Ready?"

I cleared my throat and nodded again. "Ready."

He got out and opened my door for me, then walked me to my car. I climbed behind the wheel of my Prius and pulled out of the bank parking lot with Cooper following. When we reached my townhouse, I parked and got back into his BMW.

I spent a few minutes describing the interior of my little home—as if it were actually clean. "I never got around to painting the walls, so they're all the same boring white they were when I moved in a year ago. The most interesting things about the whole place are the gleaming wood floors and the brick fireplace. Though I'm not sure if the fireplace works; I've never had a reason to use it."

He didn't seem at all bored as I went on about my stack of paperbacks and love of reading. He even sounded interested in my favorite authors, but I wasn't sure if he was just being polite.

"Okay, are you ready for the evening I have planned?" His smile threatened to split his face in two.

I couldn't imagine what he'd planned, but I was certain I was not even close to being ready for it. "I hope so."

The long cobblestone driveway, lined with dormant crepe myrtles dressed in white lights, hinted at what lay beyond. Cooper's house was sequestered behind a grove of old, twisted walnut trees. I wasn't sure what we were doing there, but when we pulled in, I realized it was the first time I could actually recall seeing the front of his house. It was magnificent... a European-style country manor in aged bricks and stone.

"Stay here," he said. Then he ducked down to quickly press his lips to mine in an all-too-quick kiss. "Don't move."

I felt as though I were returning to the scene of a crime. My only relief came from the fact that he didn't come around and open my door. *Maybe he forgot his wallet.* He disappeared through the heavy wooden front door and was gone for what seemed like an eternity but was really only a minute or two. When he came back out, he seemed nervous, as if he was holding back some sort of secret he wasn't sure I would like. He sauntered over to the car, opened my door, and offered his hand.

I automatically took it, but I was instantly terrified and fought to keep the hysteria from my voice. "Are we having dinner here?" I was prepared for a crowded restaurant, even an intimate one, but definitely somewhere with people. Not his house. Not completely alone. I wouldn't have the excuse of being drunk. I wouldn't have the gut-wrenching vomiting to save me from myself.

He froze. "Would you rather not eat here?"

I felt his anxiety. One word of rejection, and I would shatter him. I was sure of it. I forced a smile. "No, this is fine. I'm just surprised. I didn't know you could cook."

"I didn't cook. I hired a good caterer." He pulled me against him, wrapping his arm around my waist, and led me through the front door.

"Okay, now I don't want you to jump to any conclusions." He closed the door behind us. "No matter how it may seem on the surface, nothing about tonight is meant to be anything other than dinner. I don't want to scare you off, and I'm not trying to seduce you." He paused for an impossibly long moment. "Not that I wouldn't love to, but I'm perfectly capable of being a gentleman. I promise. I just wanted you all to myself tonight, with no prying eyes or people eavesdropping." He let his hand slide from my waist and down over my hip for a brief moment before drawing it back. "And your wonderful dress gave me the idea."

"My dress?" I squeaked, trying not to be afraid. I told myself to be brave, but he was leading me toward the stairs, and I knew what was up there.

"Mm-hmm."

Stomach flip. Big time. He had a nice moan.

"What about my dress gave you the idea?"

He kissed my cheek. "I'll tell you later."

Music played softly somewhere in the house—Chopin, one of my favorite nocturnes. I stole a quick glance at him. He was holding back a smile, but at the same time, his eyes searched mine as if he might be afraid of my reaction. As soon as we hit the upstairs landing, I smelled food aromas, only recognizing a few: fresh-baked bread and herbs, seafood and succulent fruits, fresh bacon—a wonderful blend I could almost taste. I relaxed a little, knowing there was actually a dinner planned. I wasn't even worried that the hallway wasn't lit. A glow came from the floor below, and a hint of moonlight shone through a window.

He let go of my waist and took my hand, towing me down the hall with childlike eagerness. I could feel the excitement pouring off him in waves. That bolstered my nerves, as well. He stopped at the closed door at the end of the hallway and turned to face me.

He placed his fingers under my chin and tipped my face up so he could look into my eyes. "This is just dinner." Then he kissed me lightly and turned back to the door, pushing it open.

Oh. My. God.

It was... was... "Beautiful."

"Do you really like it?" he asked, pushing his other hand into his hair.

"I have no words." I dropped his hand and stepped all the way into the room. I blinked back tears, pressing my hand against my lips to keep my mouth from falling open.

The cozy little sitting room that led to his bedroom had been transformed into something I could've only imagined in one of my books. He had moved the sofas—to where, I had no idea—and in their place, two chairs faced a round table draped in a floor-length white tablecloth and topped with fine china and a silver candelabra complete with flickering white tapers. The fireplace blazed with crackling logs, the smell of oak blending with the bacon, and a row of white votive candles burned in clear glass cups along the mantel. A rolling cart like the ones used in fine hotels was stacked with silver-covered dishes, and a bottle of wine chilled in a silver bucket.

White orchids covered every available surface. In little pots. In vases. The petals blanketed the table and the floor. Magical.

"This is right out of a book." I turned to face him and had to fight back the tears again as a scene from *Blood Everlasting* came to mind. "Did Silvia give you this idea?"

He flashed his lopsided grin. "No, this was all me."

"How did you do all this?"

He laughed. "It wasn't easy. After spending half the afternoon working up the nerve to ask you, I was devastated when you said no."

I knew it. I could tell the date had been important to him. "And you're sure Silvia didn't give you the idea?" I teased.

"Positive," he said with a bit of irritation.

"Well, that's good. I was going to say if Silvia had given you this idea, you would to have to do a little better than send her roses."

"Better than roses?"

"Diamonds at the very least." I looked up at him from under my eyelashes.

"Would it make you uncomfortable if I kissed you?" He glanced through the french doors at the bedroom beyond. "Being this close to the bed and all?" His voice was low and husky.

I hadn't thought of the bedroom in at least a whole minute. But amazingly, it didn't frighten me. I'd been completely transported to a place where fear did not exist. "No. It wouldn't make me uncomfortable."

He carefully took my face in his hands and stared into my eyes. I didn't know if I was breathing anymore; I couldn't tell. I was completely lost in his gaze. I could feel the electricity crackling between us as his lips got closer.

He hesitated for longer than I could stand, but I didn't want the sweet anticipation to end. So I kept myself still and closed my eyes, desperate for the moment when his hot lips would press against mine again. I had become addicted in such a short time. And yet I felt as though I had fallen for him a long time ago. We'd danced around our relationship for more than a year, playing at business when what we were really doing was simply delaying the inevitable.

When his lips finally touched mine, the sensation was so exquisite I moaned into his mouth. He responded by dragging my body harder against his and stroking my face. I could feel him trembling slightly, and it made me want him all the more. I almost wished for him to let go of his resolve and forget to be a gentleman for a little while, just long enough for me to be completely swept into the current.

I worked my hands into his hair, something I'd wanted to do since the first time I'd seen his disheveled look. A growl built deep in his chest as I tasted his lips, sliding my tongue over first his top and then his bottom lip, feeling the peppermint tingle everywhere I touched.

"Katie."

I felt rather than heard him whisper against my mouth, and the intimacy of my preferred name on his lips for the first time was enough to cause my knees to buckle. He held me tighter as he trailed kisses from my chin down my neck, causing the silky softness of the cashmere to caress my skin where he touched.

My head was swimming, and I gasped for air.

He groaned. "I love that reaction. You have no idea."

"Hmmm." I held tightly to him, worried if I let go, I would slip to the floor in a puddle.

"I suppose I should feed you if you don't have the strength to stand," he said playfully.

But I definitely heard the satisfaction in his voice. If he only knew what else was weak. If he hadn't stopped kissing me when he did, I would have steered him into the bedroom on my own. "I *am* very hungry."

THE FOOD OF LOVE

"BREATHTAKING. I'VE SAID IT BEFORE, but it bears mentioning again." He pushed a bit of my hair back away from my face, brushing my cheek with his fingertips.

My skin tingled where he touched, and I drew in a shaky breath.

"Sit," he ordered, giving me his best serious look and pointing to the dark walnut bistro chair beside me.

I did as I was told, curious to see what else he had in store for me.

"Close your eyes," he said.

I closed them and shivered with anticipation.

With his lips close to my ear, he whispered, "Okay, now open your mouth."

I bit my lip and paused for the briefest of moments before I obeyed. I felt his body heat as he leaned in closer, and I detected the faint aroma of fresh bacon. His fingers touched my lips, and the first thing I tasted was saltiness. I bit down on the morsel he placed on my tongue, and the flavor exploded in my mouth—bacon, a burst of fruit, and the tangy sweetness of cheese and crunch of roasted nuts.

I couldn't help it; I moaned. It was so good. More than the food, it was the experience. With my eyes closed, I was focusing with my other senses, and nothing I had done ever felt as intimate, as erotic.

I opened my eyes to see his face lit up in a wide smile. "What was that?" I asked once I'd swallowed.

"Did you like it?"

"Did you not hear me moan? I don't usually moan for food, so yes, I liked it." I licked the salt from my lips.

"Yeah." He chuckled. "I liked the moaning."

"So? What was that? And do you have any more?"

"That... was a halved fig wrapped in bacon, stuffed with goat cheese, and topped with slivered almonds. And yes, there's more." He reached behind him and pulled another fig from a tray and brought it to my lips.

I opened my mouth obediently and let him feed it to me. The butterflies in my stomach swarmed. I moaned again. I wasn't sure whether the goose bumps on my arms came from the exhilarating flavors or the electrifying current passing between us. "What's next?" I asked eagerly.

He flashed a crooked smile, eyeing the tray behind him. "Hmmm. What shall I choose next? Ah, yes..." He turned around, concealing his choice.

I closed my eyes again and opened my mouth without being asked. Something wet dripped onto my tongue before I registered the sweetness or the fragrance. It was fruity, but like nothing I'd ever tasted before. The juice was slippery and sticky at the same time, and as I bit down, it dripped down my chin. Before I could wipe it away, Cooper caught my hand in his. I opened my eyes in time to see him bend down and run his tongue across my chin. Then he pressed his lips against the same spot in a trail that led to my mouth and a breathtaking kiss.

He pulled me to my feet, his arms wrapping around me as he continued to ravage my mouth. I was devastated when he stopped. He flushed, clearly embarrassed. He had promised to be a gentleman, but I wasn't going to hold him to it.

He held the chair for me to sit again, and I did. The wine was placed in front of me next. The liquid was a pale gold color and terrified me more than anything else that night. I was not to be trusted with alcohol after Friday.

He must have seen the look on my face because he said, "Just a sip. You'll be fine."

I let him put the glass to my lips and carefully took a sip. It was nice and light and brought back the flavors from the sticky fruit.

"Are you ready for dinner?" he asked.

"Yes." I was ready for anything he wanted to give me.

Why did it have to be a Tuesday night? How was I supposed to stay up all night talking to Cooper if I had to get up and go to work in the morning? It was nearly eleven o'clock, and I wasn't remotely ready to go. Cooper didn't seem to want me to leave either, which thrilled me to no end. Time had flown since dinner.

We sat across from each other on the thick carpet at the foot of Cooper's bed, drinking the last of the wine from the same glass and talking about anything and everything.

"So you still haven't named the imaginary cat?" His lips twitched with a smile. "It's been over a year. Don't you think it's about time you did?"

I rolled my eyes. "Go ahead and laugh. I'm fully aware of how pathetic that sounds."

He tilted his head. "No, it's not pathetic at all. I've never been a cat person myself, but if I was going to get a cat, I might start out with an imaginary one first. Still, I think even an imaginary cat deserves a name. No wonder he doesn't come when you call."

"And what do you think I should name him?"

"Oh, I don't know. Something regal, I would think. Claude du Chat?"

I let out a giggle. "Claude? I don't think so. Maybe Henry?"

His eyebrows perked up. "Henry?"

"A character in a book I read. Henry, the Earl of Devonshire. It's a mouthful, I know."

"I like it, a lot... but how about Henry, the Earl of Catnip? More fitting for feline aristocracy, don't you think?"

"You're being way too nice. Or you're making fun of me. I can't quite tell."

"I'm not." He leaned in to steal a quick kiss. "I actually love your imagination."

"You may change your mind about that. My imagination can be a scary place." I laughed, reaching for the wine glass. "Enough about my *cat*... and my boring existence. I want to know what makes Cooper Maxwell tick."

"There's absolutely nothing *boring* about you." Cooper watched me intently as I took a sip from the glass and waited until I held it out for him. "But I *would* like to know why you work so hard to avoid your mother."

"Oh, you noticed that?"

"I've noticed you ignoring her calls almost every time I'm in your office. How many broken cell phone excuses are you up to now? Five? Six?"

"Six." I paused for a moment, carefully choosing my words. "She just makes me..."

"Makes you what?"

My laughter sounded hollow. "Makes me feel like I'm back in high school or something, except she keeps reminding me that I'm not getting any younger. As far as she's concerned, I'll never be smart enough, pretty enough... *thin* enough. For my birthday, she sent me a gift certificate for a local plastic surgeon, someone she met at one of my dad's medical conferences. Oh, and a list of suggested procedures I should have done. I'm thinking of having it framed as a reminder of how *not* to parent if I ever have children of my own. She never lets me forget all the ways I fall short. Unlike my sister, I'm a constant disappointment to her."

His eyebrows shot up. "You *obviously* don't see yourself the way I do. I've spent the better part of a year watching you across your desk as you managed my small fortune." He winked. "You're clearly smart enough to find your way around my muddled finances. In fact, your intelligence was one of the first things that drew me to you. And as far as *pretty* enough, or for heaven's sake, *thin* enough..." He nuzzled his nose against my ear. "If you had *any idea* what you do to me, just being this close to you, you wouldn't say such things."

I had to force myself not focus on his words, or *my* words would have been gibberish. Besides, when he looked at me like that, I felt I could tell him almost anything. "But you don't understand. My mother is everything I'm not. She's slender and elegant and stunningly beautiful... even at her age. She doesn't trip over air or struggle for the right words in a social setting or live vicariously through fictional characters."

"Well, I haven't met your mother, but I can tell you I find your clumsiness to be endearing. I *like* feeling as if you might need me to catch you when you fall. I look forward to listening to you stumble over your words for the right thing to say, because to me, that means what you're saying is honest and comes from right in here." He laid his hand over my heart. "And I can promise you, I am *not* a fictional character. One day, *very* soon, I'm going to show you how much I adore your body *exactly* the way it is." Cooper leaned in, capturing my lips with his, causing my panties to ignite.

"I think you're trying to distract me," I said, pulling in a few jagged breaths as I attempted to get my libido under control.

Cooper smirked. "You caught me. So tell me more about the nutty bunch you work with. Besides Vicky, who else should I be wary of?" He held my hand to his lips and kissed my palm gently.

"Well..." I tipped my face to the ceiling as I thought. "Silvia can be dangerous."

"Dangerous? How do you mean?"

I bit back a smile. "No one crosses Silvia. I'm serious. I might not have come tonight if she hadn't set me straight. I think *I* might owe her a dozen roses too."

He sighed. "Just a dozen? I was thinking at least two or three."

My eyes widened. "That many?"

He ducked in to press his lips against mine in a quick kiss. "You're definitely worth it."

The music ended, and he jumped up to start it again. I took our glass and downed the last swallow of wine.

"What would you like to listen to now? I think we've exhausted my supply of classical music, but I may have some old jazz if you're game."

I pulled myself off the floor and sat on the side of the bed. "When you say old jazz, do you mean Nina Simone? Because that would be nice." I leaned back until I was lying flat, staring up at the carved crown molding along the ceiling.

He laughed. "I think you have overestimated my feminine side."

"Oh." I giggled. "I'm glad you don't have too much of a feminine side. I sort of like that you're a man."

"I was hoping you'd noticed."

"Cooper?"

"Hmm?"

"Tell me why my dress gave you the idea for dinner?" I closed my eyes to listen to the music.

"When I saw you wearing it, I knew the fabric must feel wonderful against your skin. I wanted to do this—" He sat beside me and ran his hand from my waist to my thigh. "—the whole time I sat across from you. It reminded me of Friday night when you told me you thought my sheets would feel magnificent against bare skin." He pulled in a ragged breath and stood up, quickly putting a little distance between us. He slid back to the floor, crossing his legs in front of him. "I knew the most romantic place I could take you to dinner would be the same place I kissed you for the first time."

"I have no idea what to say," I whispered, lowering

myself to the floor so I could sit across from him. I took his hand and pressed it to my heart. "Can you feel how fast my heart is beating? Are you sure you're real?"

"I'm real," he replied, taking a deep breath.

"Sometimes I wonder." I sighed. "I've never met anyone like you before."

"I could say the same, you know. You are someone very special, Kate."

We were quiet for a minute. Then I shifted my weight so I was sitting closer to him. "Okay, it's your turn to tell me about your job. I don't know anything about what you do."

Cooper dropped his hand in his lap. "I just don't like talking about it," he muttered, his voice thick.

"Is it something bad?" I didn't know what made me ask that question, but his blank expression made my heart pick up its pace.

He hesitated, and his eyes tightened. "I'll tell you someday... soon."

I nodded absently. "Is there anything you *can* tell me?"

"I know how to milk a cow." He ducked his head and blushed crimson. "And I'm a closet video game nerd. I used to have the arcade high score playing Time Crisis."

"Time Crisis?"

"It's a shooting game. I have impeccable aim."

"Oh really?" I bit my lip. "You're good with a loaded weapon?"

"Yes. And now that I've shared some of my most embarrassing secrets, are you going to need me to knock off the competition with my first-rate shooting skills?"

"You mean Dean?" I teased.

He grimaced. "Right. Dean. I almost forgot."

"What about poor me?" I stared at my lap. "I have to watch all of those beautiful women drooling over you, and wonder why in the world you would want to be here with me when you have so many other choices."

Cooper gently cupped my chin and tipped up my face. "There's nowhere I'd rather be at this moment, Katie."

My breath caught in my throat when I heard him say "Katie." Cooper smiled as he dipped his head down to kiss me.

"Katie?" he whispered against my lips, and the butterflies in my stomach went crazy.

"Hmmm..."

"I can either take you home right this minute..." He paused to push my hair back behind my ear.

"Or?" I asked with a shiver.

"Or I don't think I'll be strong enough to take you home at all."

Breathe. In and out. It's easy. "I don't want to go," I whispered.

"I want you to stay, but I think I should take you home. When this happens... and it will—" Cooper tipped his head down and touched his forehead to mine. "—I want it to be perfect."

"Tonight *has* been perfect," I said.

"And there will be plenty of time for more perfect nights."

We just sat there like that, our breathing staggered, our hearts racing, until the music ended again. The room was too quiet then. Cooper stood first and pulled me to my feet. He wrapped his arms around me in a crushing hug. I could feel his lips in my hair, and I knew he was whispering something, but I couldn't hear the words over the pounding in my chest.

He groaned. "I think we'd better go."

I nodded halfheartedly. He was right, but it didn't make me happy. I wanted to stay and talk all night. But if we stayed like that much longer, we would stop talking, and if we stopped talking, we would start kissing. Kissing wasn't bad. I really liked kissing. I liked kissing Cooper more than I had ever liked kissing anyone else. But kissing was a prelude, not a finale, and in a totally technical sense, we were on our first date. Good girls didn't reach the finale on the first date.

Damn it! Sometimes being a good girl is really inconvenient.

"Are you ready?" he asked as he helped me to my feet.

The little voice in my head screamed *no,* but I said, "Yes."

Time moved too quickly after that. One minute, I was in his arms, standing beside his king-size bed, warring with my hormones and my heart. And in the next, he was pulling his car into my driveway. He held my hand across the center console on the drive home. I could feel his pulse racing along with mine. I kept running every moment of the evening through my head like a slow-motion movie. I stopped to rewind at all the kissing parts and the parts where he spoke my name.

Then he said, "We're here."

My heart sank. I had to say goodbye and let him go. I'd never dreaded a goodbye as much. The silly thing was I knew I would see him the next day. He had asked me to lunch. But lunch was so far away, and I wasn't ready for goodnight.

"Yep, we're here," I said.

He laughed lightly. "There aren't words to describe how I feel about tonight, but you're stalling."

Caught. "I know. So sue me."

He angled himself so he faced me in his seat. He brought my hand, still entwined with his, to his lips and slowly kissed the tips of each of my fingers. "It's almost midnight. You need sleep." He let go of my hand and opened his door.

I waited for him to come around and open my door. The chivalry was so simple and old-fashioned. I loved it.

He pulled my door open, and I let him guide me out of the car. I dug my keys from my purse, taking a few seconds longer than necessary. He took the keys and unlocked my front door, then slipped them back into my hand.

"Cooper..." I was finally *living* one of the books scattered around my bed, and it was so much better in real life.

"I know," he breathed against my hair.

I staggered in his arms.

He took my chin in his fingers and tilted my face up until he could press his lips against mine in the lightest of kisses. "Goodnight, Katie. Sleep well."

I HAVE ABSOLUTELY NOTHING TO WEAR

I WOKE UP WITH A JOLT and blinked out the sunshine while my head cleared. I had no idea what time it was. Or what day it was, for that matter. The last thing I remembered before falling asleep was replaying dinner in my head. The mere memory did something to my poor stomach. Not that I was really complaining. If that feeling could be bottled, I'd buy it.

I lightly touched my lips, certain they were still swollen from all of the kissing. Who was the girl that only days ago swore she was perfectly content with a fantasy guy trapped within the pages of a book? I didn't know her anymore. Rolling over, I buried my face in my pillow and let out a squeal worthy of a teenage girl. Real kisses were so much better. There were no words to describe how much better. Not even in the best book.

I reached toward the nightstand to dig for the clock. It was buried under the outfit I'd worn yesterday.

Seven forty-five. *Crap.*

I disentangled myself from my twisted blankets and jumped out of bed to survey my clothing situation. It was bad. All the clean clothes that had been on the bed were lying on the floor where I had shoved them last night, right along with my shoes, several dust bunnies, and who knew what other creepy crawlies might be hiding out in a pile of dark clothing on the floor.

Damn. Damn. Damn.

I was tempted to call in sick, but that would be worse. If I didn't show up, the assumption would be I had stayed with Cooper all night. And although I would have loved to have stayed with Cooper all night, if I was going to be accused of that, I would have much rather it were true.

I had to stop myself from imagining that scenario. No time to hyperventilate.

I ran to my closet in the unlikely hope I'd left some work-appropriate clothes hanging there. But I knew the answer before I reached the door. There was nothing left in the closet other than the scary outfit Silvia had bought me for my birthday. And even at my most desperate, I wouldn't wear *that* to work.

Reluctantly, I pulled open my emergency drawer and stared with acute remorse at what I would be forced to wear—my last-resort outfit, reserved exclusively for when I was bloated, on my period, or sick. Those three things usually occurred simultaneously.

My father had gotten the pantsuit for me for Christmas several years ago, and I couldn't bring myself to throw it away. If it had come from my mother, it would have donated to the nearest Goodwill, but I couldn't bear to part with a gift from my dad... even if he'd failed to consult with my fashionista mother before buying it. But I also couldn't force myself to wear it except in an emergency.

I halfheartedly gathered the dreadful outfit in my arms and sprinted into the bathroom. After most likely setting a new record for showering, even though I shaved my legs—I wasn't leaving anything to chance—I pulled on the wretched black and white paisley, elastic band trousers and the equally hideous, matching beaded sweater. When I looked in the mirror, it was worse than I expected. After last night, I'd been certain the pathetic girl who lived in her books had been replaced by a breathtaking, sophisticated woman.

I was wrong. The woman staring back at me looked absolutely nothing like the woman who had worn the cashmere dress.

I was wearing curtains! I wanted to cry, but I was too frantic to take the time.

I pulled on my dangerous boots for the second day in a row, hoping the four-inch heels would somehow distract from everything north of them. It wasn't likely. I wondered if I had time to stop at the mall on the way to work. *Right. I don't even have time to stop at Starbucks for coffee.*

My cell started ringing, but I had no clue where it was. I ran to the bedroom, dug through the blankets on my bed, then kicked through the clothes on the floor, finally finding the phone in a shoe near the nightstand.

Out of breath, I flipped it open after the fifth ring. "Hello?"

"Did you sleep well?"

"Cooper! Actually, I had a hard time falling asleep, and then I didn't wake up on time." I tried to laugh, but even to my own ears, it sounded a little hysterical.

"I thought I might drive you in today... if you'd like. That way, I have an excuse to see you after work too." He sounded hopeful.

I swallowed a string of obscenities. I had obviously done something very bad in a past life. On the one day I looked worse than the before picture on an episode of *What Not to Wear*, the man of my dreams wanted to pick me up and drive me to work. Life just wasn't fair.

"Cooper, that sounds wonderful, but I think I should drive myself today. You know they'll all assume I didn't go home last night if you drive me." *And I'll die if you see me dressed like this.*

"Oh. I hadn't thought of that. You're probably right. Well, can I at least get a quick kiss before I go?"

Huh? "What do you mean?"

"I'm in your driveway. I wanted to surprise you."

Oh. My. God. "Oh!" I couldn't hide the shock in my

voice. I didn't even try. I knew it would be futile. "I'd love that, but I'm not dressed yet." I looked down at my ugly outfit and grimaced. The relationship was bordering on obsessive if I was even *considering* kissing him while wearing this outfit.

"That's okay with me," he teased.

My stomach jumped. "I'll be right down." I snapped my phone shut, yanked the sweater over my head, pulled off the dangerous boots, then slipped out of the elastic pants and tossed them onto the bed with the sweater. I caught my reflection in the mirror and laughed. Even my daisy underwear was embarrassing.

I shook my damp hair until it looked as though I'd just rolled out of bed and grabbed the only clean towel I had. *Come on, Katie. You're a strong—*gulp*—confident woman. If Bridget Jones can kiss Mark Darcy in the* snow *in her* underwear*, you can kiss Cooper in a towel.* I realized that part of me really wanted to take a chance and see the light in his eyes when he saw me there with only a thin layer of non-Egyptian cotton covering me.

Wrapping the towel around me and hoping it covered enough, I scurried down the stairs to the front door. I cracked it open, squinting at him in the bright sunshine.

Cooper's mouth fell open, and his eyes roamed over my body before settling on my face. "You weren't kidding, were you?"

I was lying... not kidding. *That's not the same thing. But who's keeping track?* "I'm running really late." I really, really wanted to ride to work with him, but unless I wore the damn towel all day, that wasn't going to happen.

"Can I come in? I don't want you coming out dressed, or rather, undressed like that." He spoke carefully, as if unsure of what I might say.

I quickly stepped behind the door and opened it wider so he could squeeze through. He looked phenomenal, as usual, wearing jeans and a black turtleneck sweater under his leather coat. I would have bet he never threw all of *his* clothes on the floor in frustration.

"I shouldn't have kept you out so late last night." He cupped my cheek in his palm. "You look tired."

"I'm not too tired." *Another lie.* If I hadn't been pumped full of adrenaline at that moment, I would've probably dropped to the floor.

"Well, I won't keep you out so late on a work night again. It's an eleven o'clock bedtime for you." Cooper dipped his head down, and his lips smashed against mine in a very hot, but too brief kiss. "You'd better go get dressed before I decide I'm not going to let you."

My insides melted, and he kissed my open lips once more before slipping out the door and shutting it behind him. He even made sure to turn the lock on his way out. I wouldn't have thought to do that. I was still frozen in place, mouth open like a fish, staring at the closed door. I gave my head a quick shake as I heard his car rumble to life.

"Peppermint." I sighed, touching my fingertips to my lips.

I had officially crossed the line into desperate measures. I gave one last cursory look at my reflection in the window before twisting my key in the lock and letting myself into the bank.

After my dangerous run-in with Cooper that morning, I was too afraid to wear the hideous emergency outfit for fear he might decide to surprise me at the bank for another stolen kiss. Instead, I sank to a level only Vicky had ever reached and wore the inappropriate leather skirt and the dangerous boots, but not the horrible see-through blouse. Luckily, I'd found a white button-down shirt hanging in the laundry room. Topped with a menswear vest, the outfit was almost acceptable.

I hurried into my office before anyone could take more than a passing notice of me, or at least, I thought I did. I was apparently not fast enough to avoid detection.

"Hey, James? Is that you? Muy caliente," Phil called out approvingly before I could close my door.

Great. *Now* Phil was officially behaving like a man. He would choose the wrong day to decide he wasn't one of the girls.

"Thanks, Phil," I shot back, pushing my door shut as if that would keep anyone out.

It didn't.

The rest of my "fans" soon discovered I was there, and before long, they queued up outside my office like groupies at a pop concert. I figured I should just get it over with, so I took a deep breath and opened the door to take questions... like Lady Gaga facing the paparazzi.

Silvia was first, of course—no one would dare challenge her place in the pecking order. She slipped her little reader glasses down her nose and peered over them. "How was dinner?" She kept it simple on the surface, but I spoke Silvia. She was really asking, *Did you see him naked?*

I crossed my arms over my chest. "It was nice. We had something with lobster in it. French, I think." *Keep it simple.*

"That *is* nice," Silvia said with a forced smile. But she obviously didn't think it was nice at all. She was trying to read between the lines.

"Did you see him naked?" Vicky blurted.

I didn't speak Vicky, but it wasn't hard to decipher. *Did you have sex with him?*

I probably shouldn't have been surprised, but her question caught me off guard. I snorted out a laugh. "No! It was just dinner." *Cooper's words from last night.*

"Did he kiss you?" June asked.

"Once. It was very sweet." He had kissed me sweetly at least once.

They all squealed, and I had to cover my ears. I felt as if I were back in high school as they shouted at me to spill the details.

"Start at the beginning and don't leave anything out," Silvia commanded, grabbing my elbow and dragging me out of my office.

"Is his body as hot up close as it is from a distance?" Vicky asked.

"Is he a good kisser?" June questioned.

"Um, I hate to disrupt the important, work-related interrogation going on over here, but it's time to open, and someone just pulled up with a delivery." Phil pointed at the FTD delivery truck parked in front of the building.

My heart sputtered to a halt for a few seconds until I saw the driver carrying the first of what I knew would be several dozen red roses. I started to laugh. They all looked at me like I was crazy, but they had no idea.

Those flowers weren't for me.

A ROSE BY ANY OTHER NAME WOULD STILL BE AS FUNNY

Cooper sat across from me with his feet up on my desk. His fingers were laced behind his head, and he was tilted so far back in the chair I was afraid he would tip over and fall to the floor.

I could tell from his expression he was thrilled with himself. And it was funny to watch him struggle, torn between the devilish grin he wore and the pure sexual longing I had almost gotten used to in the past few days.

He'd arrived not fifteen minutes after the roses. My suspicions about his surprise visit had been dead on.

"Have I told you how sexy you are today?" The hungry look was back.

I rolled my eyes. "Three times."

"Not often enough," he murmured, staring a hole in me.

I had to restart my heart again. I was very glad no one else could see the way he was looking at me. Silvia was too busy admiring her roses and gloating that she was the only one who got flowers to even notice Cooper at all.

She *had* spent several minutes thanking him when he first arrived. His premonition of needing to be protected from Silvia wasn't that far off the mark. She fawned all over him. I wasn't worried about her, though. And her attention guaranteed Vicky wouldn't have an opportunity to get close to him.

Cooper righted himself in the chair and leaned toward

me. "Tell me again what happened when the delivery guy said the flowers were for her." He smiled the megawatt smile that made me breathless.

His mood was contagious. I found myself having as much fun as he was. "Well..." I started. He had already heard the story once, but I had a hard time getting through it without laughing. "Okay, at first, she just popped up her eyebrows and stared at the guy. For, like, at least two whole silent minutes, she just stared at him with this shocked look. And then she asked him, 'Who are these flowers for?'" I covered my mouth to stifle another round of giggles.

"He said her name three times—" I held up three fingers. "—before she acknowledged him. Then she said..." I paused to jam my hands on my hips in my best Silvia impression. "'You have got to be shitting me.'"

His grin widened. "And the driver said?"

"The driver said, 'Lady, I can I assure you that I shit you not. Now, do you want your damn flowers or what?'"

He roared with laughter. It was, for lack of a better word, the *cutest* thing I had ever heard. It was easy to forget he was a grown man when he laughed like that. Yet the sound did things to my body that reminded me how much of a grown man he was.

He took my hand and played with my fingers. "I wish I'd gotten here sooner."

"No, I think your timing was perfect. I'll need to be very careful around you. You have a sneaky streak in you, Mr. Maxwell."

"It's all in the name of love, Miss James."

I froze, and for an instant, my heart stopped. He said *love*. I told myself I was being silly. He didn't say he loved *me*; he just said the word. But my heart was having a hard time maintaining its rhythm, and my ears were ringing. Or was that my phone?

"Did I scare you?"

I tried to act nonchalant. "No."

"Katie, you have to know I've been in love with you for months."

Breathe, Katie. Breathe. I wasn't sure what hit me the hardest, my name, like a caress on his lips or... I couldn't even think it. I couldn't think at all with the ringing in my ears. I reached over to my desk phone to silence it and automatically picked up the receiver with a shaky hand. I heard a muffled, "Hello?" but I was much more concerned with Cooper as he stood up to walk around the desk.

He frowned and leaned over me to tuck a piece of my hair behind my ear. "Surely none of your other clients spend as much time in your office asking stupid questions and stumbling around with balancing their checkbooks. At least, I hope none of them do."

I heard the voice on the phone say, "Hello?" again, and I absently put the receiver to my ear. "Hello?" I said, gazing into Cooper's uneasy eyes.

"Ah, there's my best girl. I've been calling you all morning. I need help with something."

"I'm sorry," I said. "Who is this?"

"It's Dean," he boomed over the line. "Isn't this Katie, my best girl?"

Cooper grimaced. "*His* girl?" he mouthed.

My eyebrows furrowed together as I shook my head. "Oh, hi, Dean. I have someone in my office right now. Can I call you back?" I smiled at Cooper, who wrinkled his nose as if he'd smelled something bad.

"Who could possibly be more important than me?" Dean asked.

I ignored his question, but Cooper clearly heard it and reached for the phone in my hand.

I moved it out of his reach and said, "I'm right in the middle of something. Can you give me thirty minutes?"

"I'll just come down there," Dean replied.

"No! I mean... don't come here. I'll call you back in

thirty—" Cooper pulled the phone from my ear, and I had to shout to be heard. "Make that forty-five!"

Cooper replaced the receiver and raised an eyebrow at me.

"I didn't think you'd noticed me," I muttered.

He shook his head with a look of utter exasperation and pushed his hand through his hair until it stuck up. "How could you think I didn't notice you? I couldn't sit still when you were around. And I found any excuse to see you."

My heart was flying in my chest again. His face was just a few inches from mine, and I was getting dizzy from the proximity.

"Oh." Speechless.

"Can I kiss you?" He put a hand on each arm of my chair and leaned down again, his eyes softening and turning hungry.

I knew he wasn't asking permission to kiss me; he had kissed me enough times to know he didn't need permission. He was asking if it was okay to kiss me *here.*

He saw my hesitation and pulled back slightly, a strained smile on his lips. "Not here."

"Not here," I mouthed, shaking my head.

"Not a problem." He stood up straight and held out his hand.

I took it hesitantly and let him lead me out of the office.

Once we were in the lobby, he spoke loud enough so anyone nearby could hear. "Katie, I think I may need a new safe deposit box. Would you mind if I compare a few different sizes?" He kept his face smooth, but I recognized the quiver of his smile threatening to destroy the illusion.

"Sure, Cooper," I said, trying to play along. I wasn't sure anyone was convinced, but I wasn't about to argue with him. "Hang on. I'll be right back."

I went to my office and got my keys for the vault. I jingled them for everyone to see as I crossed the lobby, and he bit back a smile. We walked together to the door, and I twisted the key in the lock. He held the door open for me. Once on the other side, I let loose a nervous laugh. For just a moment my thoughts flashed to the dream I'd had about Cooper in the vault, and I felt that familiar jolt of electricity surge through me. If he only knew...

He put his arm around my waist, checking behind him as he hurried me through the thick walled opening of the secure vault. The area was out of view from the lobby, and no one could walk in without unlocking the door. We would hear anyone before they saw us.

Once we were alone, he gently pushed me against the metal wall and put a hand on either side of my shoulders, caging me in. "Can I kiss you now?"

"If you don't, my heart may stop beating," I whispered.

"Well..." He kissed my forehead. "I have a vested interest in your heart beating, so—" A kiss on my nose. "—I guess I know what I have to do." He nuzzled my neck, nibbling and kissing his way across my chin, sending goose bumps up and down my arms.

"I'm going to pass out. I'm not kidding." I panted for air.

He shook lightly with laughter but didn't stop his slow attack. "I'll revive you," he whispered against my lips, teasing them with his tongue.

I let my head fall back, and it hit the metal wall with a dull thud. "Ouch," I said with a giggle.

He stopped teasing my mouth and looked at me with wide eyes. "Are you okay?"

"Mmm-hmm," I purred.

He shuddered against me. I liked that I could make his body react in the same way he made mine go crazy. He went back to causing shivers of electricity to shoot through me, making my limbs turn to jelly. He kissed his way from my chin down my neck and back up again, finally finding his way to my mouth.

"You're *my* girl," he practically growled, molding his

lips with mine and sending his peppermint breath into my lungs. He pressed the length of his tall frame against me, trapping me between the hard metal wall and his muscular body. If it weren't for the pressure on both sides of me, I would have collapsed to the floor.

He murmured my name between kisses, having clearly discovered the power it had over me. I was sure I didn't disappoint. Every time I felt my name on his lips, I shuddered. And each time I shuddered, he trembled. The power I had over him quickly became obvious. It was intoxicating.

I had no idea how long we stood in the vault getting drunk off each other, but I thought people would start getting suspicious. "Cooper..."

"Katie," he teased, reveling in the way my traitorous body reacted to my name on his lips.

I rested my hands on his chest as I struggled to catch my breath, ready to shove him away if he didn't cooperate. *Oh my God.* "The cameras!"

"Mmm," he murmured, obviously unconcerned, then slid his hands under my shirt, bringing them halfway up my bare back.

"I'll get fired."

He paused as if thinking it through—then went back to his silent assault. "I'll find you another job," he whispered.

"Okay," I relented, twining my arms around his neck.

We both flinched at the sound of someone putting a key in the lock and jumped apart, quickly smoothing our hair and clothes like a pair of guilty teenagers. Phil poked his head into the vault as I was pretending to point out a box size Cooper didn't already have. I flashed Phil an innocent look. I knew he wasn't buying the act, but he didn't say anything about our obvious make-out session.

"James, the natives are getting restless. No one is going to get anything done if you two are in the building. For some reason—that I can promise you I *will* get to the bottom of—you have no appointments scheduled for this afternoon, so why don't you get out of here for lunch? Call it a client meeting, but don't even think of expensing it." He turned to Cooper and nodded. "Nice job with the flowers. I wish I'd known that was all it took to shut Silvia up. I would have sent her roses a long time ago." Phil laughed, then turned and left.

Cooper drove me thirty miles away to his favorite restaurant, a place called Rustique. During the drive, he raved about the food as if it rivaled kissing. He didn't actually say that, and I wasn't going to offer the comparison—I couldn't imagine anything being better than Cooper's kisses—but the way he talked about it made me all tingly. Unlike French cuisine with its calorie-laden sauces, kissing was allowed on my diet.

When we finally got there, we were escorted through a quaint dining room with rough-hewn beamed ceilings and aged stone walls to a small, candle-lit table isolated in a dark back corner. The aromas of fresh bread, lavender, and rosemary were strong. I had never been there, but I instantly knew it was where last night's dinner had come from. I was right to get the tingles. Being there was like having Pavlov ring the dinner bell. And although the food didn't rival our kissing, it came very close. The conversation came close as well. I discovered wonderful new things about the man I was falling for.

"… so that's it in a nutshell. A few months ago, my parents chucked their highbrow lifestyle, took their names off the guest list for every upcoming society ball and cotillion, packed up the house in the city, and moved to Dorchester, in the English countryside, where they bought a dilapidated manor house and converted the grounds to an organic farm. They live like hippies, raising cows, sheep, and chickens. That's how I learned how to milk a cow, but trust me, it's not something I share with just anyone." He winked.

"I had no idea you're from London," I said, tearing a piece of bread from the loaf. "You never said... and you don't sound... I mean, you can't tell."

"I moved here when I was young," he explained. "But my parents speak with a very pronounced, very posh, English accent. I don't notice it. But I'm sure you would."

"So you're not an American citizen?" Not that it mattered, but I was curious.

He chuckled. "Yes. I am. I'm actually both. Although I hardly ever go back to England, I have dual citizenship. My parents moved back after I graduated from college, but I never had any desire to leave America. I'm very glad I stayed." He said the last part without inflection, but I hoped I was part of the reason he was happy with his decision.

"How often do you see your parents? I don't believe you've ever mentioned them."

"I used to visit them several times a year, but lately I only go back for Christmas. I hate making the trip. They come here frequently, though. I adore them, of course, but they're very... um... *private* people, and I suppose I've fallen into the habit of respecting that by not talking about them." He picked up my hand and played with my fingers. "That's just how it's always been."

I knew we were abusing the liberty Phil had given me, but I couldn't find it in myself to worry. Better Phil's wrath than Silvia's, anyhow. Besides, when it came to accounts, Cooper's was the biggest one we had. Phil could afford to give me a little latitude. If only I could have stopped thinking about the very unsexy underwear I was wearing and how the law of averages said I would need something better in a hurry.

My thirty-minute lunch had stretched out over two hours by the time we got back to the bank. Cooper held the door for me as we entered the lobby, and we hadn't gotten even half-way across the small space when we both stopped dead in our tracks.

Phil was in my office, sitting in my chair. Cooper stood behind me, and I turned to look at him. He wore the same confused look on his face as I imagined I did. The entire wordless conversation lasted less than fifteen seconds. Then I heard a familiar sound—the melodic timbre of a deep tenor singing—and everything fell into place.

Dean. Apparently, because I wasn't in my office when he arrived, Phil was dealing with him. I was certain Dean would never be satisfied with that arrangement. I would be expected to take over. That would be both good and bad. Good—because Dean was actually pretty fun to be around. And bad—because I was pretty sure Cooper had already formed an opinion about him, and it wasn't a good one. Not that I could blame him.

Phil looked up and saw me. He hurried out of my office to meet me in the lobby. "Well, hello. You do still work here, don't you? Did you forget Dean was coming in to see you?"

My eyes darted from Phil to my office, where Dean was rocking back in the chair across from mine. "He wasn't supposed to come in. I told him I'd call him back... oh." I groaned. "I forgot to call him back. I guess you want *me* to talk to him."

Phil smirked. "Ya think?"

I was torn. Cooper still had a tight grip on my elbow, like a jealous boyfriend, but Phil was staring me down like... well, like my boss.

"I get this little thing between you two. I really do." Phil waved a finger between us. "But I sort of need you to do some actual work for at least *part* of the day."

I nodded, blowing out the breath I'd been holding.

Cooper slowly let go of my elbow. "Remind me again why getting you fired was a bad idea?" he whispered, planting a quick kiss on my temple.

I flashed him a smile. "Maybe you should try harder to convince me... next time."

Cooper winked. "I'll be back at the stroke of five." Then he turned and walked out the door.

Phil rolled his eyes.

I watched Cooper drive out of the parking lot before stalking off toward my office. "I'm going," I said over my shoulder.

"There's my best girl," Dean crooned as I dropped into my chair with a great big fake smile.

"Hi, Dean," I said in my cheery voice. "What brings you in today?"

"I was hoping I could ask you a few stupid questions while we stumble around balancing my checkbook."

My heart skipped as I recognized Cooper's words from earlier.

A wide smile split Dean's face. "Come on, Katie. That was funny."

"That was a private conversation," I muttered.

"You probably shouldn't have private conversations and take phone calls at the same time."

Touché. I folded my arms in front of me.

Dean leaned across the desk. "Oh, don't be mad. I'm only trying to look out for you."

"Look out for me?"

"I'd hate to see you lose your heart to a *scoundrel.*"

I laughed. "Cooper's hardly a scoundrel."

"We never really know someone as well as we think, do we?"

THE ELEVEN O'CLOCK BEDTIME

ILVIA CALLED MY NAME, AND I looked at the clock. *The stroke of five.* Cooper had arrived.

I hurried to the door, careful not to fall in my dangerous boots, and opened it for Cooper. Atlanta should not be so cold in January. I had moved there to escape the cold... and my mother. Too bad I hadn't actually been able to escape either.

"Wow," I said as he swept me into an embrace. "It's freezing out there."

"The weatherman said to expect flurries, but I'll keep you warm," he whispered, laying his forehead against mine. "We could start a fire," he added with a naughty grin, and I shivered, but not from the cold.

Silvia came around the corner, and he pulled his face away from mine.

"Are you taking your flowers home?" he asked her sweetly. He was probably messing with her stomach too.

She barked out a laugh. "No, I think I'll keep them here so everyone can enjoy them."

I looked sideways at Cooper. We both knew why she was leaving them—so everyone else would be reminded he sent them to *her*. And who could blame her? If Cooper had sent *me* flowers, I'd have left them for the world to see, too.

"Time to go," I said. "We don't want to be here when the snow hits." Roughly translated... *I have better things to do.*

"Well, get going then," Silvia snapped playfully.

I hoped she was still too caught up in her flowers to

go back to paying attention to every look Cooper gave me. That hungry look was back in his eyes, and he was towing me toward the door.

Cooper waited for Silvia to flip the lock before he opened the door. A blast of arctic air blew in, sending a new wave of shivers through me.

He frowned. "Where's your coat?"

I shrugged. "In Connecticut."

He quickly slipped out of his leather coat and held it out for me to slide my arms into the warm sleeves. He smiled then, satisfied, and opened the door again. Silvia rolled her eyes, and I bit back a smile of my own. Leaving her to lock the doors behind us, I got into Cooper's car, wrapping his coat around me and breathing in his cologne.

Cooper slid into the driver's seat and pulled on his seatbelt. We were both very aware that Silvia had not yet moved from her spot behind the glass door, which gave her direct view of where he'd parked. I was sure she was sitting there waiting to catch a glimpse of some action.

"Hungry?" He raised one eyebrow, and I knew he wasn't referring to food.

I suppressed a giggle. I was always ravenous around him. In fact, I was amazed we had been able to hold out so long in that department.

"Actually," I looked up at him from under my eyelashes, "I need to do something."

His eyes widened. "What?"

"I need to go to the mall."

Cooper waited outside the dressing room while I tried on another ensemble. He seemed to be amused, which was good. I definitely didn't want him to be bored. He took every opportunity to run his hands over the fabric of each outfit as I modeled them, and I suspected it was just an excuse to touch me. Not that I was complaining.

When I came out, he appeared to be staring at a rack of summer dresses a few yards away, but then I realized he was on the phone. I caught part of what was obviously a private conversation.

"No, I seriously don't care about that anymore. I just can't keep up this double life much longer. The illusion is getting thinner and thinner every day." His free hand pushed into his hair, gripping it in a clenched fist. "So help me God, if you screw this up for me, it won't be her I drain of every last drop of blood from. It'll be you. In fact, I'll kill you, dig you up, reanimate you, and then kill you again, just for the fun of it."

I gasped, and he spun around to face me, his mouth falling open as he did a double take.

His eyes roamed over my body before locking onto mine as he stalked toward me, disconnecting his call without saying goodbye. "Wow."

He tugged me into his arms and attacked my surprised lips with a mind-numbing, toe-curling kiss. Just as my lungs began to scream for oxygen, he released me and motioned for me to spin all the way around. I felt like a ballerina in a music box, twirling to music only we could hear.

"You have to get that. I didn't mind the other things you picked out, but this is... *hot*." He slid his hand across my shoulder, down my back, and up again, setting my skin on fire everywhere he touched.

His phone vibrated in his hand.

"Do you need to take that?" I asked.

He shook his head. "No, it's just my assistant. She drives me a little crazy sometimes, but nothing is as important as spending time with you."

With a deep breath, I processed his words. I'd overreacted. It was just his assistant. He wasn't *really* threatening to kill someone. That was ridiculous to even imagine. I mean, how many times had I plotted Vicky's demise?

He nodded toward my cleavage. "So will you wear that bra with this blouse?"

"Would that be bad?" I pulled my lip between my teeth. The lingerie I had picked out was a little... *delicate.* As in barely there.

"No," he growled. "That would be good."

The heat in his eyes made my knees a little weak. We seemed to be engaged in foreplay rather than shopping, which may have been why he'd agreed to come in the first place.

"Okay." I tried desperately to steady myself. "I'm ready to go when you are."

"Oh, Katie... I've been *ready.*" He leaned in and gave me a quick kiss. "Now go change before I do something in this department store that could get us both arrested."

We sat in my driveway with the motor running for almost an hour, just talking and watching the snow flurries blowing in the dark sky.

"Would you like to come in?" My voice trembled.

He turned in his seat and took my face in his hands. "Katie, you're shaking. What's wrong?"

"It's nothing," I lied.

"If you don't tell me, I'll assume it's because you don't want to be with me."

My eyes went wide. "No, it's not that. Definitely not that."

"Then what?"

I looked away. "It's silly."

"You're blushing." He leaned his forehead against mine and closed his eyes. "Please tell me."

I sighed. "I'm nervous."

He opened his eyes. "Nervous?"

I took a deep breath. "You say you want to be with me tonight, and I want that too. I even bought all that lingerie, but I had no idea how I was going to put it on without you noticing. And you said it was an eleven o'clock bedtime for me, but I have no idea if I'm going to bed by myself or if you're coming with me, and if you are, well, I don't actually look that good when I wake up in the morning, so I'll be mortified the next day, and what if I've forgotten how to...? Well, you know. It's been a really long time." The words flew from my lips in an incoherent blur.

He stroked my cheek. "Please don't worry about that, Katie. I have no doubt it will be... *earth-shattering* when you're ready. But when I said you had an eleven o'clock bedtime tonight, I really meant I was going to take you home in time for you to be in bed, quite alone, by eleven so you could get a good night's rest. I have absolutely no intention of starting something I would have to interrupt for sleep."

"But—"

He put a finger to my lips. "I want to be with you, more than anything. But when that finally happens, I don't want to have to stop just because you have work in the morning."

Before I knew what I was doing, I wound my arms around his neck and attacked him with a reckless kiss. He shuddered as my tongue touched his, and I moaned into his mouth. I pulled away, pressing my forehead against his with a nervous laugh.

Cooper took a lock of my hair and twirled it around his fingers. "Your hair looks pretty like this. I don't think I ever said so."

"Thank you." I reached up, sank my fingers into his hair, and gave it a good shake. "I like yours like *this*, too. It's very sexy."

"So..." he said, still teasing my hair with his fingers, "what were you thinking when I walked into the bar Friday night?"

That question took me completely by surprise. "What?"

"What were you thinking?" He didn't look at my face. Instead, he studied my hair, which I hoped was shining in the moonlight.

How was I supposed to answer that question? I knew the answer, of course, but could I tell him I nearly melted into a puddle up on that stage? "I was very... surprised." *Understatement of the year.*

He glanced at my face. "How so?" His voice sounded so innocent, but I had a feeling he'd been saving that line of questioning for a while.

"Well..." I had to think fast. "I just thought you looked really good." I was still holding back, and I was sure he knew.

He started playing with the hair at the base of my neck, which sent shivers down my spine. "Explain." He kept his voice even, but he sounded determined to get an answer.

I let out an exasperated sigh and launched into the best explanation I could come up with without sliding under my seat in embarrassment. "I was used to seeing you so buttoned up."

"Buttoned up?"

"Yes, buttoned up. So very appropriate to the point of being unapproachable, in a way. But Friday night, you walked in and looked relaxed in your own skin. Your hair wasn't perfectly combed, and your face wasn't perfectly shaved, and your clothes were a little rumpled." I was remembering that night as I described it, and I could feel my heart speed up. "There was something a little dangerous about the way you looked. Like I was going to be in trouble." And I was.

He smiled.

"What are you thinking right now?" I demanded.

"I was thinking your description could also apply to you that night." He flashed his lopsided grin. "Except for the part about not shaving. You were stunning, but not in the reserved way I was accustomed to seeing you. The clothes were... well, they were ridiculous." He laughed. "But the tentative way you carried yourself in them made *my* knees a little weak."

"You liked me thinking I might fall on my ass?"

Cooper let out a throaty laugh. "No. But I told you yesterday, I *like* catching you when you trip. I want to be with someone who needs me like I need them." He stopped to nuzzle his face into my hair. "I was already in love with you, of course, so it was quite a shock to me that I could fall for you harder than I already had."

"I always thought you were gorgeous. Shallow, I know." I coughed out a laugh. I wasn't ready to confess that I was secretly so infatuated with him I had completely given up men altogether for the sort that I could find strictly in paperback. Hell, I'd given up *living* to wall myself into my fortress of fiction. That made me sound pathetic, and I wasn't going to be that girl anymore. "But I didn't expect you to be so... *sexy*." I felt the heat move up my neck into my face. "I was hearing little voices all evening long urging me to kiss you."

"I'm not surprised you were hearing voices. You were pretty drunk."

We laughed. And then he kissed me. I wondered if I would ever really get used to him kissing me. I hoped it would always feel like new.

My cell phone rang. *If it's not one thing, it's my mother.* I didn't want to answer it, but I knew her. If I didn't, she would just keep calling. I had already used up my allotment of broken cell phone excuses for the year, so I gave Cooper an apologetic look and flipped open my phone.

"Hi, Mom."

"Katie, I'm almost surprised you answered. Did you get a new phone?"

"Yes." I hadn't had a new phone in over a year.

"You are *not* going to believe what happened to me at the spa this afternoon. I went to get my—"

I knew it would be a long, drawn out story of waxing gone wrong or other assorted fashion faux pas. "Are you okay?" I interrupted, interjecting as much concern into my voice as I could muster. The simple fact that she was telling me the story told me she was okay.

"Oh, I'm fine, but you have to hear this. It's quite frightening, really."

"Mom, I'd love to hear your story, but I'm on a date." I figured that little bit of information would stop her in her tracks. She would be delighted I was out with an actual man.

"Is that right?"

If I closed my eyes, I could see my mother's red lips pursed as she smoothed her platinum hair behind her ears. A dead giveaway to head for an exit.

"Yes, he's right here with me." I looked over at Cooper and rolled my eyes.

My mother paused for a long time. "You know, if you didn't want to hear my story, you could have just said so. You didn't need to lie to me. Did you actually think I was going to believe you were on a date? I mean, really!" And she hung up.

I burst out laughing.

Cooper tilted his head to look at me. "What?"

"She didn't believe me. She hung up." I knew I would have to call her back and explain. Apparently, she believed I was a lost cause even while she was trying to convince me to try. Wouldn't she be surprised when she realized I was telling the truth?

Cooper tapped his watch and made a face. As much as I hated to do it, I had to stop talking to him and go in. I didn't know enough yet. I wanted to hear more about his childhood, or his favorite ice cream, or anything. I wondered for just a moment if he *wanted* me to go so he could do something more exciting. I had no idea what he did when he wasn't with me, and that bothered me. I'm sure people would think I'd learned some of that over the past year he'd been my client, but those kinds of things just never seemed to come up.

He got out and retrieved my packages from the trunk before coming around to open my door. I handed him my keys as I had done the night before, and he took my hand and led me to the front door. When he unlocked and opened it, we stepped inside and stood in the shadows. He carefully laid my packages on the floor and backed me against the wall.

The desire with which he kissed me erased any shred of doubt as to how he felt about me. It was as if he thought he would never see me again, but we both knew he would. We had made definite plans for Friday night. I knew I wouldn't see him at work the next day, but that was probably necessary if I was going to be able to do my job with any degree of competency.

And yet, he seemed frantic at having to go a whole day without me—as if he always spent every day at my side. It was slightly irrational, but I felt the same way. In the back of my mind, I *knew* I had just traded one obsession for another, but at least I was living. For the first time in my adult life, I was allowing myself to exist outside of work... or fiction.

When it seemed he was certain he had thoroughly kissed me senseless, he stopped and—of all things—laughed. I couldn't help but laugh with him, though I had no idea what we were laughing at.

He stepped back. "I dare you to think about anything else for the rest of the night." And then he left.

He didn't play fair.

"So much for being competent at work tomorrow," I muttered.

THE MYSTERIOUS WIRE TRANSFER

THURSDAY MORNING, I WOKE UP with plenty of time to get ready. I even took the time to run through my torturous exercise routine, which I had neglected to do since Friday. After thoroughly battering my body with lunges, crunches, and curls, I showered slowly, savoring the feel of hot water running through my hair and over my skin.

I had shaved my legs the day before, but I shaved them again, making certain they were smooth all the way up. I remembered not to neglect the bikini area, because according to Vicky, no one ever should. I shaved under my arms too, for good measure. I wasn't taking any chances. Cooper could have changed his mind after that magnificent kiss and decided to show up at the bank. Surely, he would have thought about me the entire night too.

I dressed in new clothes, not the outfit Cooper liked so much, but another one he'd seemed to like almost as well. I wanted to save his favorite for Friday's date.

I still didn't have a coat, but I did have Cooper's. He'd forgotten to take it, and as I wrapped it around me, I was very glad. It still smelled of his spicy citrus cologne and even a little bit like peppermint. I ransacked the pockets, trying to find the source of the mysterious peppermint breath, but was disappointed when I came up empty.

I was never the first one to arrive in the mornings. I wasn't actually first that day either, but I was second, and that was almost as rare. When I let myself in, Phil stood in the middle of the lobby, staring at me as if I'd grown a tail.

I laughed at his shocked expression. "Good morning, Phil."

"What the hell happened to you?" he asked.

I had no idea what he meant. "Um... nothing?" I held up my hands in mock surrender.

"Uh, no, James, there is definitely something different about you." He was still staring, and it made me feel a little self-conscious.

I scurried to the restroom, where I stared at my reflection in the mirror for a full minute. I turned as far around as I could to look at my backside. I couldn't see anything out of the ordinary. In fact, I thought I looked pretty damn good.

I marched back into the lobby and stared Phil down, hands on my hips. "There is absolutely nothing wrong with the way I look," I said with more attitude than I had intended.

Phil just rolled his eyes. "I never said there was anything *wrong* with the way you look. I'm just a little amazed at how put together you are these days. This is the third day in a row you've put me at risk of saying something I shouldn't. Are you trying to get me fired for sexual harassment?"

I made a sour face, shaking off the image that brought with it. "Oh, ewww, Phil. I like you better when you're just one of the girls."

"What? Save the boozing for Friday nights. We're on the clock here."

I didn't stick around to explain why there was something very wrong with what he'd just said. I made a beeline to my office to wait for the others to arrive. I'd never been so anxious to see Vicky in all the time I'd worked there. After my recent shopping trip, and heaping dose of confidence, courtesy of Cooper, I felt as if I could finally give her a run for her money in the sexy department.

It didn't take me long to remember why I was never excited to see Vicky. She slipped into my office while I was reading emails and plopped down in the chair across from me. *Cooper's chair*, a little voice told me. I shook it off and focused on Vicky.

"What?" I asked when she didn't say anything.

"I'm trying to see if you look different." She pinched her eyebrows together and stared at me.

I glared back with total incomprehension. "Why would I look different?"

"Phil said you look different. But I don't see it. I figured I would be able to tell if you'd done Cooper yet, but you don't look any different to me. Maybe a little more fashionable." She gestured toward my new outfit. "Same vacant expression in your eyes, though. You definitely haven't had sex in a very long time." When she was satisfied she had figured me out, she got up and walked out the door.

Just to walk back in less than thirty seconds later. "You have kissed him, though. So it's only a matter of time. I may have to let you have him. He looks like a lovesick puppy around you, anyway." The disgust was evident in her tone.

"You know, Vicky, some of us prefer to build up the mystery a little before opening our legs. You should try it."

"Mystery, shmystery... you're simply a prude. But really, it's okay, Katie. I get it. It's your thing. And obviously Cooper likes that sort of *thing* if he keeps sniffing around. I'm over it."

Good. I wasn't going to share him regardless. It would be better if she just gave up and moved on. She could always have Dean. I laughed at the visual of Vicky and Dean making out in the vault.

Just before nine, I decided to venture out to see what everyone was up to. I was no longer current news. Phil had given me a slight resurgence after telling everyone I had somehow *changed* since yesterday. But Vicky reassured everyone I was as pathetic as always, just a bit more polished.

And as some sort of cosmic exclamation point to punctuate that sentiment, I managed to trip coming around the corner and nearly rammed my head into a wall. After that, no one paid me much attention. Everyone knew Cooper never came in on Thursdays.

I debated whether or not to call him. Just to say "Hi." Surely that was allowed? Wasn't it just yesterday he told me he was in love with me? Maybe I should have told him how I felt. No, not *maybe,* I *should* have told him, and I regretted not doing it.

Everyone sat around the giant news monitor in the lobby, watching something unfold. It was local, so I plopped down across from June and pretended to care. I wasn't really interested. I was too busy wondering what Cooper was doing and if he was thinking about me. I was still so very pathetic.

"Katie, did you see that?" June asked. "Someone killed a superior court judge downtown. They said it was some kind of mob hit. That's the second one in less than a week."

"Killers on the loose in Atlanta. Wooooo." Vicky waggled her fingers at June.

"I wonder who paid for *that.* I imagine it's very expensive to knock off a judge, even in Atlanta." Only Silvia would think of the financial aspects of murder.

"Speaking of money," Vicky interjected, "Katie, did you see the large deposit that went into Cooper's account today?"

My mouth fell open. "Why are you poking around in Cooper's accounts?" I was flabbergasted, but honestly not that surprised. This *is* Vicky we're talking about.

She shrugged. "I was just curious. Why didn't he come in today?"

I shook my head. "You know he never comes in on Thursdays."

"I just figured now that you two are an *item.*" She made quotation marks in the air.

"Why should that matter?" I said defensively as I stood

up, brushing imaginary lint from my pants. Why did that irritate me so much? He said he would be working. He must need to work sometimes.

"Does he normally deposit money without going through you?" She wouldn't let it go.

"Not normally," I muttered. It was strange he wouldn't have me do the deposit.

"How much do you think someone would pay to knock off a judge?" Silvia asked, changing the subject back to the news. I didn't think she was paying much attention to the separate conversation going on between Vicky and me.

"At least a hundred grand," Phil answered.

"Only a hundred grand? Cooper's deposit was *twice* that amount. Maybe now that you're dating, he'll want someone else to handle things for him." Vicky's bright blue eyes sparkled with enthusiasm. "It really was an awful lot of money. He might not want you knowing how much he has now that you're *involved*."

"I know everything I need to know about Cooper." When had I become such a prolific liar?

"You could have fooled me," she said, turning back to the TV.

I was desperate to know exactly how much money Cooper had deposited and why he was making deposits I didn't know about when I was his banker, but I felt inordinately guilty about checking. And I was definitely going to check. It was still my job, and I couldn't imagine him asking me to give his account to someone else.

The story on the news was rapidly getting under my skin, so I hurried into my office and closed the door behind me. I needed to hear his voice. I dialed before I was fully seated and waited impatiently while it rang. After several rings, someone picked up, but it wasn't Cooper. *Voicemail.*

I slammed the phone down without leaving a message and pulled up CNN on my computer. There were no new details about the mob killings in the city.

I was being silly. Did I really think Cooper was a hired assassin just because I couldn't reach him on his cell? Or because he'd received a huge deposit on the day of a murder? Or because he refused to tell me what he did for a living? Or because I heard him threatening to kill someone just *last night?*

What was the only thing he *would* say about his job? *I'm an international man of mystery... a contracted employee of a large organization.*

I pulled up his accounts on my screen and did a search for deposits. *Holy crap. Two hundred thousand dollars!* But why hadn't he gone through me? Because it was a wire transfer from a bank in New York, of course.

Somehow that didn't make me feel better. I tried to remember the last time he'd had funds wired into his account. I couldn't recall anything, so I did a quick search of his record to find the information. It took a little digging, but I discovered a transfer of almost the same amount six months ago.

Feeling a little ridiculous, I did a cross reference with CNN to see if any other high-profile murders had occurred in Atlanta around the same time. I found four. The dates weren't exact, but close. Could I ignore the coincidence?

I shook my head. *This is all because of that phone call I overheard last night. Who am I kidding? This is all because of that last kiss.* He'd left me with a desperate feeling that carried over to the next day. I was going to give him a piece of my mind... if he'd ever answer his phone. I was being paranoid. I needed to forget the whole crazy idea and get back to my job.

"Katie, did you hear what I said?" my three o'clock appointment asked, rapping her knuckles on the desk.

I sat across from Christine Craig, shaking myself back from wherever I'd been, and tried to give a crap about what she was telling me. "I'm sorry." I blinked at her a few times. "I was just trying to decide what would be best for your needs." All right, I lied. It was becoming painfully obvious my quality of work was slipping. I needed her account.

"Oh, okay," she said, apparently content with my explanation.

I managed to open a full package of accounts and pushed her out of my office just after four. I took a deep breath. It had been the longest day of my career. Cooper hadn't called.

I packed up my briefcase and logged off my computer, even though I knew I still had almost an hour before I could leave. I didn't really care. I had satisfied the one requirement Phil had given me for the day—opening a new account. And technically, I was doing pretty well, thanks to Cooper's mysterious wire. I was measured as much by my existing accounts growing their deposits as I was by bringing in new ones.

So Phil could kiss my ass. I was going home early. I had a headache.

Not really. But that would be my *official* statement. *Katie had a terrible headache and had to go home. Katie was going to do some laundry tonight and maybe even clean her house, and if she didn't hear from Cooper by dinner time, she might even buy a new book, or maybe... a cat.*

I rolled my eyes at my own absurdity. How likely was it I would do laundry?

"James, are you still here?" Phil asked as he passed my office.

I looked at the clock, expecting it to be inching toward four thirty, but it was just after five. I had no idea where the time had gone.

I jumped up, pulled on Cooper's jacket, and grabbed my bags. "Nope, Phil, I'm gone."

THE CABERNET FLU

FRIDAY MORNING, I WOKE UP feeling like crap. My formerly phony headache pounded behind my eyes, and I was cold. I would have thought it was karma, but I'd never actually *used* the headache excuse.

Through the window, I saw a sliver of daylight beginning to crest the horizon, but it hadn't managed to lighten the sky yet. I'd stayed up way too late, hoping Cooper would call. I knew I was being silly, but I didn't expect him to ignore me for the entire day. That was probably why I'd drunk a whole bottle of wine by myself, and if the taste in my mouth was any indication, I'd eaten that cat I didn't own.

Who does this? Katie James, that's who. I was clearly being ridiculous. I used to get along perfectly well without a man in my life, so why was I suddenly unable to make it through a single evening without a phone call? What did Cooper even see in me besides a pathetic girl with nothing better to do on a Thursday night than read romance novels and make up imaginary pets?

I rolled over to look at the clock upside down on the nightstand. If my eyes could be trusted, it was just before seven. With a hand pressed to each side of my head, I sat up. I had to make a decision: either get up and go to work or call in sick. I fell back against the pillows and stared out the window. The light was spreading upward, and a pale blue color took the place of the dark purple.

I had expected my mother to call me last night, too. I left

her four messages from work telling her I really did have a date the other night. I knew I would regret it later, but I wanted my mother to know I was actually happy, especially since I finally fit within her definition of happiness. But that was before I didn't hear from him all night.

I reached for my phone to call Phil and let him know I had the cabernet flu, but my cell wasn't on the nightstand. I fished under my pillows, but it wasn't there either. I rolled to the side of the bed and looked on the floor. No cell phone.

Crap! I had to actually get out of the bed.

It was cold... the kind of cold I thought only existed in Connecticut with my mother. I was horrified to admit, even to myself, that I'd hoped Cooper would show up at my door late last night in search of a goodnight kiss. I'd wanted to be dressed in something thoroughly unforgettable, so I'd fallen asleep in Cooper's coat and one of my new bra and panty sets. Well, I was certain *I* would never forget my stupidity, thinking he would care enough to come see me.

I pulled his jacket tightly around me and climbed out of bed in search of my missing cell phone. I tried to remember when I'd seen it last. I knew I had it when I came home. I thought so, anyway. I checked my purse, but it wasn't there.

Finally, I fished through the pockets of Cooper's coat. *Bingo!* I'd had it all along. I flipped it open to call Phil, and to my horror, I had twenty-four missed calls. I clicked on the call log and scrolled down to view the times. There were five missed calls from my mother.

The rest were from Cooper. My heart sank. He'd started calling me at five thirty and stopped just after one in the morning. I had gotten drunk alone for no reason. Not that there was *ever* a good reason for that, but there went my bad reason, too.

Now, I really feel sick.

I couldn't imagine why I hadn't heard the phone

ring, even if it was in the jacket pocket. *Leather isn't exactly soundproof.*

I flipped through the menus on my phone and shook my head as I discovered the problem. I had turned off my ringer and never turned it back on. I didn't remember turning it off. Maybe someone else did it as a prank. It was not a funny prank, if they did.

Damn. Damn. Damn. I was afraid to listen to my voicemail, so I just highlighted Cooper's number and hit Send.

He answered on the first ring. "Katie?" he said in a frantic tone.

"Hi," I replied in my familiar pathetic girl voice.

"I've been worried sick about you. Where have you been?"

I sighed. "It's a really long story," I said, feeling incredibly guilty for doubting him. "Basically, I forgot to turn my cell phone ringer back on, and I missed all of your calls. Plus five from my mother, but she suspects I don't know how to operate a cell phone anyway. And I drank an entire bottle of cabernet, thinking you didn't want to talk to me." The tears came, and I didn't even try to stop them.

"Of course I wanted to talk to you. I've been worried sick. I even came by your house a few times and rang the doorbell, but there was no answer."

"Really?" I didn't know how to feel about that. I was happy he wanted to see me so badly, but I was on the verge of tears knowing he had been ringing my stupid broken doorbell while I was lying in my bed, curled up in his coat, wearing sexy lingerie and drinking really bad wine.

"Really," he said gently. "Why didn't you answer the door?"

"My doorbell doesn't work." More tears spilled out.

"Katie, don't cry. We have lots of evenings ahead of us. Don't be upset about one missed opportunity."

"But I'm wearing lingerie." A sob shook me.

"I'm on my way over," he teased. At least, I thought he was teasing. "Are you going to work today?"

"I'm calling in sick," I said, reining in the tears. "I feel sort of horrible." I climbed back into my warm bed and placed the phone between my head and the pillow.

"Would you like it if I came over?"

"Uh huh." I didn't really care anymore if he noticed how pathetic I was. Being sophisticated and sexy all the time was hard work. Besides, before I drank all the wine and ate the damn cat, I'd cleaned my townhouse so I wouldn't be embarrassed about that. I even washed my sheets.

"Cooper, where are you?" I asked in my sexiest voice, although I was pretty certain I already knew. He was probably still in bed.

"I'm in the car, almost to your house."

"What?" I sat up too quickly and immediately regretted it. I held one hand to the side of my head.

"Didn't you say you wanted me to come over?" I could almost hear his lopsided grin.

"Yes, but I didn't think you were on the way." I jumped out of the bed and sprinted into the bathroom to find my toothbrush. I couldn't have cat breath when I was certain he would smell of peppermint, as usual.

"I'll be there in about three minutes. Come let me in." He hung up.

I squeezed a large blob of toothpaste onto my toothbrush and checked out my reflection as I brushed my teeth. Dark rings of mascara circled my eyes, and with the foam bubbling out of my mouth, I was a full-on rabid raccoon. Once I'd rinsed off the makeup, I didn't look half bad. My hair was tousled in a sort of sexy way, and I was wearing the sexiest underwear I owned. Thank God—and Vicky—I'd shaved yesterday.

I slipped out of his warm jacket and snatched the blanket off the bed to wrap it around me like a cape as I flew down the stairs. I opened the door, and there he was. "Hi."

"Hi back," he said in a sleepy voice.

I stepped behind the door as he came in then closed and locked it behind him.

He wrapped his arms all the way around me, pulling me into a tight embrace. He held me there for a long moment before releasing me. "I was so worried about you."

I winced. "I'm sorry."

He bent down and kissed me softly. "It's okay... now that I know you're safe."

"The only danger to me was myself, I'm afraid." I managed to laugh as I tugged the blanket further around me. "You look like you didn't sleep. Is that my fault?"

He shrugged.

"Maybe you should lie down." I bit my lip.

He seemed to notice the blanket wrapped around me for the first time and raised an eyebrow.

I smirked. "If you can handle it."

"I think I can *handle* it fine."

I only barely caught his double entendre. I led the way up the stairs to my room and sat down on the edge of the bed. "Have you noticed we don't do living rooms?"

He gave me a quizzical look.

"I've been to your house twice, and I've only seen the inside of your bedroom, and you come to my house, and we end up in the bedroom."

He laughed. "I hadn't noticed until you mentioned it. I guess we're good in the bedroom."

I arched an eyebrow. "That remains to be seen."

He sat beside me. "Is that a challenge?"

"I don't know." I blushed. "Phil!" I shouted.

He frowned. "That was... unexpected."

"Ewww." I laughed. "I need to call Phil to tell him I'm sick."

I reached behind me to grab my phone, and I rolled onto my stomach while I dialed. It took a few rings for him to pick up. "Hey, it's Katie. I'm not feeling well today. I think I might have the flu." I laughed nervously. *The cabernet flu.*

"I guess that put a damper on your romantic plans for last night. I'm sure Prince Charming was devastated."

I glanced over my shoulder at Cooper. "Not really. I didn't hear from him all evening."

"Well, color me shocked. Should I fill him in if he shows up here looking for you?"

"Sure, if he comes in, you can tell him I'm sick."

"Feel better, and tell Maxwell I said hi."

"Uh... thanks. I'll see you Monday. Bye." I snapped my phone shut and tucked it under my pillow. I giggled and rolled until I was on my side with my head propped up with one arm. "Phil said hi."

His eyes widened. "Does he know I'm here?"

"I can't really be sure, but it doesn't matter. I'm not going to work today. Besides, he won't care. I refuse to tell him this, but he's always been more than fair with me. It's a good thing, too. I was supposed to see Dean again today. Phil thinks he has a major crush on me," I added for good measure.

"I'm sure Dean isn't the only one." Cooper's eyes darkened, and his jaw tensed.

"Don't worry. It's pretty obvious my heart belongs to someone else." That was as close as I could get to saying what he wanted to hear. But it seemed enough because he got that hungry look in his eyes again.

"Is that so?" he asked.

When I nodded, he reached down to hook my wrist with one hand and pulled me upright again, barely brushing his lips against mine. "I almost forgot." He fished into his pocket. "I got this for you." He pulled out a gold bangle as wide as one of his fingers with a small silver bell-shaped charm dangling from the clasp.

"What's this?" I asked, taking it and trying to make out the swirly inscription across the top. "Hen... Henry, Earl of Catnip?" My eyes shot up to his. I was rendered speechless.

He swept a tendril of hair away from my face, tucking

it behind my ear. "Since your imaginary cat now has a name, I decided he also needed a collar to keep him safe. But since imaginary cats have no place to *wear* a collar, I figured you could wear it for him." A faint blush colored his cheeks.

"This is too much. I can't—"

"Please, I want you to have it." He coaxed the bracelet from my fingers, slid it over my wrist, and locked it into place with a smile. "Besides, it's already engraved, so unless someone else has a cat with the same name, we're kind of stuck with it."

"Cooper, it's beautiful. I... I don't know what to say." My eyes roamed over his face, pausing on his lips.

"You know I'm going to kiss you now, right?" he growled.

I almost gasped from the intensity of the stomach ripple that followed. "I had hoped." I managed a whisper, but my breathing wasn't even, and my heart had picked up speed.

"Katie, if I kiss you right now, I don't think I'll be able to stop at just kissing, especially with you wearing this." He tugged lightly on the blanket.

I knew he wasn't referring to my taste in bedding, but what I was wearing under it. And he hadn't even seen it yet. I let the blanket fall off my shoulder, exposing the top swell of one breast and the sheer lace encasing it.

He let out a moan and closed his eyes for a moment as if trying to gain control of himself. He whispered my name.

That undid me further, so I let the blanket fall all the way to my waist, giving him a view of the entire lace bra and its contents. I shivered and became intimately aware of what the cold was doing to my body and how he would react to that.

"Damn." He closed the space between us, crushing his lips against mine in a kiss that sucked the oxygen from my lungs in a violent rush.

I found myself gasping for breath as his tongue tangled with mine in the most sensual kiss I had ever experienced.

His hands slid down my arms, lightly grazing the sides of my breasts, as mine slid up his back. I felt his hands splayed out over my waist. My breath came out in little pants as I waited impatiently for him to explore further, but he managed to maintain some control even while I tangled my fingers into his hair, pulling his face harder against mine.

I nipped at his lips with my teeth, and he moaned into my mouth. I had no idea how he was holding on to that reserved control—I had already abandoned mine even before he touched me. I wanted him to lose control. So much. I snaked one hand between us to undo the buttons on his shirt.

He pulled my hand away. "Not so fast," he whispered against my lips.

It wasn't fair. I needed the feel of his skin against mine.

He slid his hand across my stomach and rested it against the swell of my breast. He continued to kiss me until I was half delirious. He sucked on my bottom lip, then released it to tangle his tongue with mine. I thought he was trying to kill me.

"Take me now, Cooper," I whispered in desperation.

He chuckled hoarsely. "I'm getting to that."

I couldn't help it. I found that funny and laughed. It was going to be a slow death. Well, if I was going to die, at least I was with him. A surge of emotion coursed through me, and I knew exactly what I had to do.

"Cooper?" I murmured.

"Hmm?"

"I love you."

To my horror, he stopped kissing me. He pulled away and stared into my eyes for a long minute. "What did you say?"

"I said... I love you." I sucked in a steadying breath and smiled. "I love you. I love you. I love you. I know we've only been a couple... *officially*, for a few days, but I do, I love you."

Those three little words seemed to shatter every bit of his control. With one yank, the buttons on his white shirt flew in every direction. He pulled it from his shoulders and tossed it to the floor. His mouth found mine again, and his skin was hot where it touched me. His hands explored up and down my body, only briefly pausing to slide the lace away and toss it aside.

I squirmed beneath him, unable to meet his eyes as I lay across my bed wearing absolutely nothing. He hovered above me in only his gray slacks.

"God..." His breath hitched. "You're beautiful."

I splayed my hands against his chest and slid them down to his flat stomach, feeling a shudder go through him as I fumbled to unbuckle his belt. Then my shaky fingers slipped under the waistband of his pants to unfasten the button.

His lips trailed from my collarbone down to my breasts and over my stomach. I was dizzy and close to tears.

I reached down and knotted my hands in his hair again, jerking his face up to mine. "I promise we can do this again later, I just need you... inside me... right now." It was so very true, self-evident really, that I surprised myself by feeling no embarrassment in saying it. So I said it again. "Take me, Cooper."

His lips turned up in a beautiful smile, and he kissed me as he slid his pants down his legs until I could feel the length of him pressing against me. He grabbed my leg to hitch it up against his hip and, with a deep growl, filled me completely.

His fingers curled around my shoulders, anchoring him to me. "My beautiful Katie, can you feel what you do to me? How crazy you make me?" he whispered as he made earthshattering love to me.

INQUIRING MINDS WANT TO KNOW

I F I HAD BEEN RELEGATED to old news on Thursday, by Monday, I was back to being the front page headline. Thanks to Vicky.

"Stop right there!" Vicky shouted from across the bank as soon as I stepped through the door.

I froze in place, but I wasn't sure why. I imagined some enormous spider dangling in my path and Vicky trying to prevent me from stepping into its web. There was no spider. No spider web. Only Vicky's web of suspicion.

She walked up to me and held her hands up for me to stay still while she circled slowly, checking me out from every angle. I expected her to say, "Nice outfit." But instead, she took my wrist in her hand. Was she checking my pulse?

"What's this?" Vicky yanked my wrist toward her face examining my bracelet. "Who's Henry? Cheating on Cooper already?"

Speechless, I stared her down. Then she sniffed the air around me.

I instinctively alternated raising each arm to check my armpits. I thought I smelled pretty good—Shower Fresh Secret and gardenia perfume. Vicky continued with her inspection, and I felt as if I were showing at Westminster. Maybe she could confer with Silvia, and should they decide me worthy, they could present me with Best in Show.

Next, she felt my forehead. Did she think I looked sick? Despite a little soreness in my previously under-used nether regions, I thought I positively glowed. I may not have gotten much sleep, but I couldn't possibly be more satisfied if I tried. I almost never left the bed all weekend.

Vicky frowned and clicked her tongue as she made some sort of mental observations. I wondered where she'd left her clipboard. Finally, she stood back from me and just stared into my eyes, a deep crease forming between her brows. Her scrutiny gave me chills, in a creepy sort of way.

She shook her head with a look of absolute disgust frozen on her otherwise pretty face. "When Phil said you were sick on Friday, I thought maybe, just maybe, you had the flu. But..."

I waited but she didn't continue. "No flu?"

"No flu," she stated. "You've been having sex!"

I felt the flush of embarrassment immediately burning into my cheeks as everyone in the bank raised their heads and looked at me. Did she have to say it so loudly? I hadn't really believed she would be able to tell, or I would have tried to avoid her. She was a proverbial bloodhound.

I knew it was more than just the smell. I had showered several times over the weekend. It was as if she could see it in my eyes. Because of course she could smell Cooper on me. I could smell him myself. I was wearing his coat.

The weather was much better, but I wore it anyway. I slung it over the back of my chair, so I could discreetly sniff it throughout the day.

I know. Pathetic. But in a very romantic way. Being in love made it somehow acceptable to be pathetic all of a sudden.

Vicky looked at me funny the rest of the morning. I expected her to grill me for details, and it was almost eerie that she didn't. I knew I was being over the top, but who could blame me? After what could possibly be the longest drought in history, I'd finally had sex. *Amazing* sex. But seriously, was I really being judged by a woman who probably took on the Flying Wallendas over the weekend? I was sure she'd break her silence soon enough.

I had worn Cooper's favorite of my new outfits—the brown pants and the champagne blouse—knowing I would see him that evening. He'd caught a plane for New York on Sunday night. It was some mysterious business trip, and although I hated it, he made it somehow tolerable by keeping me on the phone last night until I fell asleep to the sound of his voice. And he'd sent me almost constant text messages since I'd gotten up that morning.

Cooper: Good morning sweetheart. I hope you slept well. I miss you already.

Cooper: Wake up sleepy head.

Cooper: Forgotten me already?

Katie: Don't be silly. Stayed awake all night. Couldn't sleep without you. Come home soon.

After my shower...

Cooper: You should be awake at all times pining for my return.

Everything changed for us on Friday. Aside from the obvious *having sex* part of it, we had truly become a couple. He even called me his girlfriend—not to me, to someone on the phone. But still, he said it. And it was a lot nicer than I would have dreamed.

We had been snuggled together in my bed, drifting in and out of sleep, when his iPhone rang, startling me with the chorus of "Don't Fear the Reaper" playing in a loop. *"Don't Fear the Reaper"? Really?*

He looked at the caller ID and slid out of my arms to step away from the bed. He thought I was asleep, and I guessed it was sort of dishonest to pretend I was, but I did.

"Hello?" He paused for a long time. "Yeah, well, I can't really talk about that now; I'm at my girlfriend's house." He said *girlfriend,* and it sounded like he was bursting to say it.

He paused for another heartbeat. "Thanks," he said, sarcasm dripping from his voice.

I wanted to open my eyes to see his expression, but I didn't want to give myself away.

"You know I can't do that." Three beats. "You know why."

I didn't know why, but I didn't know what he was talking about either. I guessed that it was work related, and since he wasn't interested in telling me what he did for a living, I tried not to worry about it. *Okay, so I pretended not to worry about it.*

"Can I call you later?" Five beats. "Okay, thanks."

He slid back into bed, pulled me into his arms, and proceeded to wake me up.

At work, my morning was filled with little more than texting Cooper.

Katie: Wearing your favorite outfit today, better not miss your flight.

Cooper: With the sexy underwear?

Katie: Of course!

Cooper: Leaving for the airport now.

I knew he was kidding, but it still made my stomach flip. I'd always wanted to be a wanton temptress like my favorite fictional heroines.

I shared every minute with him as if he were sitting in his chair across from me. With all the texting back and forth, I hadn't done much work at all. And I couldn't wipe the smile off my face if I tried.

And I tried. Everyone was hovering in the lobby, staring at me since Vicky announced I'd slept with Cooper.

Katie: Everyone knows.

Cooper: Good. Easier than marking my territory.

Marking his territory? That was the second dog reference in one day. I laughed out loud, and everyone in the lobby looked at me like I was crazy.

Silvia poked her head into my office. "I have no doubt you had a *stimulating* weekend. You may as well tell me all about it."

My mouth fell open. "I'm not telling you about my... about *that.*"

"Oh, come on, Katie. We've been waiting a year for something exciting to happen in your life. You can't just leave us hanging now that it has."

"I beg to differ. I can, and I *will*, totally leave you hanging. This is not up for debate. Sorry. If you want smut, go talk to Vicky." I shooed her away with both hands. "Now go. I need to call my mom. She left me at least a hundred messages this weekend." *Hey, one little white lie never hurt anyone.* I picked up the phone. My finger hovering over the buttons, I raised an eyebrow.

"You're no fun, Katie James," she grumbled as she wandered out of my office.

Phil shook his head as Silvia passed him, and I wondered how long he'd been lingering outside my office.

Replacing my phone handset to the base, I stared at Phil's unreadable expression.

He tilted his head and squinted at me as if he was deciphering some secret code, then stuck his head in and smiled. "Dean's on the phone. Could you please pause your texting long enough to pick up your line?"

"Sure thing." *As soon as I tell Cooper.*

I couldn't have been on the call more than five minutes, but when I hung up and flipped open my cell, there were three frantic messages in my inbox. And two missed calls.

Cooper: Last message cut off... is Dean there?

Cooper: Where the hell are you?

Cooper: Is everything ok? Pick up your damn phone!

I quickly keyed in a reply.

Katie: I'm fine! Phil made me answer a PHONE CALL from Dean. I had no idea you were such a jealous boyfriend. ☺

Cooper: Something about that guy doesn't sit right with me. Can't explain it. Just booked an earlier flight home.

I caught myself smiling as I reread his message. I had no idea he was as quick to freak out as I was. The man was seriously jealous. But for some crazy reason, I couldn't find it in me to be bothered by that fact, especially if it meant he was coming back sooner. It would appear I'd found Cooper's one flaw... okay so his *other* flaw, the major one being secrecy. *But no one's perfect, right?*

Oh, I have it bad.

I glanced out my door, and Phil was squinting at me with that slightly bewildered expression. I wished I knew what he was thinking. Then again, maybe I didn't want to know.

Silvia milled around outside my office. I would have thought she would be excited about my foray into teenage behavior, but I was beginning to think they were taking turns interrupting my texting.

She stuck her head in and peered at me over her glasses. "No flowers?" She smirked. "I didn't even have sex with him, and I got flowers."

Katie: Silvia wants to know why she got flowers for that stupid outfit but I didn't get any for sex.

Cooper: Oops!

I fell into a spasm of uncontrollable laughter. Silvia rolled her eyes and walked back into the lobby.

I knew I should be working, even as I held my phone, keying in message after message. An hour later, June meandered by. Apparently, it was her turn.

She poked her head in and stared at me until I was forced to ask, "What?"

"We were just wondering... are you sexting?"

Et tu, June? I just frowned at her and relayed her question to Cooper.

Cooper: Hadn't thought of that. You start.

Katie: How do I start?

Cooper: Tell me what you're doing right now.

Katie: Pretending to work while I text you.

Phil was starting to give me dirty looks, and I knew it would only be a matter of time before he said something about my slacking off all day.

Katie: Will probably be fired. I haven't done a bit of work today.

Cooper: You can work for me. Balancing my checkbook... naked.

Katie: Does that pay well?

Cooper: Not really. But there are exceptional benefits. But back to sexting. Seriously, you're going to have to try harder.

Sensing the exasperation oozing out of Phil, I put my phone on my lap, under my desk, and pulled a stack of papers from the pile I'd been ignoring. Pretending to look them over, I continued to watch Phil from my peripheral vision until my phone vibrated. I glanced down at the new message.

You have yet to respond to me. So, what do you have to say for yourself?

Someone was getting very impatient. I decided to give sexting my best shot. I hoped he was in a meeting or somewhere he would have to struggle to hide his reaction.

Katie: I'm thinking about you naked and all the naughty things I'm going to do to you with my tongue.

I snapped my phone shut and went back to shuffling papers so Phil wouldn't know I'd been texting again. My phone vibrated again a few minutes later. I flipped it open in my lap and sneaked a peak.

Mom: Katherine Grace James! What in the world is wrong with you?

Crap! Crap! Crap! I'd just sexted my mother.

I tried to call her from my desk phone. She didn't pick up. I waited and tried again. I tried three times before giving up. Maybe tomorrow. She couldn't stay mad at me forever.

I thought about dialing my mother one more time when Vicky walked in with her typical smirk. "You know, I've been thinking."

"Did you need an aspirin?"

"Very funny." She scowled. "No, I was thinking you need to do a little digging."

"Digging?"

"Yeah, digging. If Cooper *is* involved in something illegal, surely you would see evidence of it somewhere. My dad had this old saying, 'If you walk around the barnyard long enough, you're bound to step in shit.' So I imagine a killer would eventually end up with a little blood on his shoes. Have you ever looked at Cooper's shoes? Dean says you can tell a lot about a guy by his footwear... how the soles wear, stuff like that. Mark my words, Katie. You need to dig through the guy's closet to see what you can find. Just watch out for skeletons while you're at it."

I stared open-mouthed at the doorway long after she'd vanished from view. She actually wanted me to search for bloody shoes in Cooper's closet? The worst part about her suggestion was I actually thought it might be a good idea... for all of five minutes, until I shook it off and considered the source. In just a few hours, Cooper would walk through that door, and everything would be perfect. I wasn't about to let Vicky ruin my happy day.

For the next hour, I actually did some work, since Phil had started watching me a little too closely. I hadn't seen him hovering in several minutes, though, and then I realized I hadn't seen anyone in a while. They didn't know Cooper was on a plane. Had they gotten bored already? I could only hope.

I stood and walked to my door. Everyone was paying rapt attention to the parking lot. Not that I was complaining. I was just curious as to what would draw all of them away from the spectacle that was *me*. I stepped out into the lobby. There was a mini traffic jam in our tiny lot. I counted three... no, *four* delivery vans parked in front of the building.

"Well..." Silvia glanced over at me. "I guess that settles it."

"Hmmm?" I was too busy watching the dozens of white orchids being unloaded from each of the four vans. My mouth fell open, and I covered it with my hand. I was a little dazed.

"I guess he likes you better," Silvia said.

When I met Cooper in the lobby, he tried for a welcome home kiss. Much to his disappointment, I put a damper on that. I only permitted an innocent embrace while I was still under the constant scrutiny of my coworkers. I wouldn't even entertain his attempts to drag me into the vault for covert necking.

I thanked him with a careful kiss once we were alone in my office. "The flowers are beautiful."

"So are you," he said softly, playing with a small potted orchid as he gazed at me from across the desk.

"Silvia has decided you must like me better."

He raised his eyebrows. "And it took a truckload of orchids for her to draw that conclusion?"

"Several truckloads of orchids," I corrected. "But you did send her an awful lot of roses."

There were orchids literally everywhere. I had three on my desk, and they lined the floor against the wall and along the top of the cabinets above my desk. And that wasn't counting the rest of them scattered all over the bank. I was fairly certain we wouldn't be able to get a fraction of them in the car with us.

I realized while I had been mooning over the flowers, he hadn't said anything. "You're quiet."

He shrugged.

"Work?"

"I don't want to bore you with the details."

"Okay, but that's what a relationship is about, boring each other with details."

He was almost too still as he sat there watching me.

But I didn't have to wonder what he was thinking; there was no question as to where his eyes were focused.

"You like this blouse." It wasn't a question. I could see the flash of heat in his eyes when he looked at it.

"I'd like it better if you weren't wearing it." He rubbed the light stubble on his chin and grinned at me. His smile still had the power to take my breath away.

"That can be arranged," I teased.

"Now?" He almost leered at me.

I laughed and rolled my eyes. "Oh, absolutely! I think that would go over big, if I got undressed right here in my office with everyone watching. Phil would love that."

He frowned. "I don't think I like Phil anymore."

"Cooper, why don't you like Phil?"

"He's trying to force you to work with Dean. I don't trust Dean. There's something very strange about that guy." He pulled one of the fragile petals from the little orchid and almost immediately flashed an apologetic grin. He was definitely in a strange mood after his New York trip.

I reached for his hand. "I'm not even remotely interested in Dean. He's no Cooper Maxwell."

He laughed, twining his fingers in mine across the desk. "Can you leave yet?"

"Soon."

"How's your mother?" he asked straight-faced, but I knew he was fighting a smile.

I cleared my throat and kept my face serious. "Probably still wondering whose naked body I was planning to ravage with my tongue."

His eyes widened. I could tell by the look on his face he was picturing it in graphic detail.

I was somewhat satisfied with his temporary punishment for bringing up my disastrous sexting incident. "How was New York?"

"Cold and lonely without you." Cooper leaned back in the chair, letting my hand go to push his into his hair. As he lifted his arm, I noticed a stain on his shirt.

Ordinarily, I wouldn't be the least bit concerned with a stain. I personally found it impossible to make it through an entire meal without dropping something on my clothes. But Cooper was impeccably neat. And the particular stain I was scrutinizing was on the underside of his sleeve between his wrist and his elbow, and it looked remarkably like dried blood. My thoughts immediately flashed to Vicky... and shoes.

"You have something on your shirt," I pointed out cautiously.

He twisted his wrist around to see. "Oh."

"Did you cut yourself?" I asked, trying to keep my voice steady.

His cheeks flamed. "It's probably just sauce. I never go to New York without getting a chili dog from a street vendor. I must have put my sleeve in the chili."

My head bobbed as I forced my lips into a smile. Guilt shot through me at my suspicion.

He put his arm down. "So I thought we would go to your house first and pack a bag for you. My bed is infinitely more comfortable than yours, and we're sleeping there tonight."

I told myself chili dog sauce was a perfectly reasonable excuse for having a dark red stain on his shirt. And when I didn't believe it, I told myself again, and again. And I reminded myself it was Vicky who had put those traitorous thoughts in my head. As far as where I would sleep that night, I couldn't argue with him. I'd slept in his bed before, and it was scrumptious. I would be perfectly safe and blissfully happy in Cooper's bed. *What could I possibly have to worry about?*

"Then dinner. I'll let you choose that." He leaned in to close half the distance between us. "Because you are going to need your strength tonight." And he flashed his lopsided grin, making my stomach flip again.

"Well, then," I said, trying to breathe, "I suppose we have a busy evening ahead of us. We shouldn't waste any time. I'm ready when you are."

"I was ready when I got here." He came around the desk and held his black leather jacket for me to slip my arms into the sleeves. Then he grabbed my briefcase from the floor behind me, bending to brush his lips against mine in what would be the first of many kisses that night.

A TRIATHLON

"**C**OOPER, DO YOU HAVE A hairdryer?" I asked. He sat on the edge of my bed, waiting patiently for me to pack. He'd picked up one of the books from the floor and was flipping through the pages. "Don't be silly," he shot back, but I didn't know if that meant "Don't be silly, of course I do," or "Don't be silly, why would I own a hairdryer?"

"Yes or no? I'm trying to hurry. Don't confuse me."

"Yes." He laughed. "I have shampoo and soap and towels and... what else might you need?"

"Peppermint toothpaste?" I poked my head out of the bathroom to see his reaction.

"Now you're being ridiculous." I wasn't sure if he was referring to the toothpaste comment or the sticky note he plucked from the pages of the book. "What's with the Post-its?"

"Oh... um..." I felt the heat flash from my chest to my hairline. "I like to mark my favorite parts, so I can read them again. It's silly."

"Not silly. I do that sometimes." His head bobbed as he examined my tattered paperback with a smirk. "You must really like this book."

A sudden twinge of guilt propelled me across the room. Watching Cooper flip through the pages of one of my *Immortal Blood* books was like watching him confront a former lover. I expected to see his serene expression twist with jealousy. *Ridiculous.*

"Mmm-hmm." I eased the book out of his hand and tucked it under my pillow, avoiding eye contact. "Elizabeth Jayne is my favorite author. I've been known to read her books more than once."

"There's nothing wrong with that. I think I read my copy of *The Bourne Identity* until it disintegrated." He stood up, cupped my chin and tipped my face up to his. "Hey, don't be embarrassed. I love that you read. It's something else we have in common."

I gave him a quick nod and tossed the rest of my things into my bag, anxious to get him out of my bedroom before he discovered anything more embarrassing. "I'm ready." I started for the stairs.

He caught up and took the bag from my shoulder. "Where would you like to eat?"

We stopped for fast food on the way, wasting no time before heading back to his place where we could be alone. As he pulled his car into his driveway, I asked if I'd get to see more of his house.

"You've already seen all the best parts." He winked before getting out and unloading my bag from the trunk.

I was acutely aware of the fact that he still kept a great deal of himself hidden from me. I thought of our first date—was it only a week ago?—when he asked if I was intentionally keeping him from seeing my home. "Cooper, are you intentionally trying to keep things from me?"

Something dark crossed his features, and he frowned. "I don't *want* to keep anything from you."

I recognized he didn't say he *wasn't* keeping things from me. Just that he didn't want to. Hardly the same thing. "Why won't you show me your living room?"

He relaxed almost instantly and laughed. "I will gladly show you my living room, and the kitchen too if you like. Would you like to see the dining room? I never go in there.

I spend most of my time in my sitting room and bedroom. The house is really too big for just me.”

I was reminded of the first night I'd been there, when he sounded almost embarrassed by the lushness of his bathroom. I wondered why he lived in such an opulent house if he didn't like it.

His garage opened into what I suspected was a mudroom, but it could only be described as pristine. The black slate floors were spotless. Open, floor-length wood cabinets lined the wall on one side, and other than a single gray wool overcoat, nothing hung on the hooks. Cooper ushered me straight through to the kitchen, and I gasped.

He looked at me funny and rolled his eyes. “It's just a kitchen, Katie. I almost never cook in here. I think there's cereal in the pantry. No milk, I'm afraid, but I may have a bag of marshmallows somewhere, too.” There was that embarrassment again.

No matter what he said, it was more than just a kitchen. It was a work of art, something straight out of a Tuscan winery. Dark, distressed walnut cabinets surrounded golden granite counters. His stove—the one he never used—was a high-end commercial number in shiny stainless steel, just like the enormous refrigerator. A huge copper sink was set in the counter along one wall and a smaller matching one in the island. He may not like cooking, but if he would let me, I could cook up a storm in there.

Beyond the kitchen was a keeping room that looked as though it had been set up for a magazine photo shoot. Not a thing was out of place. Not a speck of dust on anything.

“How long have you lived here? You don't have any pictures... of anyone... anywhere that I've seen. No magazines, no mail sitting out. It's like a real estate model.”

He shrugged. “I've lived here a long time. But I guess I never had a reason to make it more personal. I'd hang your picture... if I had one.”

I dropped the interrogation for the moment. I would come back to it later. I didn't know when, but I knew it wasn't the right time. He was slipping into melancholy, and I definitely didn't want that.

He led me into the next room. "This is the main living room. There is another one in the front of the house near the formal dining room, but this one is my favorite. I don't really use any of them, but if I did, I would use this one."

"I like your sofa. Is it comfortable?" I tried to infuse my voice with the longing I felt for him.

"Why would you ask about the sofa when you know how wonderful the bed is?"

"I was just thinking I didn't want to wait until we got upstairs." I took a tentative step closer to him and pulled my bottom lip between my teeth.

He smiled, putting down my bag, and reached out to take my hand. "Why didn't you just say so?"

He tugged on my hand until I almost tripped into his arms, and he wound them around me, burying his face in my hair. His lips brushed against my ear, and a chill ran through me. He must have felt the tremor because he groaned and ran his tongue over my earlobe. My body responded by melting into him, and my shaky hands found their way under his shirt, smoothing over his muscled chest and flat stomach.

He grabbed me around the waist and lifted me slightly, towing me the few feet to the sofa in question. He put me down and, with a devilish grin, pushed against my shoulders until I fell into the plush sofa with a giggle.

I watched as he slowly unbuttoned his shirt and tossed it aside, and then he dropped to his knees in front of me and reached up to undo the buttons on the blouse he was so fond of. He took great care, and way too much time, to remove and gently lay it over a chair before kissing his way from my lips to my chest and back.

He was going to torture me again. He seemed to love

dragging things out until I couldn't breathe. All I wanted was to feel him as close to me as possible.

"Time for more earth-shattering love?" I whispered against his ear as he nuzzled my neck.

"You always rush me. I'm taking my time tonight."

I let my head fall back against the sofa and groaned softly. "Then you'd better take me up to your bed. This sofa wasn't made for marathons."

He kissed his way down to the delicate lace covering my breasts. "I was thinking of a triathlon, actually. The sofa is just the first leg. We'll get to the bed all in good time."

I shuddered hard, and that just drove him to step up his assault. He was going to kill me. There was no question. My poor heart hammered in my chest, and his ear was close enough to hear that. But it wasn't his ear I was concentrating on at that moment. His mouth had found its way beneath the lace and was torturing me in a wonderful way. My hands slid up his back and twisted into his hair, holding his head in place. The sensations were intense and wonderful and still full of surprises. I wasn't paying attention to his hands. I should have been.

I gasped with delicious surprise. "What did you just do?"

"Did you like that?"

I moaned my answer, and I could feel his lopsided grin against my skin. Then he did it again and again until I almost begged him to stop.

"I think I like triathlons," I said as we lounged in the claw foot tub a few hours later. His arms were wrapped around me from behind, and my head rested on his hard chest.

"I knew you would."

"You surprised me a little. I had no idea you have so many tricks up your sleeve." I knew he couldn't see my face, but I couldn't help but smile anyway.

"You would never give me the opportunity. You like to rush too much."

I shrugged. "I get impatient."

He bent down and put his lips to my ear. "You need to learn patience."

"I guess you'll have to teach me."

"Hmmm. I suppose that might be fun."

We were quiet for a long moment before I spoke again. "You know, tomorrow is Tuesday."

"Yes, it generally comes after Monday."

"Smartass." I swatted his hand. "I mean, you have a standing appointment on Tuesday."

"Yes, to... um... balance my checkbook." He kept his voice even, but we were both aware of the humor in that.

"I will be wearing clothes at the office, you know."

"Oh, I insist."

"I could always balance your checkbook at home," I suggested.

He rested his chin on the top of my head. "I can actually balance my own checkbook, you know."

I pulled myself up slightly to turn around and look at him. "Are you going to start balancing your checkbook yourself?"

"And miss out on an opportunity to watch you do it? Perish the thought."

I settled back in with my head cradled against his chest. "You had me worried for a minute. Vicky suggested you might want to replace me as your banker because we were dating."

"Don't be ridiculous. Does she think I'll be asking *her* to manage my accounts now?" He laughed, but it was cold.

I was immediately relieved. Vicky had tried to convince me of exactly that.

"Besides, what we're doing is much more than dating." He ran his fingertips lightly down my arms as if to emphasize his point. "I think of the past year as our dating phase. It may have been somewhat unorthodox, but I always considered every appointment with you to be a date."

He thought of our appointments as dates? And here

I'd convinced myself he just hated accountants like so many of my other clients. All the worries I had bottled up instantly vanished when he explained his reasoning. It made perfect sense. I had always prepared for his appointments the way I would prepare for a date. I dressed a little nicer on those days, wore my expensive perfume. I got nervous. I played with my hair and chewed on my lips and generally didn't relax until he was gone. I would replay every nuance of our conversations back in my head later to analyze their meaning.

I just didn't know he was doing the same thing. I had no idea that while I was thinking of him as some unattainable prize, forever outside my grasp, he was in turn planning his next move to woo me.

"So what made you decide to go completely rogue and pursue me?" I almost felt silly asking, but the question had been burning a hole in my brain since my birthday.

He shifted beneath me. "Well..." He smoothed his hands through his damp hair.

"Please tell me." I forced myself to stay still, barely stirring the warm water with my fingers. I didn't want to make him more nervous by looking at him, despite the fact I was dying to see his expression.

"It came to my attention that perhaps I was being just a bit too subtle in my approach, and so I decided to crash your birthday party in an attempt to see if maybe a more obvious tactic would catch your eye. When it appeared you might actually be interested in me, I just couldn't rein it in anymore. I became a man on a mission."

I wasn't sure which part of it flagged my attention more: the fact that he had intentionally crashed my party or that information about me was being brought to his attention. I assumed someone was feeding him information, but I wasn't entirely sure if it was by design or accident. "So someone told you to change your hair and dress all rumpled?"

He hesitated for a moment. "I was simply going for

the opposite of my previous approach, which had been to impress you with my neatness."

I suppressed a giggle. "I actually was impressed by your neatness."

"But not driven to lust."

"Maybe not as much," I admitted. "So how did you find out about my party?" I turned to look at him.

He bit back a smile.

"Silvia," we both said at the same time.

I raised an eyebrow. "So her roses were for more than just that silly outfit. Or was that all a part of the plan? Get Katie dressed up in something completely embarrassing to distract her?" I was almost angry when that possibility flashed to mind.

"No. Don't be ridiculous. I would've never chosen for you to wear that out if it had been my decision. Silvia picked that on her own."

"Hmm." I turned back around and cuddled against him again, then shivered.

"You're cold."

"I'm not." I didn't want to get out of the tub. I was very much enjoying the closeness and the conversation.

"You're a bad liar," he teased and pulled me up with him to stand.

He got out first and helped me step over the side. Then he grabbed an enormous towel from a metal rack and tucked it around both of us. It was fresh-out-of-the-dryer warm, and I liked being cocooned with him. He wrapped his arms around me under the towel and lifted me awkwardly off the floor.

"This should be interesting." He laughed as he carried me to the bedroom.

He set me down on the carpet and proceeded to dry me without unwrapping us. All it really managed to do was to press the front of me to the front of him in a way that put the hungry look back in his eyes.

"Haven't you had enough?" I murmured.

He flashed me that lopsided grin before whispering his lips down my moist neck. "Could there ever be enough of you?"

A SEA OF ORCHIDS

I woke up early Tuesday morning and for a fraction of a second forgot where I was. Despite the limited amount of time I'd actually spent sleeping, I felt amazingly rested. I attributed that to the magnificent bed and the wonderful sheets. And, of course, to the exquisite triathlon that had put me to sleep completely relaxed.

Cooper was out cold, his face buried in one of the sumptuous pillows and his arm resting lightly over my waist. Just like in my dream all those nights ago, I stared at him sleeping. He was gorgeous... puddle of drool and all. And he was mine.

I carefully slid out from under his arm and went into the CRWAT, closing the door behind me. His bathroom didn't seem nearly as intimidating as on that first night. I turned the handle on the shower and waited only a moment for the water to heat up. I stepped into the numerous sprays of the multiple showerheads and closed my eyes as the hot water flowed over me. I was almost sad to go to work. I'd always loved my job, but I hadn't had anything else worthwhile in my life, so it was an easy relationship. Since Cooper, I felt as if my job was competing for time with him, and I didn't want to give up a precious moment for something as trivial as work. The relationship was moving too fast to be normal, but I was also too invested—okay, too obsessed—to give a damn.

I squeezed a glob of shampoo into my hand and lathered my hair. The smell of lavender and mint made me smile as I thought of Cooper.

I sensed rather than heard him step into the spray and struggled with a knee-jerk reaction to cover myself before I remembered he'd already seen me naked. *A lot.* Up close. And he'd certainly reacted positively. Fortunately, the shower was enormous, and the water surging out from every angle muffled my squeal.

"Allow me." His hands slid into my hair, and I was more than willing to surrender the task to him. "You got up early."

"I have to go to work," I said with a moan as he massaged my scalp.

"Not for almost two hours."

I turned to face him, but he kept his hands in my hair, working up a serious lather. I felt the suds slipping down my body.

"Well, I figured I might need to take a shower."

"You *are* taking a shower."

I looked up at him from under wet eyelashes. "I thought I might need to take another one."

His eyes flashed down my body. "My thoughts exactly."

Later, Cooper drove me to work and kissed me goodbye without getting out of the car. We both agreed I would never get anything done if he came in. I was really going to get fired if I didn't start doing my job. The entertainment value of my love life was only worth so much. I figured Phil had been pushed as far as I dared.

Besides, Cooper had an appointment with me at ten thirty, just like every other Tuesday. And much to my delight and his, Phil couldn't do much about the fact that I would be wasting an hour of my day with Cooper when I had been wasting that same hour twice a week for the past year. I wondered how long everyone but me had known his appointments had nothing to do with banking and everything to do with love.

I laughed at myself when I thought about how I had honestly believed he needed my help to balance his checkbook. It was easy to see in hindsight. No one in his right mind would open so many CD accounts just to close them down again a month later.

And all those safe deposit boxes. He finally admitted that he didn't have anything in three of the four boxes he had rented. He only kept them so he would have a reason to see me.

I only thought about Cooper every other minute instead of every single minute. I almost felt like things were back to normal, except for the fact I was still literally tripping over all the orchids in my office, not to mention the ones scattered around the lobby. It sort of looked like someone was getting married in the bank. We had taken several to Cooper's house, but that hadn't put a dent in them.

I picked up one of the pots I'd tripped on and put it on the desk. It occurred to me that it was a good thing orchids didn't have a fragrance. If they did, between those and Silvia's roses, the place would have smelled like a funeral home.

I dropped into my chair and figured it was a good time to call my mother. And surprise, surprise, she even answered. "Hi, Mom."

"Katherine." She only said my full name when I was in deep trouble.

Still, I was encouraged that she even took my call. I decided to go straight for her soft spot and hope for the best. "So have you heard the wonderful news?"

"And what news would that be?"

"I have a boyfriend." I let my genuine excitement color my tone in hope she would actually believe me.

"I don't find humor in your attempts to shock and confuse me. Your sister would never treat me this way."

My sister was a much better liar than I was. "Mom, I'm not being funny. I really do have a boyfriend. He's one of my clients. Can you believe it? He asked me out after a year of secretly liking me." I hoped the truth would draw her out of her icy mood.

"So where is this *alleged* boyfriend?" I could almost hear one of her perfectly arched brows raise in suspicion.

"Well, he's not here now. I'm at work. But he has an appointment at ten thirty to talk about his accounts. I'm still his banker, after all."

"Isn't that a bit of a conflict of interest?"

Was the woman trying to torture me? All those phone calls nagging me relentlessly to find a nice man, and when I did, she was worried about a conflict of interest? She didn't even pick up on the fact that, as one of my clients, he must have money. And I knew my mother's preference for her daughters marrying money.

"Mom, just be happy for me, okay?"

"Well..." She paused for an impossibly long time. I thought for a second I'd lost the call. "We'll see. If you still have the boyfriend in a month, do let me know."

I should have known she was still irritated with me. But I didn't expect her to be downright mean. "Okay. Well, I'd better go. Still on the clock here. I'll talk to you later." I tried to sound cheery. I was pretty happy, after all. I only had to get through the next thirty minutes to see Cooper again.

I wandered into the lobby, feeling a little like a Christian at the Coliseum. I wondered where all the lions were hiding.

"Well, good morning, Katie. I didn't expect to see you in today," Vicky said, her claws only barely concealed.

I had no idea what I'd done to provoke her ire, probably something to do with sex. Maybe because I had gotten to Cooper first. Maybe just because she wasn't the only one having great sex anymore. I didn't know about Silvia's, June's, or Phil's sex lives. They had the good sense to keep it to themselves. And thank God for small miracles.

I forced a smile. "Morning, Vicky. Why would you think I wasn't coming to work?"

"No reason."

"How's that piercing working out for you?"

Her face lit up in a genuine smile. "Fabulous, actually. I had no idea a woman could have that many orgasms in a row."

I toyed with the idea of telling her I was well aware. But I was afraid that conversation would send us down a path I wasn't prepared to go down. So instead I just said, "Wow."

"Wow is an understatement. I climaxed seven times last night. My husband said I'm positively wearing him out. I may need to bring in a fourth-quarter substitution." She gave me a wink, and I winced.

I knew who she had in mind for her fourth-quarter whatever, and I stamped down my fury. "Well, good luck with that."

"Hmm."

I saw Silvia coming out of her office and headed toward her with long strides. "Silvia, I hear you've been playing matchmaker."

She gave me a sly smile. "Matchmaker? Ha! More like babysitter." She waved me off and scurried toward the vault.

What a peculiar day. It was entirely possible everyone had quite had their fill of my love life. I was hopeful, but at the same time—and I would never tell *them*—I was just a little sad. I certainly didn't want them to continue following me around like bargain-basement paparazzi, but I sort of missed the attention. For a minute. Maybe.

I decided to venture into the back, where I found that June and Phil were going at it again. I didn't know what had happened, but it was a good bet Phil had done or said something wrong.

June wagged a finger at him. "You've really done it this time. You have exceeded my expectations of how low you could stoop."

"How many steps away am I today, June?" Phil taunted.

"Steps? There are no more steps, *Philip.* You have officially reached the basement."

Phil choked out a nervous laugh. "What did I do?"

"You know what you did." June spit her words out in a huff and stormed out of the room.

I actually felt a little sorry for Phil. I thought it was rather amusing too. Silvia blew into the room to confront Phil. She had a really hard time keeping a severe expression because he was still grinning like an idiot.

"I can't..." Her hand flew up to hold back a laugh, and that set Phil off again into his own spasm of hysterics.

I started to lose it too and quickly got out of there. A few minutes later, Silvia stopped off at my office to fill me in, and I was still laughing when Cooper walked through the door.

"What's so funny?" he asked.

I succumbed to a fit of giggles just looking at his questioning face. "Nothing," I managed on a deep breath.

"Katie..."

"I'm sorry. It's too funny. I can't say it." I put my hand over my mouth to hold back the laughter.

He pulled his brows together in a deep furrow.

"Okay. Okay." I pulled in a breath. "June got mad at Phil." I paused, trying to rein myself in.

He nodded. "I can see why June would get mad at Phil."

"Wait. You have to let me finish." I was having a really hard time not breaking up again.

"Fine." He finally gave in and cracked a wide smile.

"Okay. June got mad at Phil for saying he felt like he was locked in a room with a million tiny vaginas." I pointed at the orchid.

"Oh." He studied the flower for a minute. "I never noticed. They *do* look like tiny vaginas."

The look on his face was so innocent and confused, I was instantly overcome with hysterics again. Thankfully, my hysteria was contagious, and he started to laugh with me.

"So, I was thinking..." I said as soon as we both stopped laughing enough to continue. "Do you really want to balance your checkbook here... now?"

A slow grin spread across his lips. "I'm intrigued. Continue."

"Well..." I could feel the heat stain my cheeks. "I was thinking about what you said before."

"I've said so many things. Remind me."

He couldn't make it easy for me. Oh, no. Not Cooper. "You know," I whispered. "Balancing your checkbook... naked?"

He reached across my desk and stroked his thumb against the back of my hand. "It's a stimulating suggestion. I might be inclined to agree..."

"But?"

"Not *but*, more of an *if*."

I captured my bottom lip in my teeth. "If what?"

"Well, *if* I'm allowed to *distract* you while you're balancing. That might make it more fun for me."

The absolute look of lust that flashed across his face made my heart stop for a beat. When it started again, it was racing. I knew at that moment I would not be able to work if he stayed a minute longer. "Cooper. You know I love you. But you have to go. I can't do my job if my legs are too weak for me to stand."

"It's not really fair to punish me for your weakness, is it? I still have forty-five minutes left."

I laughed at his playful expression. "You have the whole evening. I don't have my car, so I have no doubt you'll be here before the doors lock at four to watch me do paperwork for an hour."

"Don't be silly. I'll be here at lunch. You need to keep up your strength with those weak legs and all."

"Okay. *Fine*. Lunch. But that definitely means you have to go now." I stood and wobbled around the desk to grab him by the arm. I tugged until he was on his feet. "Besides, I can't miss you if you don't leave."

"See you soon." He pressed his lips to mine in a lingering kiss before sauntering across the lobby like the cat that ate the canary.

Leaning against my doorframe, I watched as he climbed into his car and backed out.

"Sacking the quarterback while on the clock, Katie?" Vicky sneered.

I rolled my eyes. "What is it with all the football references?"

"Phil's right about you. You're such a novice. It's playoff season. Say it with me... Roll Tide!"

I had no idea what laundry detergent and football had in common, but I wasn't going to ask. Instead, I turned to escape back to my desk.

"Oh, Katie?"

"Yes?"

"I've been wondering... did you ever ask Cooper where that two hundred grand came from?"

I looked around to see if we were alone then motioned her closer with my index finger. "It just so happens, I did."

"Well?"

"He's... you can't tell anyone, okay?"

Vicky was on the verge of bursting. "Oh, for Pete's sake, just tell me already."

I leaned in to whisper in her ear. "He found a golden ticket in a chocolate bar and was made the sole owner of a candy factory."

"Ahh!" Vicky pushed away from me, her face as red as her hair. "When did you become such a bitch?"

"Right around the same time you started harassing me about my boyfriend's source of income." I glared at her. "Keep your nose out of other people's business."

"Bitch." She started to walk away, and I was certain I would be rid of her for at least the next half hour, but she stopped dead in her tracks and spun back around to face me. "Did you hear about the murder in New York yesterday? It was someone fairly important. The news said it was a mob thing. Isn't that a crazy coincidence? Someone in Atlanta gets themselves killed by the mob and then, someone in New York gets killed."

"You mean, with New York being so famous for its crime-free streets? People get killed all the time, Vicky, especially in major cities. The world is a scary place. You should stop watching the news if it bothers you so much."

She had an odd expression on her face, almost triumphant. "Didn't you say Cooper was in New York yesterday?"

Crap! So much for getting any work done today.

YOU CAN GOOGLE JUST ABOUT ANYTHING

I SPENT THE NEXT HOUR SURFING the internet, looking for information on the mob hit in New York. The victim was a wealthy business owner living in an upscale section of Manhattan.

It's just a coincidence. Damn Vicky! She was trying to get me worked up and paranoid for absolutely no reason. I was pretty sure millions of people lived and breathed in New York City. Any one of them could have killed that businessman. I knew better than to think Cooper was capable of such a horrible thing. I knew everything I needed to know about him. *Almost everything.*

Of course, I started with a Google search of Cooper Maxwell. I found a doctor in Hawaii and a hair salon in Toronto. There was absolutely nothing listed about *my* Cooper. He didn't even have a Facebook page. Even *I* had a Facebook page. How could anyone have as much money as Cooper and not have a single mention on the internet?

I tried to clear Vicky's smug expression out of my head as I clicked back through the story about the murder. I certainly couldn't imagine him shooting someone while talking to me on the phone or between text messages. *Oh hey, Katie. Love you. Miss you. Disabling security cameras is a pain! Be right back while I shoot someone. Did you get your flowers?*

I closed the internet window and rocked back in my

chair. Was I supposed to ask him outright? *Oh, honey, I was wondering... was that really chili sauce on your sleeve or was that blood from your latest hit?* I knew I was being ridiculous.

I dialed Cooper's cell phone.

"Katie?" He sounded surprised to hear from me.

"Hi," I squeaked out.

"Is something wrong?"

"Missed hearing your voice." And I did. I was sure talking to him would completely dispel any of the crazy notions Vicky had been trying to force into my paranoid, pathetic skull.

"What happened to work?"

"I'm still working." I hadn't done a single bit of work since Vicky.

"Well, you'd better stick to it. I don't want to be accused of distracting you from your job." I could hear his lopsided grin.

I nodded, forgetting he couldn't see me.

"Katie? Are you still there?"

"I'm here. I miss you. I'll see you at lunch, okay?"

I still felt anxious as I dropped into the passenger seat. "Hi, you," I said.

"Hi yourself."

"Did you find time to miss me?"

He leaned in for a quick kiss. "I did nothing else the entire time I've been gone."

"Certainly you must have done something else. Didn't you have work to do?" I forced a big smile.

Cooper tipped his head. "Maybe a little."

"Hmm. I did a little work before I got distracted." I glanced out the windshield at my coworkers inside the bank, then back to Cooper's face. "I checked your accounts after you left. You know, to prepare myself for balancing." I watched his expression, and for a fleeting second, I saw a smile touch his lips. "Anyway, we should talk about what you'd like to do with that extra two hundred thousand dollars."

"Oh." His forehead furrowed for a second before smoothing out again. "I wasn't expecting it so soon. It's too much to be sitting in my checking account, isn't it?"

My lips curved up in another forced smile. "Yes. It is. You don't get wires very often. Is that why you went to New York?"

"Sort of." He adjusted the rearview mirror. "I had business there."

"Oh." I turned back to the window. I needed another approach. "So where are you taking me to lunch?"

"That depends. How hungry are you?"

"Not very." I was actually starving.

"Would you rather do something else?" He flashed a crooked grin.

"Actually, I would." I faced him and swallowed hard.

"What?" He laughed, but it came out as a nervous sound.

"Well, you've seen me at work so many times..." I laced my fingers together on my lap and squeezed. "I'd like to see where *you* work."

"Okay." Cooper drew the word out slowly.

"Perfect." My face split in a wide smile.

"So..."

"So?"

"Why so curious today?"

Just wondering if you've been out killing people lately, honey. I shrugged.

"No special reason?" He raised his eyebrows. "Talking to Vicky maybe?"

I felt guilty for being suspicious. I had to hand it to Vicky... being sneaky was hard work. But I'd read a lot of romantic suspense. I was sure I could pull it off. "So where are we headed?"

"Back to the house."

I looked at him sideways. "Your house?"

Cooper nodded slowly. "My office is at my house, but there's nothing much to see. A desk and chair, that's basically it. My job doesn't exactly chain me to one place. I've even been known to work at the kitchen table. It really just depends on if I'm under the gun or not."

Under the gun? My body went rigid. "Oh. You know what...?" I ran a list of scenarios through my head. If Cooper worked from home, there was an easier way. "Let's go eat Italian instead. I think my appetite's back."

And I'm going to need my strength.

THIS NEVER HAPPENED
TO NANCY DREW

EN ARE, AT THEIR CORE, fairly simple creatures. Even wonderfully kind, gentle, brilliant men could be tricked by really good sex. It made a woman feel powerful. Or in my case, slightly guilty.

Cooper had finally fallen asleep. I didn't really *want* to trick him. Even if I did have a good reason. And I definitely had a very good reason. We'd talked for hours about everything and nothing, but not once in that time did he offer up a single shred of information about his career. Not the slightest detail. So I decided to resuscitate the terrible plan I'd hatched at lunch.

On the surface, it seemed like a pretty good idea. For over three glorious, mind-blowing hours, I encouraged him to try several very strenuous, almost decadent sexual positions in the hope he would pass out from exhaustion. He was thrilled. We started on the sofa and ended up on the bed, and I believed we may have been everywhere in between.

I really should have passed out right along with him after that last intense round. He was incredible, and his stamina was impressive, but I was running on pure adrenaline. I was a woman on a mission. I felt there would be no reasonable excuse to keep his profession from me unless he had something to hide. Exactly *what* he was hiding remained to be seen.

I carefully slithered out of bed and grabbed his shirt from the floor. I slipped it on and buttoned most of the buttons. I couldn't go creeping around his massive house in the middle of the night wearing absolutely nothing.

I stood perfectly still for a moment, waiting to see if he would stir. He didn't. His face was buried in his pillow, his arm tucked over the other pillow I'd put in my place. His breathing was deep and even. He was definitely asleep.

I had to restrain myself from bending down and pressing my lips against his tousled hair. Instead, I grabbed my cell phone from the nightstand and slinked out of the room. I gently closed the door behind me and practiced in my head what I would say if I was caught sneaking around in the dark.

I was looking for something to drink. Then I remembered the bottled water he kept in the mini fridge in the sitting room. *I was craving a midnight snack.* Right, because I always wake up in the middle of the night, hungry for marshmallows. I knew he didn't have anything else to eat in his kitchen.

I heard a strange noise. And he would believe I was brave enough to investigate on my own? Ridiculous.

Even I wouldn't believe any of those excuses, and according to Phil, I'm a complete novice. I would just have to cop to the crime and say I couldn't sleep and was—not *snooping* because that sounded too dishonest— investigating my surroundings.

I was looking for a book. That might actually convince him. He knew I loved books.

I crept down the stairs very carefully because the only light came from the faint glow of the moon. I waited until I reached the bottom before I flipped open my cell phone for light.

Cooper had said he worked from just about anywhere, so I decided to start in the keeping room. I had officially been introduced to that part of the house the other night, so I knew the layout. I was extremely familiar with the sofa and blushed as I walked by it... *leg one of our triathlon.* The things he'd done to me on that sofa were definitely taboo. I took one last look around the room and didn't see anything that might be a clue.

I still didn't want to turn on the lights as I made my way into the kitchen. Somehow, I felt safer cloaked in darkness as I nosed around. I pointed the glow from my phone toward the counter, but it wasn't enough to see. I opened the refrigerator to shed more light on the room and proceeded to investigate.

His drawers were stocked with the usual things—flatware, napkins, potholders, rolls of aluminum foil, plastic wrap, boxes of zipper bags—all useless items in a kitchen with no food. His upper cabinets housed very nice glassware and china. Other shelves revealed a full set of stainless steel pots and pans, large ceramic mixing bowls, and measuring cups and spoons.

In his pantry was nothing but a single bag of marshmallows, the big fluffy ones, and amazingly, still soft. As it turned out, I *was* sort of hungry, and since breakfast was still hours away, I stuffed one into my mouth. The instant the powdery sweetness touched my tongue, I let out a tiny groan of pleasure. I should have eaten more at dinner.

Just as I was about to pop in a second one, I spotted a row of hooks on the inside of one of the pantry doors. On each hook was a key. I turned my phone to shine a little more light on the faint printing above each one: garage, spare house, car, file cabinet. *Bingo!*

I grabbed the bag of marshmallows because they were too tasty to leave behind and reached for the filing cabinet key. I heard the sound of footsteps behind me and froze.

Someone who was definitely *not* Cooper barked, "Don't *move!*"

So obviously, I did the exact opposite. I screamed and

threw the bag of marshmallows straight up into the air. The puffy white confections scattered like giant snowflakes.

"Down on the floor, lady," the man demanded.

I heard the click of what could only be some sort of gun and imagined it pointing right at me. Prepared to hit the deck as ordered, I remembered I wasn't wearing anything under Cooper's shirt. I wavered for a moment, trying to decide would I rather die of embarrassment or of a gunshot wound.

"I said get down on the floor. On your knees. *Now!*" His voice echoed in the empty room.

A thundering noise built behind my ears like the sound of rain hammering against a tin roof, and a sharp jolt of panic rose from the pit of my empty stomach, threatening to send the marshmallow back up. Did Cooper know? Had he ordered a hit on me? Was I about to die for stealing a bag of marshmallows?

I wasn't even aware tears were tumbling from my eyes until I tasted the saltiness on my lips. I thought I heard yelling from somewhere in the house. I wasn't really sure because the roaring in my ears was almost deafening. I heard the timbre of a new voice, but I was too afraid to turn and look. And as far as I knew, the man with the gun trained on my head—or wherever he had it pointed—was still there, waiting for me to drop to my knees.

Then I distinctly heard Cooper's furious voice. "What are you doing in my kitchen?"

"I-I was h-hu-hungry, and—"

"Stop!" Cooper yelled.

It was the end of my poor, pathetic little life; I just knew it. I felt myself falling apart as violent sobs shook me. Someone grabbed my shoulders from behind, and I screamed.

"It's okay, you're safe." Cooper pulled me tightly against his chest, enveloping me in his arms. "Get that fucking gun out of my girlfriend's face!"

"Who the hell are *you*?" the man asked.

"I'm the guy who pays your fucking salary," Cooper shot back. Then he turned to me. "Oh, Katie, I'm so sorry. I should have warned you about the motion detectors on the security system. Don't move. I'll be right back. I need to reset it so they'll leave."

Security system? Motion detectors? A new wave of sobs shook me. He probably thought I was crying because I was freaked out, which I was, but my new bout of tears was for another reason entirely. I was a terrible detective. A total failure. No detective in any book I had ever read would fail to disable the security system.

A few minutes later, Cooper scooped me into his arms again, and we stood quietly in the corner of the kitchen while we waited for the security team to leave. I felt the tension pouring from him as he held me.

"You came down looking for food? But you knew I don't have anything in the house." He cradled me tighter against his chest and kissed my hair.

I looked at the marshmallows scattered around the counter and floor. I still had the sweet taste of them on my lips, so I lied brilliantly. "You had these." I reached for the closest marshmallow and held it up for inspection.

He paused, staring at the sugary treat for an impossibly long minute. "I'll have the kitchen stocked by the time you get off work tomorrow."

"I don't think that was really the issue this time." I nodded in the direction of the exiting men with guns.

"Yes, well. They're gone now, and I'll see to it you have the codes for the alarm system in the morning."

"You don't have to do that. This is all my fault." A fresh batch of tears escaped my puffy eyes. "I shouldn't have been sneaking around your house. I knew better. You told me you didn't have any food. I was just seeing what I could dig up."

"No. I want you to feel at home here." He brushed

my tears away with his thumbs. "You should be able to rummage through my kitchen if you're hungry. You'd be able to do that at your own house."

"Maybe I should just stay at my own house." I hoped he would say something like, "Don't be ridiculous," or "Absolutely not."

"Do you *want* to go home? I wouldn't blame you if you did after being accosted in the night by armed men." He surveyed my appearance for the first time since he'd saved me from being shot. "And you aren't even wearing very much, are you? You'd think that would have been their first indication you belonged here. This is unacceptable. I should have been more careful. I'm not used to having anyone here other than myself. It's no excuse, but it's all I have."

I felt even guiltier. And I'd already been feeling pretty guilty before he started blaming himself. I had been the one creeping around in the dark, doing reconnaissance without underwear. "It's not your fault, Cooper. I should have told you I was hungry. I know you would have come down here and scavenged for marshmallows for me." I used my best *sexy voice,* which oddly enough, I was getting pretty good at.

"Of course I would have. I would have probably gone out and gotten you something a little more nutritious than marshmallows if you wanted. I was just thinking of you standing here wearing nothing but my shirt, which looks amazing on you, by the way." He took in my state of undress again with a shadow of his lopsided grin, then shook his head. "I feel horrible that you had a gun pointed at you while I was lying in bed, thinking you were sleeping beside me."

"I guess it's a good thing I screamed." I was pretty sure that was an understatement.

"Yes. A very good thing." He kissed the top of my head. "Are you still hungry, my little forager?"

I shook my head. "No, I think I've had it scared out of me."

"Can we go back to bed then?" He slipped his arm around my waist and tugged me against him.

I was glad he did. The adrenaline was starting to wear off, and I thought I might fall down. "I don't know if I can sleep yet."

"I was counting on that."

SPY GAMES

I WAS LATE FOR WORK. VERY late. *Again*. Cooper decided my middle of the night ordeal, followed by another exquisite sex session, earned me extra time in bed and turned off my alarm. He let me sleep until almost nine and didn't understand why I would be irritated with him. Ridiculous, over-protective man. Then he informed me I'd have to drive myself to work because he had an afternoon appointment across town and wouldn't make it back in time to pick me up.

When I finally got to the bank at ten fifteen, Vicky was waiting for me in the lobby. "Nice going, Katie. Leave it to you to almost get arrested." She looked infinitely pleased with herself.

My mouth fell open, and I stood there staring at her.

She laughed. "Stop looking at me like I'm psychic. Cooper called to say you would be late, and he told Phil what happened."

"I did *not* almost get arrested. I just set off an alarm." I didn't mention how close I had come to getting shot or how I had been dressed or any of the other sordid details, for that matter. And I could only hope Cooper had edited out all the truly embarrassing bits.

"Hmm," she muttered with a raised eyebrow. "I would've loved to have seen that."

"It wasn't nearly as exciting as it sounds." It was *way* worse. I had nightmares off and on for the rest of the night, but in my dreams, Cooper was holding the gun, and it was pressed against my temple.

"Well, it sounds like you had an interesting evening just the same." She walked away without a single mention of what she had done last night. I almost smiled at the thought that my evening had been more exciting to her than hers, but based on mine, I didn't think I should be proud.

Silvia came out of her office at that very moment. With a smirk, she shook her head at me. "Do I even want to know what happened?"

"Not really."

"I didn't think so. You're still alive, so I guess everything worked out in the end."

I suspected Cooper hadn't edited enough.

Silvia went back to working on some project, so when Phil strode over and parked himself directly between me and the door to my office, I knew they were taking turns. I wasn't sure if *they* knew it, but that was how it seemed.

"What I want to know is... exactly *what* were you doing that required the SWAT team to be called in?" He crossed his arms over his chest.

I tried to think of something witty to say. I had apparently used up my allotment because absolutely nothing came to mind. "I was eating marshmallows."

"Stolen marshmallows?"

"Apparently."

He didn't press for more details, so I didn't volunteer any. He just shrugged as if vaguely disappointed and wandered off to do whatever it was Phil did.

Right on schedule, as if she had been cued from behind the proverbial curtain, June walked around the corner. She didn't say anything; she just smiled in June's sweet way.

I figured maybe she was waiting for me to say something. "Hi, June."

She wasn't. She just walked over and took my hand in both of hers in a very motherly gesture. June was really the mother I'd always wanted, the one person who didn't give me grief for my every decision. She gave my hand a squeeze, pressing an orange card into my palm, and left.

"Oh, very funny! Ha, ha!" I made sure they all heard because I knew they were all in on it. It was one brand new *Get Out of Jail Free* card.

As if my morning couldn't get worse, my weekly conference call with the head office turned into a thirty-minute tirade on how badly my job performance had slipped. I'd gone from a top performer to below mid-level. I was actually more surprised I'd managed to stay above the bottom. I certainly hadn't been doing much work lately.

I leaned back in my chair and stared out the window. Searching Cooper's house in the middle of the night had been the wrong approach. But since he'd given me a key and codes for the alarm, I could search during the day.

That morning, Cooper had insisted I should be able to get into his house any time I needed to, and I definitely needed to. I had tried to remind him I had a house of my own, but he insisted that since I could fill my imaginary cat's imaginary bowl and Henry, Earl of Catnip, would be fine for several days, I really didn't have a reason to go to my house each night. He seemed completely unaware of the unwritten rules of love and dating that said we were rushing things.

I knew we were moving a little—okay, *a lot*—fast. But Cooper had made a few fairly good points using phrases like "seizing golden opportunities," "life's too short," and other popular clichés. He stated very eloquently how we had already wasted an entire year because we were too afraid to take a chance. Before I knew it, I was tucking his house key into my pocket and saving his alarm code in my cell.

Key or no key, I couldn't search Cooper's house while I was stuck at the bank, so I decided to actually get some work done. I flipped past the paperwork I didn't want to bother with quite yet and stopped at the printout from

Cooper's wire transfer. With all my plotting to search his house, I'd almost forgotten I had access to every transaction on Cooper's accounts. Yep, Nancy Drew had nothing to fear from me.

I pulled up his profile and began a systematic search for all deposits made in the past year. Some were extremely large, like the two hundred thousand he received last week. Others were more reasonable, but still, by no stretch could they be considered small.

I switched to look at the transactions going out of his account. I frowned when I saw *Le Guarde Systems* got a hefty check each month. If Cooper didn't turn out to be a hired assassin, I was definitely going to convince him to change security companies. As much time as I spent balancing his checkbook, I probably should have remembered them before I entertained thoughts of covert ops in the night.

He also employed a gardener and a housekeeper, who both got regular checks, and he paid an occasional caterer. I stopped to stare at the check he had written on the day of our first date. That was a very expensive dinner.

Holy shit! He gave fifty thousand dollars to St. Jude Children's Research Hospital.

I felt a sharp twinge of guilt. First, I was rifling through his personal things at his house, and now I was crossing the line of *need to know* with regard to his bank accounts. And all along, he was donating money to sick children. But since I'd already crossed that line, I wasn't about to stop.

Pushing back my guilt, I kept searching. I had seen most of the entries time and time again without a second thought, but with my new suspicions, they carried more weight. More power. I found a check written to someone named Vivian Allen. I went further back and discovered she was receiving monthly payments. I had no idea who the woman was, but she was paid very well.

I knew I shouldn't, but I did a quick search in our

account database for the mysterious Ms. Allen. No results. I pressed my fingers to my temples and tried to massage away the new headache. My next mission would be to find out who Vivian was and why he was paying her. My Google search netted pages upon pages of results to dig through, but nothing that immediately jumped out at me. I was acutely aware I wasn't going to find anything about her while I was at the office, so I tried to push her to the back of my mind and focused on my job.

My phone rang—Cooper. So much for focusing on my job.

I used my sexy voice to answer. "Hi, you."

"Still mad at me for letting you oversleep?"

"I was never *really* mad at you."

"Well, you might be when I tell you this. My meeting just got pushed up to an hour from now."

"So no lunch?"

"I'm afraid not. But the good news is I'll be back in time for dinner. I have something special planned."

A wide smile broke out across my face. It was as if the sky had opened up and presented me with the perfect opportunity. "I'm sure I can find something to do for lunch." And if I planned things right, I'd have just enough time to search. "I'll see you after work."

After telling Phil I needed an extra-long lunch—swearing it would be the last time ever, or for the year, whichever came first—and texting Cooper to be sure he'd left for his meeting, I made my way to his house. I pulled into his long, twisting drive, and jumped out of my car in a hurry to get inside.

"Crap!" I screamed as the car started to roll forward. I jumped back in to stamp my foot on the brake and pushed the button to engage park.

By the time I reached the side entrance, I was sweating

bullets. I turned the key in the lock and quickly slipped through the door to punch in the code for the alarm.

Not wasting any time, I skipped over the keeping room and went straight to the kitchen to retrieve the key to the file cabinet. I opened every door on the lower floor but found nothing. The rooms looked as if no one had set foot in them except to clean. I was beginning to get discouraged when an idea came to me.

I hurried to the staircase and took the steps two at a time. I had never even considered the rooms on the upper floor. Until that moment, I hadn't noticed the four other doors along the hall. I had tunnel vision when it came to that hallway.

I tried each door, opening them to well-appointed but impersonal guest rooms that could have been in expensive hotels. The last door, the one closest to Cooper's room, was locked. I jiggled the handle; it wouldn't budge. That had to be the room I was looking for, and I was determined to get in there. I asked myself what Stephanie Plum would do. With a sinking feeling in the pit of my stomach, I realized she would have been smart enough to search upstairs last night. My ordeal with the armed men had been for nothing. I shook my head, marveling at my own idiocy.

The door didn't have one of those standard bedroom locks that could be twisted open with a screwdriver. After checking the top of the door frame for the key—like I'd seen done in spy movies—I ransacked the drawers in Cooper's bedroom. *Nothing.* And time was running out.

Another brainstorming session sent me scurrying into the adjacent bedroom where I threw open the window, toying with the idea of climbing out and using a rope to reach the other room—another tactic I'd seen in the movies. One look down brought me back to my senses.

I shut the window and flopped onto the bed to stare at the ceiling. I lay there for several minutes, certain my foray into sleuthing was an utter failure. Then I noticed there were two doors on the wall shared by the locked room. I jumped up and sprinted to the first door—an empty closet. The second led to a bathroom, which had a door on the opposite end. *Jackpot!*

I crossed the tile floor and stepped into the room beyond. An office! A simple pine desk I was sure was an antique stood in one corner. Behind the desk was a comfortable-looking chair. Hundreds of books in built-in bookcases lined the walls. I spotted a low filing cabinet along the back wall behind the desk, but my elation over that discovery was muted by another one: a laptop.

The computer sat open on his desk, and I raced over to it, catching my toe on the leg of the desk on my way and falling conveniently into the swivel chair. I slid my fingers across the keys.

I stared, open-mouthed, at the flashing cursor waiting for the password. *Crap! Crap! Crap!* I had absolutely no idea what his password could be.

I tried his name and his date of birth. Then I tried London and a combination of his date of birth and name. I tried his favorite color and even my name, but nothing worked. I had no idea how long I was sitting there trying to crack his password when a tremor made me jump. I choked back a scream when I realized my cell phone was vibrating in my pocket.

I pulled out my phone and flipped it open. I knew who it was without looking.

"Miss me yet?" Cooper asked.

"I missed you before I even left this morning," I said.

"I'm just making sure you've eaten lunch. I can't have your legs going all weak on me later."

I swiveled the chair around until I was looking out the window. "My legs are always weak when I'm around you." I giggled, spinning back to the desk. A bright yellow sticky note on the corner of Cooper's desk caught my eye, and I pulled it off to read it. The note was written in his neat handwriting. *To Katie with Love.*

Cooper said something, and I sat up straight. "What did you say?"

"I said I made it halfway to the other side of town when my meeting was cancelled." He chuckled. "I guess I could've gone to lunch with you after all."

"Where are you now?" I tried not to sound anxious.

"I'm about to pull into the driveway."

I should have seen that coming! If only I read thrillers instead of romance novels. The chair tipped over as I jumped up to run. I scrambled to right it. Then I stuck the yellow note to the side of the desk again and frantically put everything in his office back to the way it was.

"Katie, are you still there?"

Oh, I'm here all right. "Yes," I squeaked, carefully closing the bathroom door behind me.

"Why is your car in the driveway?"

I bolted down the hall to Cooper's room in a panic. "I... umm... I needed to change. I ruined my blouse." I looked down at my pristine blouse and cringed.

"Oh, not my favorite one, I hope."

I wrapped my fingers around the hem and pulled. It wouldn't rip. "No, not that one," I panted, running into the bathroom to find something sharp. *Why is it you can never find a pair of scissors when you need them?*

"Well, that's a relief."

I heard a car door slam. I spotted a bottle of hair gel and quickly squeezed a glob onto my fingers. "Yeah, but I really liked this shirt." I rubbed the gel onto the front of my blouse until a greasy stain formed, then glanced at my reflection in the mirror. Yes, the large spot would be sufficient.

"I'll get you a new one," he said.

I could hear his voice through the phone and from down the hall. I turned away from the mirror, unbuttoning my shirt.

"Hi." He still held his phone as he crossed the bathroom

to where I stood. He looked positively thrilled to see me, as if we'd been away from each other for days, even weeks.

"Hi." I forced a shaky smile, my phone still pressed to my ear. I hoped my heart would return to normal before he noticed, or at least hoped he would mistake the racing heart as desire rather than panic.

I was playing a dangerous game, and as much as I knew I should stop and come clean, that wouldn't happen. I had to know his secrets. And if he was unwilling to tell me, I had no choice but to find out on my own.

He raised an eyebrow. "You're flushed. Did you run here?"

I quickly retraced my steps in my head, hopeful I'd left everything the way it had been before my search. Holding my shaky smile in place, I said, "You know I don't run unless I'm being chased... especially in these." I pointed at my dangerous boots. "Of course, I don't need to run to trip over air."

Cooper gave an understanding nod. "I like your dangerous boots with this skirt." His fingers skimmed my hip, and he grinned crookedly before nodding toward my blouse. "What did you spill? It looks sticky."

"Hmm... very sticky," I said, my fingers fumbling with the rest of the buttons. "I need to change so I can get back."

"Here, let me help you." He replaced my fingers on the buttons, undoing them slowly. "Whatever this is, it's seeping through to your skin. You should probably take a shower."

"Probably." I took an unsteady breath as he leaned in to kiss the corner of my mouth.

"I should probably help you." He smiled against my lips when I nodded. "You're going to be late getting back." He kissed down my neck as he peeled my blouse off my shoulders, dropped it to the floor, then pulled his own shirt over his head.

Cooper paused in his seduction long enough to twist

the water on in the shower. He unzipped my skirt and slid it down my legs. "Very late," he growled.

"I'll get fired," I said, tangling my fingers in his hair.

"In that case, we should stop now. I definitely don't want you to get fired," he teased between kisses.

"You're a terrible liar."

"No, that's you. I'm actually a very good liar when I want to be."

I flinched.

Cooper captured my face in his hands and locked eyes with mine. "I've never lied to you, Katie."

I nodded, letting him pull me into the shower with him, but I had to force myself to relax. His words kept playing over and over again in my head. *I'm actually a very good liar when I want to be.*

SOMETIMES THE SHOW DOESN'T HAVE TO GO ON

COOPER DROVE ME BACK TO the bank after lunch with the excuse he had to work on investing the two hundred grand wired in last week. That worked for me. I could spend more time with Cooper, and Phil couldn't fire me for slacking off with my boyfriend at work. I didn't have anyone else on my calendar, and I had absolutely no plans to work when I got back to the office anyway.

I had barely walked through the door when Dean swept me into a tight embrace. "There she is—my best girl, Katie."

I used to look forward to Dean's unannounced visits, especially the dramatic entrances. It was entertaining when he burst into my office, singing his lines as if we were players in a fabulous Broadway production. Or rather, it used to be.

Phil bounded out of my office and startled Dean just enough that he released me. Cooper's face was contorted into a deep frown as he slid his arm around my waist and tugged me sharply away from Dean. Dean grabbed both of my hands and wrenched me *almost* out of Cooper's grasp, but like a spring, I jerked back against Cooper's hard frame.

Dean's eyebrows rose sharply. Then he smiled and took a step back as if admiring me from afar. "Katie, you really look wonderful." Dean's gaze slithered down my body. "Truly scrumptious."

Cooper tightened his hold on me until it almost hurt. I could actually feel the ripples of fury rolling off him.

Phil stepped in between the two men. "Dean, you've met Katie's new boyfriend, haven't you? Dean Maynard. Cooper Maxwell." He introduced them, then walked away. *The coward.*

Any normal man would have taken that cue and behaved accordingly. Not Dean. Dean was a showman, and as any great showman knows, the show must go on. He extended a hand to Cooper, who accepted it for a tense handshake.

"Cooper, nice to meet you. You're a lucky guy. I've been trying for months to get into Katie's—"

"Gah!" I let out a gasp, certain I knew what Dean was about to say. "Dean, why don't you go have a seat in my office, and I'll be right there."

Dean gave Cooper a triumphant smirk, then winked at me before he walked off to my office and sat in the chair across from mine. I measured the fury in Cooper's eyes and patted my cheeks with both hands. They were hot.

"I know this looks bad." I shot a quick, panicked glance at Dean, who was propping his feet up on my desk. "He's just trying to be funny. Dean is harmless... really. Remember, he's an actor." I heard the hysteria in my voice as I tried to sound reassuring.

"An actor? Is that supposed to make me feel comfortable with the situation? He was just undressing you with his eyes," Cooper said, grinding his teeth.

"I don't think he got that far, really."

"Katie..."

"This is my job."

He thought about that for a minute, and I could almost see the wheels turning in his head. "Is it your job to cater to an ass like that?" Cooper waited for a second, but when I didn't answer, he added, "Go then. I'll be sitting out here, not twenty feet away, if you need me."

My insides were coiled up like an unpredictable spring,

ready to snap at any moment. I walked slowly into my office, stealing glances at Cooper sitting in the lobby, watching me. Standing in my doorway, I contemplated whether to close the door or leave it open. If I left it open, I was quite certain Dean's voice would carry far beyond the lobby where Cooper sat poised to listen. I was also sure Cooper wouldn't be pleased with anything he heard. But on the other hand, if I closed the door, Cooper would be more anxious *trying* to hear what was transpiring in my office, and with Dean's theater-ready voice, it could still be possible to hear every single word he said.

Leaving it up to fate, I bumped the door with my foot as I walked through. I figured, if it stayed open, so be it. The door fell shut, and I shuddered.

"You look a little green around the gills, Katie. Boyfriend troubles?" Dean leaned back in the chair with his feet still up on my desk and gave me the most arrogant smile I had ever seen perched on his lips.

"Don't you start with me, mister." He was having way too much fun, and I had to admit, if it wasn't at my expense, I probably would have laughed, too. But it *was*, so I glowered at him. Then with an exasperated sigh, dropped into my chair... and screamed.

Someone had adjusted the back of the seat so it would tilt back dangerously far. The chair kept tipping until it was almost completely reclined, and overcompensating for the pitch, I spilled out of the chair and landed on the floor with a thud.

Before I even registered the humiliation, my door whipped open.

Cooper scooped me off the carpet. "Are you okay?"

"You mean other than mortified with embarrassment? I'm fine." I lied. It hurt. Mostly my butt, but of course my pride. I wasn't about to tell Cooper, though, even if it was only superficial. He would freak out.

Dean was another story. Dean was cackling. He hadn't

budged from his reclined position across the desk and seemed very much amused. Cooper glared at him.

"Really, it's okay. I'm fine." I sat in my chair, careful not to lean back, and pulled up the lever that locked the back into place. "*Someone* adjusted my seat back," I said. "I tipped back too far and fell out."

Cooper tucked my hair back behind my ears. "Are you sure you're fine?"

I laughed. "I'm sure. Just a little humiliated, but I'm used to that."

"Okay, I'll be in the lobby." He turned and walked out, but I could tell he wasn't pleased about it. He left the door open, and I suspected it wasn't by accident.

I tried to pretend nothing had happened. "So what brings you to the bank today, Dean?"

A wide smile broke across Dean's face. "Serendipity, Katie. Serendipity."

"Very funny."

"You know, your guy seems to have a bit of a temper. I was speaking with the pretty redhead earlier, and she seems to think he might be—" Dean peeked over his shoulder before leaning across my desk until he was almost in my face. "—a killer."

"Vicky has a vivid imagination. Besides—" I glanced at Cooper pacing like a caged lion in the lobby. Our eyes met briefly before I turned back to Dean. "I think I'd know if I was looking into the eyes of a killer."

I laced my fingers into Cooper's. "You can deny it all you want, babe, but you were pitifully jealous today."

He led me out the bank door. "I was not—did you just call me *babe*?" He stared down at me with a surprised smile.

"I did."

"I think I might like that." The smile slipped into a serious expression. "But I wasn't jealous. I was being protective."

I rolled my eyes. "Is that what they call it now?"

"I wanted to kill him," he said casually, as if committing murder was as easy as taking out the trash.

I was speechless.

He squeezed my hand and laughed. "I wouldn't actually kill him, Katie. I'm just being hyperbolic."

"I knew that!" I forced myself to laugh with him.

Cooper pulled the door shut, and I turned the key in the lock to secure it. I had just spent the last hour with his accounts in front of me, attempting to restructure his finances to accommodate the recent influx of cash, and all I could do was wonder where it had come from.

I was ready to go home. I just wasn't sure where that was anymore. I was a little afraid to admit to myself, let alone him, that I was reluctant to go back to my boring little townhouse alone, when I could very easily let myself be drawn back to his lovely chateau in the trees.

"Are you ready to go home?" he murmured against my hair as if reading my mind.

The familiar fluttering in my stomach answered the question for me. "Yes," I whispered.

He responded by kissing me until I was dizzy. Secrets aside, I was still far too easily hypnotized by the taste of him on my lips.

Cooper pulled into the garage, and I waited until he came around the front to open my door.

He took my hand as I climbed out of the car. "You look tired."

"Yes, a little." I was exhausted. And hungry. But I was too tired to worry about being hungry. I'd had a long day after a longer night. Being a detective was grueling work.

"Do you want to go straight to bed?"

I raised my eyebrows.

"To sleep. Really."

I knew what would happen if I crawled into bed with him, and it wouldn't have anything to do with sleeping. "Can we order Chinese takeout?"

"Are you hungry?"

"Starving."

He grinned. "I could make you something."

I laughed.

"I wasn't kidding."

"But you don't have food."

He bent down and kissed the tip of my nose. "Correction. I *didn't* have food."

"And now?"

"And now I do."

"Catered?"

"I bought groceries!" His mock insult was over-the-top, but my shock was real.

"You shopped?"

He chuckled. "I paid."

I smiled. I couldn't see him pushing a shopping cart. "That sounds more like it. Who shopped?"

"That's hardly important. Come see what we have."

I didn't miss the *we* in that sentence. The man could definitely make me swoon when he wanted to, and even when he wasn't trying.

Positively glowing with delight, he entwined his fingers with mine and towed me through the spotless mudroom to the kitchen. *Cute* wasn't a strong enough word to describe him, but that was what came to my mind first.

I rounded the corner into the kitchen and came to a screeching halt in front of the massive island where an overflowing basket of fruit waited.

Cooper didn't pay that any attention. He opened the refrigerator door. "Okay, we have fresh fruit, as you can see, but we also have gruyere, brie, and other assorted imported cheeses." He pulled out random items to show me. "There's a beautiful filet in here I could grill."

"You have a grill?"

"You wound me, Katie. I have everything."

My eyes swept down his body, and I had to agree.

He turned back to the fridge and crouched down, pulling out another package. "You like fish, right? We have marinated salmon, swordfish, and sea bass. And check out these shrimp." He held up a bag of slimy gray squiggles.

"Cooper, who is going to cook all of this?"

"I am, of course," he said as if I was ridiculous for asking.

"Are you sure? This looks..." I gestured toward the cornucopia of food practically oozing out of the massive refrigerator. "It looks very complicated. Have you ever cooked before?"

"Now that's a silly question." He stood up and took my face in his hands. "Just because I choose not to cook doesn't mean I don't know how. I'm actually an excellent cook." He pressed his warm lips to mine in a tender kiss.

Major stomach flip. I had no clue his expertise extended to the kitchen. Of course, that was still in theory. I hadn't sampled anything yet. But I was weak in the knees just imagining him cooking for me.

He put his hands on my waist and lifted me up to sit on the edge of the island. "Katie." He watched my face for a reaction. When I bit my lower lip, he smiled and tilted his head down for another gentle kiss. "You like when I say your name. Why is that?"

I blushed. I didn't know how to explain the shivers that went through me when I heard my name on his lips. I just shrugged.

He kissed me again. "Tell me."

"It's silly."

"I appear to like silly things." He didn't fight fair. He pressed his lips against the hollow behind my ear and proceeded to make his way down my neck, igniting fires everywhere he touched.

"We're not going to eat, are we?" I murmured.

He froze, lips at my chin, then stood straight. "I was cooking, wasn't I?"

I giggled. "I think that was the plan."

Cooper stepped away from the island and leaned against the refrigerator. "Well, if I'm going to thrill your taste buds, you're going to have to leave the kitchen."

"Leave?"

"Yes. Out." He pointed toward the stairs.

"What will I do?"

"Why don't you go take a hot bath? You can put on something more comfortable. And then come back down and I'll feed you like the *babe* you are."

"Oh, that was horrible. I am officially forbidding you to utter the word *babe* again." I laughed, but he kept a straight face.

"Yeah, well. I may be running out of romantic things to say."

"Impossible!"

He erupted into laughter. "You'd better go before I forget I'm supposed to be cooking and decide to ravish you instead."

I rolled my eyes and jumped down from the counter. As I landed, something bright clattered to the floor at my feet.

Cooper reached down and picked up a brass key. I bit back a gasp. It was the key to his file cabinet.

He snorted. "Where did *this* come from?"

"What?" It took amazing effort for me to sound mildly interested, rather than terrified. I had put the key in my pocket before I searched the house and never returned it.

"This key." He studied it for a moment then walked to the pantry where all the other keys were hung and opened it. "It should be hanging right here." And he placed it back on its hook.

"What does it go to?" I feigned ignorance.

His eyebrows furrowed. "My file cabinet. But I can't for the life of me come up with a single reason why it was on the island. Or how it got there."

Inside, my heart was thumping and my blood had gone cold. On the outside, I hoped my face didn't betray my thoughts.

AN IMPASSE

I CLOSED MY EYES AS I soaked neck deep in the steaming tub. I didn't know how much longer I could play such a dangerous game. I loved him. I felt it more strongly every minute. But could I ignore my fears and trust him, or would I destroy everything with suspicion and doubt?

I wasn't sure anymore. What if I threatened to leave him if he didn't give me the answers I needed? Would he call my bluff? What if he told me he was a lawyer or a doctor? Would I even believe him? And what if he *was* a lawyer or doctor, and I blew the whole relationship with my doubts and insecurities? What if he was a mob lawyer or a mob doctor?

What *would* I accept as his profession? I supposed it didn't really matter as long as it wasn't something illegal. Or dangerous. And even then... would I leave him for having a risky job? I didn't think I could. I was reaching a place where it ceased to matter what he did; I just had to know.

I stepped out of the warmth of the bath and wrapped myself in a heated towel. I was determined to get my answers tonight. I prepared my weapons and started down the stairs.

He was still in the kitchen working on something at the stove with his back to me, oblivious to the fact that I was poised to attack. I clutched the still warm towel to my body and soundlessly crept up behind him. As soon as I was close enough to whisper and still be heard, I cleared my throat.

He startled slightly and turned to face me. "Look at you," he said in a low voice, eyes wide.

"Brave," I murmured.

"Brave?" He smiled, but I could see the hint of confusion.

"Definitely. I would have to be brave to dare to come down here without underwear again."

A slow grin tipped his lips up on one side, and he pushed his hand into his hair. I could tell he had been doing that a lot. His hair was pretty messed up.

"How brave are you?"

"Pretty brave." I pulled out my first weapon—my sexy voice—and looked up at him from under my lashes.

He took a step toward me. "I thought you were hungry."

"Famished."

"Taste?" He smiled and then turned to retrieve a sample from his pan.

I nodded and let him feed me from the fork. It was fabulous. Cooper was definitely an excellent cook.

My reaction must have told him I liked it. "It's good, isn't it?"

"You know it's good," I whispered, still using the sexy voice.

"I want to hear you say it."

"It's better than good. It's amazingly good."

Cooper took a bite of the filet and closed his eyes. "I am a fabulous chef."

I couldn't help but laugh. It was true, but funny. "Kiss me." I reached out, grabbed the front of his shirt, and towed him toward me.

He didn't hesitate. He swept me into a heated kiss, wrapping his arms around me.

"Cooper," I whispered against his lips. "Please tell me. I have to know."

He ran his tongue over my top lip. "Hmm?"

"How does your breath always taste like peppermint? Even after eating."

He didn't stop kissing me but shook with quiet laughter.

"Please tell me," I said.

"It's a secret."

Our lips moved together softly, but every now and then, he stopped to nip with his teeth.

"So many secrets." I slid my hand under his shirt, running my fingers low over his stomach.

He shook his head lightly, his lips still working with mine. "Just a few," he murmured between kisses. He took my roaming hand in his. "Time for food," Cooper said firmly.

"Time to share just one secret," I demanded with a pout.

"That's fair. But let's eat first."

Finally sated—at least my stomach—I was full and ready for sleep. Well... *bed.* I was getting used to the lack of sleep. We headed toward the stairs.

"Time for my secret," I coaxed.

"Why do you like it so much when I say your name?"

"Huh?" I muttered, somewhat confused by his strange change of subject.

"You've been keeping that a secret. You said you were going to share one secret. That's what I want to know." He flashed a devious smile.

"No, that's not what I meant. *You* are supposed to be telling *me* a secret."

"You never specified who would be sharing a secret. I pick you."

"Ugh! This is so *not* fair. I've been patient. I've told you everything about me..." Uh... other than my sneaky alter-ego, but he didn't need to know about her. "I don't understand why you can't tell me what you do for a living. How can that be so damn hard?" I turned without saying another word and stamped my feet all the way up the stairs, dropping the towel along the way. I scurried down the hall into his room and climbed under the magnificent sheets. I heard his uneven breathing as he followed me, and I buried my head under the covers.

"Katie?" he called as he stepped through the threshold of the bedroom. "Hey, come on. Don't hide. Talk to me." He sounded so miserable and lost. "Katie, please."

"What?" I grumbled from under the blankets.

"I thought we were playing. Why did you run from me?" He climbed onto the bed and crawled toward me.

"You won't play fair."

He suspended his short trek across the mattress and hesitated for a minute. "Why is this so important to you?"

"Because this is basic first date stuff. You know what I do. You know I have an imaginary cat. You know about my mother, my father, my sister, and every job I've ever had, with maybe the exception of the summer I waited tables, and now you know that. You know about the time I shoplifted the candy bar when I was five, too. Don't make me seem unreasonable for wanting to know what kind of work you do after multiple dates and sleeping in your bed. And it's rotten that you'd make me think you're going to tell me, then turn it into a joke at my expense."

He put a hand on my leg. "You're right. I shouldn't have teased you like that. Isn't it enough to know the depth of my feelings? You have to realize I want nothing more than to share myself with you completely, but there are some things I can't share, not yet. I'm asking you to trust me for a little while longer. I need time. I only hope you can wait, that what you already know about me is enough to keep you from walking away. Because what we have means so much to me."

I groaned. I wanted to be angry. I really did. And I tried to hold on to that as long as I could. But his words and the sadness in his voice shattered my angry mood into a million tiny pieces. I pulled the blankets back and sat up to face him. "Do you think so little of me? How could you even imagine I would walk away? I *love* you because of everything I already know about you. The things I don't know—the secrets—are what make me afraid. My imagination is a frightening thing."

He laughed. "What could you have possibly created in your head that would make you afraid?"

I frowned. "You don't want to know."

"I think I might," he said in a serious tone.

I covered my face with my hands and peeked through my fingers at him. "I'm sure you won't like it."

"Then I definitely want to know."

I pursed my lips and took in a deep breath. I knew I should just tell him what I was thinking and get it over with, but it was horrible and went against his request that I trust him. It said that I'd never fully trusted him. I only hoped he would be distracted by the fact that I was completely naked.

"Well?" He wasn't distracted. He was impatient. I understood that emotion.

"Okay, okay." I pulled myself up until I was sitting with my back against the headboard and tugged a pillow across the front of me like a shield. He raised his eyebrows— waiting—so I took another deep gulp of air and launched into it.

"It started the day you went to New York. No, wait. It was the Thursday before that. You remember... the day I turned the ringer off on my phone? I didn't talk to you all day."

"Last Thursday?"

Had it only been a week? Amazing. "Yes. Last Thursday."

"Go ahead."

"So everyone was watching this bulletin on the news about the judge who got killed downtown." I waited for him to nod. "Vicky was asking me about you and why you didn't come into the bank." I was reluctant to tell him how much Vicky had been wondering about him, and I was afraid to tell him she had been snooping in his accounts.

"I should have suspected Vicky would be involved in this somehow." He shook his head. "I never come in on Thursdays. Until we started dating, I didn't come in on Mondays or Wednesdays, for that matter. That shouldn't have been anything unusual to gossip about."

"If you're going to insist I tell the story, you'll at least need to let me finish."

"Certainly. Continue." He shifted until he, too, was leaning against the headboard, a pillow of his own tucked in front of him like a shield.

"Okay." I tried to remember where I was when he interrupted. "So Vicky was asking me where you were, and Phil and Silvia were talking about the murder and how much it would cost to kill a judge. They were totally caught up in figuring out how much someone would pay. I thought it was pretty morbid, but then I saw the wire transfer into your account, and it was a lot of money." I hesitated, waiting for him to catch up.

He didn't. "Okay. And?"

"Then on Monday, while you were in New York, there was a murder. I kept telling myself you were too busy texting me to find the time to shoot someone—"

He jolted. "Shoot someone?"

I glared at him. "You're interrupting again."

"Sorry, go ahead."

"Vicky said something about how it was a crazy coincidence how everywhere you went, people dropped dead. And when you came back from New York, you had that dark stain on your shirt that looked an awful lot like blood." I stared down at the pillow, picking a piece of down from the cover, trying desperately to imagine the look on his face but too terrified to see it for myself.

"And?"

"And every time I've asked you what you do for a living, you try to distract me." I peeked up at him from under my lashes.

His eyebrows pulled together creating a deep crease, and he pushed both hands into his already messed up hair. "So let me get this straight. You, or maybe Vicky—I haven't decided which of you—was the mastermind in this clusterfuck, but one of you came to the brilliant conclusion that I've been running around killing people?"

I shrugged. "It's possible."

"Well, that's bloody brilliant!"

It was the first time I'd noticed even a hint of a British accent in his deep silken voice. It was sort of sexy. "I'll admit it was a bit of a stretch."

"A bit?"

"Understatement?"

"Immeasurably so."

"You have to admit there certainly seemed to be too much *evidence* to ignore."

He gave me a look filled with utter incredulity. "Circumstantial at best. For Chrissakes, Katie. Is there more?"

"No."

He sat quietly, staring at me. I felt his frustration piercing me like sharp fangs on my tender throat. I wondered what he was searching for in my eyes, whether he was aware I couldn't force myself to look away.

Finally, he nodded. "I'm not angry. I'm somewhat amazed at how easily your imagination runs wild. Have you ever considered writing some of these things down?"

"I told you."

"True. You did tell me. But still. I think I have a pretty good imagination, and I doubt even *I* could have come up with that."

I flushed. He was right. There was no *logical* basis for any of my suspicions. "You're really not angry with me?"

"Really and truly." He snaked his arm around my waist and tugged me roughly into his lap. "Then again, if I say yes, will you work hard to make it up to me?"

I stared up at him from my position lying across his lap. "How hard?"

"Extremely hard." He flashed me the lopsided grin. "Amazingly hard."

"Amazing? Good description. I think I can handle that."

"Better than *handle,* I'd say. You're something of an expert if I'm any judge."

"Do we need a second opinion?"

His face went stony for a brief moment. "Absolutely not. My opinion is all that matters on that subject."

I grinned at his attempt at jealousy. "You're all that matters to me."

"Good." He dipped his face down to kiss me.

"That *is* good. I might need a second opinion, though. Kiss me again."

He kissed me again, more fervently, and I felt myself melting into him.

"I'm not wearing any clothes," I murmured between breathless kisses.

He smiled against my lips. "I know."

I was no longer capable of rational thought as his hands slipped beneath the blankets. The last thing I remembered thinking was how he'd never actually denied being an assassin.

JUST WHEN I THOUGHT THINGS COULDN'T GET ANY WORSE

I PULLED INTO MY USUAL PARKING spot with a sigh. It was Thursday, and the last one had nearly been my undoing in so many ways. Just one week ago, I had been plagued with suspicion, cabernet, and inoperable cell phones.

Not anymore. I needed to get caught up on all the work I had been ignoring. Cooper and I had settled into a lovely new existence as a couple. I wasn't going to worry about his job. I still had no idea what it was, but I wasn't going to worry about him being an assassin. And I wasn't going to fret over him finding out I had been snooping around. I would just pretend it never happened.

I had no idea how I got myself into such situations, but I'd finally managed to extricate myself from my own tangled web without any lingering effects. That was refreshing.

I got quite a bit done in my first hour. No one bothered me all morning, and I even managed to sneak into the back for a quick snack. I wasn't distracted at all. It was almost nice not having to worry about what Cooper was doing. I knew he was in his office, doing his mysterious job, while I was at the bank, doing mine.

Vicky stopped me as I made my way back from the break room. "Staring off into space again, Katie?"

"Just ignoring you," I said with a grin. It was the gloomiest winter Atlanta had seen in years, but to me, everything was sunshine, and I wasn't about to let Vicky spoil my day.

"Like you've been ignoring Dean? He's in my office now. Did you know he got a part in a big show? He said he'd like to take me to New York with him this time." She sounded like that kid who wanted everyone to be impressed with her toys.

Well, I wasn't impressed. "That's nice."

"I'm telling you, Katie, that man is so hot. I swear, the first time I saw him, it started to throb, and I got instantly wet." She was on the verge of swooning at the memory.

"It?" I was almost afraid to ask.

She rolled her eyes. "*It.*" And pointed at her crotch.

"Ewww."

She made a sour face back at me. "Did you figure out what Cooper does for his money yet?"

"He kills actors for a living."

"Funny, Katie."

I shrugged. "So how long have you been *seeing* Dean?" I asked with a smirk. I knew the only *seeing* she was doing was from a respectable distance.

"Just a few days." She frowned. "And since you're totally ignoring him today, he asked me to help him get his accounts in order. Thanks to you, they're pretty messed up." Vicky flipped her hair at me and turned to walk away.

Nope. Not even Vicky could ruin my morning. In fact, I was thrilled to see she'd moved on to a new pretend boyfriend, or first-round draft pick, as she called them.

Dean was my client, but of course, that had never stopped Vicky. And after the whole scene with Cooper, I was determined to completely avoid Dean. I honestly hadn't noticed Vicky showing that much interest in him. But he *was* cute. I had no problem acknowledging that. Vicky definitely had a thing for the cute ones. I often wondered if her husband was even aware of the things she said and did.

Phil whipped around the corner and stopped me before I reached my office. "James, did you hear I won my poker tournament last night? Oh yeah. I am richer to the tune of seven hundred dollars." He held up seven fingers and then made a circle two times with his thumb and finger. "I'm buying lunch for everyone."

"That's nice. Cooper has to work today, so I don't have any lunch plans."

"Good! You can choose anything you want from the dollar menu."

I rolled my eyes. "You're so generous."

"Yeah, I know."

On my way back to my office, my cell phone buzzed in my pocket. I checked the caller ID and cringed. My mother. Again. She was calling for the fifth time that morning, so I figured I might actually have to answer the phone. No, I needed coffee first. I doubled back to the break room and poured myself a cup of cream and added a splash of coffee and sugar to it.

I'd never really liked coffee that much. I was afraid I would need a double shot of Grand Marnier to work up the courage to talk to her.

I'd lost count of how many of her calls I'd ignored over the course of the week. I didn't have the strength to listen to her tirade over my *fake* boyfriend. She was convinced I'd made Cooper up to throw her off my trail. It wasn't a bad idea. I should have done it years ago. Maybe then she would believe me.

I traipsed into my office and let the door fall shut so I could call her without eavesdroppers, but Vicky poked her nose into my office as I dialed.

"Hey, Katie. You need to see this." She motioned toward the lobby.

"I've got to make a call. What do you need?" I held the phone to my ear and waited.

"Oh, nothing really. CNN just announced that the two murders in Atlanta are directly connected to the one in New York. I thought you'd want to know," she tossed in, letting the door fall closed as she left.

In the four rings it took for Mom to pick up, I didn't have time to process the new information, and when she did answer, the connection was bad. She sounded as though she was in a wind tunnel.

"Katherine Grace James, where in the world have you been? I've been calling you for days with no response. It's bad enough you don't answer your phone, but could you possibly have the common decency to listen to your voicemail? If you *had*, I may have a lot of money in cab fare."

I had no idea how listening to my voice mail would save my mother cab fare. *Or did I?*

I suddenly had a horrible feeling in the pit of my stomach, the same feeling I got when I ate something with mushrooms in it—that sudden urge to make a run for the bathroom. I was afraid to ask, but I had to know. "Mom? Where are you?"

She pulled the phone away from her mouth and asked, "Where exactly am I?" I heard someone speaking to her in the background, and then she said, "I am just a few miles from your bank. And when I get there..."

I stopped listening. She was still rattling on, but I couldn't hear a word she said over the rushing sound building behind my ears. My mother was just a few miles away. From the bank. From *me*. *Shit! Shit! Shit!* I dropped my face into my hands and collapsed against the back of my chair.

To my mother, I had been nothing but a supreme disappointment—creeping ever closer to thirty and yet to find a single prospective husband. Mom thought if she could marry a doctor, her daughters could too. My dad was a plastic surgeon in Connecticut, which basically meant my mother lived off the tits and faces of rich women. I found that funny.

I was determined to choose a mate based on nothing but love. It was purely by accident Cooper met every prerequisite Mom had ever imagined for me. And she was coming to visit. She would want to meet Cooper.

The phone had gone dead in my hand, so I jumped from my chair and did a frantic search of my office. I wanted to be sure there was nothing sitting out that my mother would grasp onto as some pathetic commentary on my life. There were just a few potted vaginas, but I was certain she would be oblivious to the humor in that. Once I decided I was safe from her scrutiny, I bolted from my office and ran straight to Silvia's.

"Silvia," I hissed from her doorway.

She was on her cell phone, but she must have noticed the frantic look in my eyes because she held up a finger. "Listen, sweetie. I'll have to call you back. Katie has some new catastrophe that needs my attention. I'll see you in a bit." Silvia ended her call and looked up at me with a bewildered expression. "What on God's green earth has happened to you? I saw you this morning, and you looked absolutely elated. Now you look like you did the day you stapled your blouse to the copy machine."

I glowered at her. "I didn't staple myself to the copier. I got caught on the copier's automatic stapler."

"Only you, Katie. That's all I have to say about that." She shook her head, laughing.

"Will you please pay attention? My mother is on her way here." I grabbed the long strand of pearls around my neck and wound them around my fingers, practically cutting off my circulation.

Silvia's eyebrows shot up. "Right now?"

"As in, this minute."

"Oh, this should be interesting."

"It's not funny."

"Oh yes it is." She put her hand over her mouth to hold back the fit of giggles.

"Gah!" I threw up my hands and left. *Does no one understand that Hurricane Grace is on her way to rain on my perfectly sunny day?*

I managed to clue everyone in, so they were all huddled

in the lobby waiting for the show to start. I was in my office, shooting off a text message to Cooper, the one I promised myself I would *not* send.

Katie: My mother is in town! Unannounced of course. She has come to inspect me with her own brand of sex radar. I may have to leave the country.

I sat on pins and needles until he texted me back less than thirty seconds later.

Cooper: I can have us on the next flight out! You aren't leaving without me. I'll pack the sunscreen. You bring the bikini.

I slid my phone across my desk, satisfied if things didn't go well, I could call for Cooper and make my escape. I patted my cheeks, telling myself to relax. It was only my mother. I had known her my entire life. Unfortunately, that only made me more nervous.

A few minutes later, I heard a commotion in the lobby. I knew my mother had entered the building when the temperature dropped several degrees. Okay, that was an exaggeration. The sour tone of her voice drifting over was the giveaway.

"Hello, I'm Grace James. I'm looking for my daughter Katie."

I poked my head out of my office and waved. "Hi, Mom."

As usual, my mother looked striking. She was dressed in white wool from head to toe. I knew the outfit was designer, but I had no clue which one. The vanilla pantsuit was tailor-made for her tall, slender frame and perfectly matched to the long wool coat and brushed suede boots. The only color she wore was the rich velvet red on her lips.

I could've never pulled off that outfit. She was all grace and elegance, unlike me. And she was built like the stick-figure women I always feared were Cooper's type. Even at her age, she was stunning. Except for the god-awful hat perched on her head like a dead pheasant dressed in silk.

I forced my eyes away from the taxidermist's nightmare. "Mom, what are you doing here?"

"What kind of greeting is that?" She frowned. "Come give your mother a hug."

I knew what that meant. I walked over and, holding my breath to avoid the cloud of Poison that always accompanied her, kissed the air by her cheek, never actually touching her body with mine. She would not have appreciated me wrinkling her designer suit.

"It's good to see you, Mom," I said, forcing a cheery voice. "I wish I had known you were coming."

She popped up one perfectly arched brow. She didn't have to say a word for me to hear her loud and clear. Had I answered my phone or listened to my voice mail, I would have known.

Like a statue suddenly coming to life, Silvia reached a hand toward my mother. "So, Mrs. James, what brings you to town?"

My mother responded by pursing her lips, and Silvia let her hand fall.

"Yes, Mom. What brings you to town?"

She smirked. "Isn't it obvious?"

I couldn't resist. "You missed me?"

She waved off that ridiculous notion with a flick of one long, slender hand. "I wanted to see this *boyfriend* for myself."

Amazing. She flew all that way to catch me in a lie. I was glad she didn't ask to see my new cell phone. "Well, Mom, he isn't here now. I *am* at work."

"The way I heard it, he's always at the bank."

"Never on Thursday," Vicky interjected from her spot behind Silvia.

"So he does exist then? Hmm." She appeared to run that through her platinum-blond head. "But he never comes in on Thursday? What's wrong with Thursday?"

"He's *working*." Vicky made the quotation marks in the air, and I fought the urge to slap the sarcastic look from her face.

Of course, my mother caught wind of a conspiracy and jumped right in with enthusiasm. "What exactly does he do?" She stared at me for a second, then looked back to Vicky for the answer.

I flashed a look of panic at Silvia, who nudged Vicky, but the words were already flying out of Vicky's mouth. "That's the two hundred thousand dollar question."

Bitch! Bitch! Bitch!

My mother huffed. "Exactly what are you talking about?"

"He's very private, Mom. He doesn't talk about work very much."

"Very much? It doesn't sound like he talks about work at all. Have you even asked him?"

"It's really none of my business," I muttered.

"None of your... that's the most ridiculous thing I've ever heard. What if he's into something *illegal*?" She whispered the word illegal, as if it was, well... illegal.

Vicky took a step closer to my mother, as if choosing sides for powderpuff football. "That's *exactly* what I told her!"

That figured. My mother and Vicky were going to be the best of friends. I thought I might need that one-way ticket to Brazil after all.

I decided I'd better separate the two before they had a chance to compare notes, so I poked Vicky in the shoulder. "Don't you have a client in your office?" Then, as Vicky scurried off with a scowl, I turned to my mother. "Mom, why don't you come and sit down? You look tired." I led her to my office.

"Well, it *was* a long flight." She nodded. "And just a horrible ride from the airport. You know you really should move to someplace more accessible."

That's all I need... to be somewhere more accessible to my mother. "I really like it here, Mom."

I got Mom situated in the chair across from my desk and excused myself to get her a cup of coffee. Or as I liked to refer to it, *make a break for it.* No one was in the lobby, as if they'd scattered like rats on a sinking ship. I zipped around the corner to Silvia's office and stuck my head part of the way in before I realized she wasn't there. I scanned the lobby, but I couldn't see her anywhere, so I cut through the back to see if she was in the break room.

"Where's Silvia?" I asked June.

"No clue." She smiled. "Your mom seems nice."

I rolled my eyes. "Yeah, thanks."

I turned to run back to the lobby and remembered the coffee—my whole purpose for leaving her alone in my office. I quickly poured her a cup and added exactly three Sweet'n Lows and a heavy splash of non-fat creamer.

I walked slowly back, careful not to spill on my new pants. It was my first time wearing them, so it went without saying that something would get spilled on them.

Silvia was still nowhere to be found. I made it back safely and set the cup down on my desk. My mother was sifting through the stack of papers with her reading glasses perched at the end of her nose.

"Mom, you can't read those. That's confidential information." I tried to sound assertive as I took them from her and placed them face-down out of her reach.

The smug expression on her face told me I had failed. She took off her glasses and folded them carefully in front of her. "Perhaps you shouldn't leave such *confidential* information out on your desk then." Her tone suggested I was five years old. "Oh, and you have a new text message." She nodded toward my cell phone on the desk.

I wasted no time in scooping it up and flipping it open.

Cooper: You're being awfully quiet out there. You haven't been eaten by the momster have you?

"Is that your *boyfriend*?"

"Yes," I said, delighted that she finally believed in his existence.

"He should learn to spell. He spelled monster with an M."

"Monster *is* spelled with an M."

She shook her head. "Yes, but it doesn't have two."

I re-read the text and bit back a laugh. I had missed his play on words. It didn't say monster; it said *momster*. That was funny. But I was lucky that my momster missed the joke. "Why are you reading my text messages anyway?"

"Oh, I wasn't really reading it. I just noticed it come in."

I wasn't going to argue about how the phone had to have flipped itself in order for her to view the text. I just dropped the subject and fell into my chair. "So which hotel did you book?" I was sure it would be the most expensive one in town. I was only half paying attention to her as I typed a reply to Cooper.

"I thought I might stay with you this visit."

I froze mid-text, and my mouth fell open. "With me?" I erased the entire sentence I was writing to Cooper and started over.

Katie: fuel up the jet and grab the highest SPF you can! My mother's moving in!

"Unless that's a problem?"

I had a sudden irrational worry. "Did Daddy lose his practice?"

"Katie, don't be ridiculous. I always stay with your sister. She loves having me."

My sister is a much better liar. Mom didn't look deranged, not really. But I was sure I'd heard her wrong. She couldn't actually *want* to stay with me.

"My townhouse is really small, Mom. I don't even have a bed in the guestroom. You'd have to sleep on the couch." I hoped if it sounded awful enough she would rethink the whole hotel thing.

"I would not. I'm a guest. You can take the couch."

My phone vibrated.

Cooper: I don't have a jet. But I do have a guestroom.

I wasn't sure if the guestroom comment was meant for me or my mother. Neither sounded appealing. If I was staying with Cooper, I wanted to stay in his room. And I definitely didn't want my mother anywhere near where I was having sex. But that was a dilemma I would have to worry about later.

"Gracey, come back here." I heard the light panting of the little dog Silvia was chasing. Gracey scampered in, sat up on her hind legs, and barked at my mother.

Silvia followed her. "Bad girl. We don't bark at nice people."

I *knew* that Yorkie was a smart dog.

"Whose dog is this?" Mom's nose wrinkled up as if she smelled something very bad.

"Get down, Gracey." Silvia nudged the little dog with her hand. "She's mine. My husband just dropped her off to me so I can take her to the vet on my lunch break."

My mother disliked dogs. In fact, she hated them. "You named your dog Gracey?" Mom's voice was tinged with disdain.

Silvia beamed. "Such a perfect name for a little bitch."

Mom glowered. "And they allow dogs in a bank?"

"It depends on if they have an account or not. Most do, but it's so hard to type a PIN into the ATM with their little paws."

I broke in before Mom could jump on Silvia's sarcasm. "So, Mom, would you like to go relax? I still have a good bit of the day ahead of me. We could go get lunch, and I'll drop you off at my house."

"I've already been to your house. You really need to dust more. I'll likely need to see an allergist before I fly home again. And are you aware there isn't a crumb of food in your refrigerator? I would have starved to death had I not told the cabbie to wait for me in the driveway. And if I were you, I'd find a better place to hide your spare key."

My mouth fell open as I choked on my words. I had nothing to say. I would have to worry about her snooping through my house later.

She wasn't looking at me. She was eyeing the little Yorkie with the pink bow in her hair, the same dog that was desperate to climb up her designer pant leg. She pushed at the dog with her suede boot. "What on earth is this dog after?"

I followed the path of Gracey's eyes all the way up to the hideous feather hat perched on my mother's head. The dog was clearly waiting for it to take flight. "I have no idea, Mom. She must like you." I tried not to smile, but it was really funny watching Gracey jump at my mother while Mom tried to shoo her away with those perfectly manicured hands.

"Is that...?" She slipped her glasses back on. "Oh my god! Is that dog *bleeding*?" Her face twisted into a look of revulsion.

Despite my obvious anxiety, Silvia was quite enjoying my mother's distress. "Oh, whoops. Yes, she's in heat. Didn't I mention that? We're having her inseminated today. I've always wanted a litter of puppies."

Mom jumped up from the chair as if it had bitten her and pointed down to the hem of her pants. "Do you see that? It's blood! On my Dolce & Gabbana trousers. Do you have any idea how expensive these pants are?"

Silvia rolled her eyes, and Mom must have noticed because her face got all red. I was bracing for a brawl when I heard a scream from Vicky.

Then a man yelled, "I told you I need my money now!"

My mother didn't sense the tsunami of tension that rippled through the room. She was still too outraged about her pants. "This animal has gotten its blood on my trousers."

Then I saw Dean... with a gun.

Cooper wouldn't like this at all.

FACING THE FIRING SQUAD

L *EAVE IT TO* V*ICKY TO find the one guy in the room with an actual weapon in his pants.* I would've rolled my eyes, but they were otherwise engaged in staring down the barrel of a loaded cannon. But what I'd done to make Dean go postal was beyond me. That was the second time in less than a week I'd found myself at the other end of a gun, and I wasn't overjoyed by that at all. At least I was wearing underwear.

The good news was my mother had finally shut up. Silvia was the only one of us brave enough to speak to Dean. I kept hoping it was just one of his dramatic moments, and any minute he would break out a wide smile, bow, and use that very *real* looking gun to shoot grape jelly all over my mother's pretty pants.

"Dean?" Silvia said. "What's going on?"

"I need my money!" Dean turned his focus from me and waved the gun in Silvia's face. He was sweating profusely, and a pool of foam had formed in the corner of his mouth.

Silvia kept her hands out to her sides. "Well, that shouldn't be a problem. It's your money."

"Exactly. It's my money. Why don't you tell that to Red here?"

"I-I tried. The accounts are f-frozen," Vicky stammered.

Silvia stepped slowly to Vicky's desk. "There must be some kind of mistake. I can't imagine why your accounts would be frozen. Let me try." She sat down in front of Vicky's computer and started typing.

"I knew I could count on you, Silvia." Dean smiled, and we all sighed.

Silvia's face tightened. "I can't get in. There's a fraud block on your profile."

Dean flew into another rage, waving the gun around the room before settling on me again. "I told you I needed to open new accounts. But you've been too busy with that *killer* new boyfriend of yours."

I felt the blood drain from my face. My mother was deathly silent behind me, and I worried for a second she'd stopped breathing. "Dean, I—" Great, the first time in my life I'd ever slacked off and had a little fun, and I was going to die because of it. *Karma, you're a vindictive bitch!*

"Just shut up, Katie. I can't stand to look at your face anymore. I can't stand to look at any of you." His eyes searched the room frantically, finally settling on something in the back. "Everyone into the vault. Let's go." Dean alternated pointing the gun at each of us until we were corralled into the vault, then he glared at Silvia. "Not you," he said, pulling her by the arm. "You're coming with me. The rest of you stay quiet... or else."

My knees took that opportunity to give out. He only shut the heavy door part of the way, so I could still see Silvia as he dragged her across the lobby. I blinked back tears, agonizing over the danger Silvia was in—the danger we were all in. I thought about Cooper and wondered if he was even aware of what was happening. He didn't come to the bank on Thursdays, but did he check the news? Was it even on the news yet?

I couldn't help but remember the time we'd kissed in the vault. I hoped I would live to do that again. I wasn't so sure. Dean didn't even remotely resemble the person I thought I knew.

My mother had lost all the color from her already pale skin, and she stood away from the wall, undoubtedly to avoid getting her Dolce & Gabbana pants dirty. Or dirtier.

Despite our current situation, I was sure she hadn't forgotten she'd been menstruated on by a dog.

June dropped to the floor beside me, and we sat cross-legged in our dress pants.

"We have to have faith that security called the police." I tried to stay positive. "Someone hit the silent alarm, right?"

"I did," Vicky said in a faint whisper.

"So did I," June added.

"So we're good." I knew we were far from it.

"This was the perfect day for Phil to decide to go out for lunch." June let out a strained laugh.

"Yes, and do you think he actually got us anything from the dollar menu?" I asked her.

"He'll swear he got us all something but was forced to eat it in all the commotion," she muttered.

I forced a smile. If only lunch was the worst of our worries. "The fries would be cold by now, anyhow."

"Yeah," June agreed. "There's nothing worse than cold fries."

Vicky wasn't holding up very well. She looked as if she might be going into shock, so June pulled her into her arms, rocking her gently. My mother maintained her proper façade as she continued to glare at Gracey, who was insistent on brushing up against her leg. But I could see right through Mom. She was terrified.

"Mom, why don't you come sit with us?"

"I'd rather stand. It's going to be difficult enough to get the blood out of these pants. I'd hate to see what might be on the floor in here."

Emotional support wasn't her forte. In fact, I tried to remember a single moment from my childhood where my mother had comforted me. Tending to skinned knees and broken hearts was my father's specialty. Mom was in charge of education and social graces. She was a whiz when it came to school dances, but she never quite knew what to do with her youngest daughter, who hadn't inherited a single iota of her inherent sophistication.

I suddenly had a thought. "June, do you have your phone? Mine's in my office."

My mother looked my way for a moment before darting her eyes away again. *That was odd.*

"No, as usual, bank rules bite us in the butt. It's in my purse. Probably buzzing like crazy. I have no doubt my sister's seen this on the news by now," June whispered.

I didn't ask Vicky. Even though she was never one to follow the rules, she was working on a state of hysteria even I was unfamiliar with. It wasn't really her fault. She hadn't done anything but flirt with the guy. And I was pretty sure he didn't want to shoot us over that.

I had no idea why Dean's accounts were frozen, or why he needed to access them so quickly for that matter. But whatever he had in there was exactly what our lives were worth.

"Does anyone know why there was a fraud block on Dean's accounts?" I didn't dare speak to Vicky directly, but she looked up at me.

"No," she choked out. "I called the Help Desk, but they couldn't tell me anything." She sank back into June's arms. "Do you think he'll hurt Silvia?"

I brushed imaginary dust from the front of my pants to keep from looking her in the eye. "No, he wouldn't do that." I only hoped I was right.

"Silvia will be just fine," June said. "This isn't her first rodeo. She knows what to do."

It may not have been Silvia's first bank robbery, but it was mine. And the only thing I could think to do was to find a way to reach Cooper. I looked over at my mother, who was nudging the dog away with the toe of her expensive boot. I caught her sliding something shiny into one of the deep pockets of her coat.

"Mom?"

She looked at me and raised her eyebrows.

"Is that a cell phone?" I held out my hand. "Let me have it."

"Are you stupid?" she hissed. "There is a man out there with a gun."

"I'm not going to call anyone. I'm going to send a text."

"I don't think now is the best time for *that*. Do you?" Even in a low whisper, her voice dripped sarcasm. She glowered at me, obviously remembering the last text I'd sent her.

I snapped my fingers. "Just give it to me."

She glanced toward the door as she dipped her hand into her pocket and pulled out a shiny black phone. She slid it to me along the floor.

I scooped it up and keyed in Cooper's number.

Grace James: At bank using mom's phone. Held hostage. Don't call. Text me back. Katie.

I flipped through my mother's complicated phone menu to find the silent setting, then tucked the phone under my leg. I didn't need Dean taking the only lifeline we had to the outside.

Mom was using her fancy feathered hat to shoo the dog away, but Gracey was even more entertained by that and continued to jump at her. "Would someone please take this dog?" Her voice was tinged with disgust, and I burst out laughing.

Dean's voice, along with the tap, tap of metal on metal, echoed off the steel walls. "Keep it down in there. There's nothing funny about this."

I froze. It *wasn't* funny. I was scared. I had actually managed to forget about the gun for half a second. I saw a small flash of light and glanced down at the phone display—a new message. I clicked on it, keeping my hand cupped around the screen.

Cooper: Is your mother holding you hostage? Is she still mad about the sexting? Where's your phone?

He had no idea what was happening. He either hadn't seen the news, or we hadn't made the news. I keyed in a quick reply.

Katie: Turn on news. Dean holding us hostage w/ gun. I'm ok. I think police are outside.

In less than a minute, he replied.

Cooper: I knew I should have taken that guy out last week when I had the chance.

My insides dropped sharply.

Katie: What???

Cooper: I mean I couldn't bear it if anything happened to you. I should have never let you out of bed this morning. I'm on my way. I love you.

Katie: Love you too. See you soon.

I really hoped that I would see him soon. The sooner the better.

An hour later, the dead pheasant had long since been sacrificed to the dog to keep her occupied. It had worked, but iridescent green and gray feathers lay everywhere. I was amazed by the number of feathers in such a small hat.

My mother had finally deigned to sit on the floor, and we all leaned against one another for comfort. No one had to say they were scared; we all knew it, especially when Vicky began praying.

Dean was still out there somewhere, doing who knew what. He checked on us more frequently, which had me a little worried. I was afraid he might suspect we had a phone. That didn't stop me from texting—just seeing Cooper's words on the small screen made me feel almost as if he were with me—but it did slow me down.

"Katie, you need to put that away." Mom reached for her phone, but I turned my shoulders so she couldn't reach.

"I'm just trying to find out what's going on out there."

Cooper: What's happening. You haven't written in a while.

Katie: Busy singing show tunes. Know anything from Kiss Me Kate?

Cooper: Not funny.

Under any other circumstances, that would have been

funny. I wished the only thing I had to worry about was jealousy.

Katie: What's happening out there?

Cooper: I don't know. But Phil said to tell you he ate your lunch. The fries were getting cold.

Dean began shouting obscenities and banging on what I assumed was the giant plate glass window in the lobby.

"We're going to die, aren't we?" Vicky hiccupped, wiping streaks of black mascara across her cheeks.

I flinched. Why did she have to put into words what I was dreading?

"We're not going to die," Mom said. "I have a spa appointment on Tuesday. You have *no* idea how long it takes to get those appointments. I'm certainly not missing *mine.*" She brushed another feather from her white pants.

"Katie, did Cooper say anything about what the police are doing?" Vicky's eyes were red and swollen from crying, which actually made me feel sorry for her.

"No," I whispered.

"Why hasn't he told you?" my mother blurted.

"Maybe he doesn't know what the police are doing, Mom," I snapped.

"I don't mean the police. I mean, why is it you don't seem to know what he does for a living?"

Great. Only my mother could ignore a crisis to bring up a passing comment made over an hour ago. I shook my head. "I'm sure it would bore me to tears."

A faint smile played on June's lips. "I can't imagine *anything* Cooper does is boring."

"It really doesn't matter what he does, Mom. I love him," I stated firmly.

Mom huffed. "For all you know he could be a *murderer.*"

That pulled Vicky from her frenzied state. She threw her hands up in the air. "That's what I've been telling her!"

"He's not a murderer." If I said it often enough, I might actually believe it. "But Vicky tried to get me to date the guy holding us hostage."

Vicky smirked. "At least I'm not cheating on Cooper with some guy named Henry."

My mother waved her hand through the air, dismissing the last comment. "It's hard enough for me to accept my daughter managed to ensnare one man. You can't expect me to believe there are two."

"Well, then..." Vicky grabbed my wrist and held up my arm, exposing my bracelet. "Explain this."

"It was a gift from Cooper. Henry is my cat."

Mom scoffed. "You don't have a cat. I was just in your house today. I would have smelled if you had a cat."

"He's a very clean cat. Even I barely know he's there."

"Enough about this imaginary cat. You should investigate a little," Mom whispered.

I wasn't going to admit anything, especially not my failed attempts at sleuthing.

Mom sat staring off into space—probably plotting her next move. And then she brushed a loose feather from her pants and grimaced at the dog. "Well, I don't think you should let it go," she said finally.

Vicky seemed bound and determined to share every one of her conspiracy theories about Cooper with the only other person I knew who was more bent on ruining my happiness than she was. She relayed the information about Cooper's wire transfer, making the whole thing sound as seedy as possible.

"That much money?" my mother asked.

"That's confidential," June muttered.

I was contemplating running into the lobby. I would have rather faced Dean and his shiny gun than sit there with my mother, Vicky, and their suspicions.

My mother's phone lit up, and I glanced down at the screen. *Perfect timing.* "Cooper said the police are coming in. We need to stay as far away from the door as possible," I whispered.

We all shifted as close together as possible, and I listened for any noises out front.

A few minutes later, Dean barked out a string of obscenities, followed by the loudest crack I'd ever heard. Silvia let loose a bloodcurdling scream. The resulting silence brought my heart to a screeching halt as I feared the worst.

For what seemed like an eternity, my heart stilled in my chest, then sputtered to life again as a series of loud pops and the sound of glass breaking shattered the silence. Gracey yipped. Mom covered her ears as the rest of us clung to each other. Hot tears ran down my cheeks as I thought of Silvia either dead or dying out there.

An explosion of sounds vibrated off the walls, and what I imagined was a rushing stampede was nearly drowned out by the hammering of my own pulse beating in my ears, making me unsure if what I heard was even real. But I *was* certain there were multiple voices shouting in the lobby.

Silvia, her face bright red and streaked with mascara, burst into the vault. Vicky let out an ear-piercing shriek.

"Good lord, Vicky," Silvia said, pressing her hand to her chest. "I may never hear again."

"Silvia!" we screamed, clambering to our feet.

Silvia scooped up her little dog and surveyed the sea of feathers. "What on earth happened in here?"

"Your dog ate my hat," my mother said quietly, obviously not recovered enough from her ordeal to manage anything more sarcastic. I was sure she'd rebound quickly. "It was quite costly. I'll send you the bill."

And there's the mother I know and love. "Oh, Silvia, I was so worried." I wrapped my arms around her and squeezed.

"I'm fine, sweetie. I managed to duck under the desk before the SWAT team came rushing in. I just can't believe Dean would do something so horrible." She shook her head. "Come on. We need to get out of here."

"Dean… is he…"

Silvia shook her head again. "I didn't see what happened to him."

After several tense minutes spent waiting for the police to clear us to leave, we were led out of the vault.

"Wait for me. I've got to get my purse!" I called over my shoulder as I hurried back to retrieve it.

The lobby was filled with white smoke, and I could barely see my hands in front of my face. Navigating by memory, I ducked into my office to grab my purse and my things before heading for the door. I'd taken that route at least a hundred times... before the SWAT team had descended on the building, upending chairs and other debris now directly in my path.

I tripped over what was probably a chair and ended up sprawled face down on the carpet.

Cooper came rushing to my side, Phil close on his heels. "Katie! Are you hurt?" He turned to yell over his shoulder. "Someone call an ambulance!"

From somewhere to my left, my mother said, "She doesn't need an ambulance. She just tripped again."

I raised my head from the floor and could feel the unshed tears in my eyes as I flashed a weak smile at Cooper. "You're here," I squeaked.

"Of course I'm here. I never left." He slid his arms beneath me and hauled me up, kissing his way from my hair to my forehead, and finally to my lips.

Mom said, "Katie, you're so clumsy, I often wonder if the babies were switched in the hospital."

"Cooper, have you met my mother?" I cringed, fully aware I had stepped out of the proverbial frying pan and directly into the fire.

GUESS WHO'S COMING TO DINNER

HE LONGEST AFTERNOON OF MY life started out as a terror-filled ordeal in the bank, followed by an endless series of police interviews, and finally twisted into something even more frightening. My mother and I never once discussed Dean or the hostage situation, which would, at first glance, seem like a blessing. Instead, after a brief stop at my townhouse to grab her suitcase, Mom spent the entire evening spinning her melodramatic yarns about my less-than-stellar childhood, followed by even more horrifying tales about my near-catastrophic adolescence. I'd heard all the stories, but never in rapid succession, with every skinned knee scrutinized and dissected in gruesome detail, until it would be crystal clear to anyone listening I was the most unbearable disappointment a parent could possibly have in a child.

She managed to toss in a few nice stories. But those weren't nearly as exciting as the tales of disaster. If I hadn't lived them, I would have felt sorry for me. I knew she was exaggerating everything, but I was afraid Cooper would accept them at face value.

For his part, he smiled and laughed in the appropriate places. He held my hand all through dinner, giving it a supportive squeeze each time a story reached an embarrassing point. Every bit the gentleman, he never disagreed with my mother's assessment of me, but he managed to toss in his own impressions—telling my mother how smart I was. He never once sank to Mom's level and shared a single embarrassing moment he'd witnessed.

Once my mother disappeared into the guest room to freshen up, I helped him with the dinner dishes, and we plopped down on the sofa to wait for her to resurface. It was still early. I hadn't fooled myself into thinking she was done for the night.

"That was interesting," he said.

I laughed. "That isn't the word I would have used."

"I was trying to be nice."

"I see that. You managed to win her over."

He put his arm around me. "Why do you say that?"

I raised an eyebrow. "You didn't see her face when we pulled into your driveway."

"True. What did I miss?"

I bit back a smile. "She was very impressed. You may regret having invited her to stay here, especially once she discovers we're sleeping in the same room." I shuddered. "I fully expect her to start planning our wedding any day now. If she hasn't already."

He froze, and I regretted saying the word *wedding*.

"Does she think we're getting *married*?" Cooper shifted beside me.

Crap! Crap! Crap! I sensed his eyes analyzing my face for some sort of answer. I must have looked like a deer in the headlights. "I'm sure she hopes so," I whispered and turned to look away. I'd never once thought of marrying Cooper. Well, I guess I had, but not consciously.

I'd dreamt it. But that was before we'd even kissed. Since our first kiss, I had been too caught up in the whirlwind of our romance to consider the possibility of marriage. I certainly didn't want him to think I was shopping for dresses. He would think I was as bad as my mother.

She was beyond delighted he was rich, as evidenced by her not asking about his job. *Slaughters kittens for feline snuff films? Fine with her!* I almost wished he wasn't wealthy, though. If he had been just a normal guy struggling to make ends meet, I wouldn't have felt so much like a gold digger.

"I never said anything to her about marriage." I tried to keep my breathing shallow, so I wouldn't start to cry, but my traitorous eyes started to prick with fresh tears. I jumped up from the sofa and wandered back to the kitchen, pretending to rinse the sink out again. I refused to cry. He would most definitely take it the wrong way. And why would I cry, anyway? I hadn't been thinking about marriage. Had I?

"Katie..." he murmured as he came up behind me.

He tried to pull me around to face him, but I held my ground. I knew if I looked him in the eyes, I wouldn't be able to stop the tears.

"Would you please look at me?" There was something in his voice. Agony maybe? I wasn't sure.

"I can't," I said on a shaky breath.

He wrapped his arms around me and rested his chin on the top of my head. "Have *you* ever thought of marriage?"

I gulped. "What do you mean by *thought of*?" I pushed my hair behind my ears.

He let out a nervous chuckle, and his peppermint breath washed over me from above. "As in, do you even *believe* in marriage?"

Oh. He didn't believe in marriage, and he was mortified I might. How did I not see that? He never wanted to get married. Was I just a fling then? Oh. My. God!

I was just a fling! I closed my eyes and took a deep breath. I wasn't going to lie. If he didn't want marriage... ever—if I was just temporary—I may as well find out now rather than later. I would have to end things if that was how he felt. How could I continue if we weren't going anywhere?

"I do believe in marriage... if two people really love each other." I let out the breath I was holding and waited.

Although I had never consciously thought about marriage, I was certain—unequivocally, unquestionably—I wanted to be married. Someday. I wouldn't let myself think about being married to Cooper. It would hurt too much if he rejected me.

"Hmmm." He kissed the top of my head. "What do you think your mother would like to do this evening?" He didn't wait for me to reply. "You should probably go check on her to see if she's settled in yet."

"Okay." I sighed. "I'll go see what *she'd* like to do." As if I actually cared what she wanted.

I ran up the stairs, taking two at a time, until I tripped and fell with a thud. I looked around to see if Cooper would come running, but he didn't. Either he didn't hear me stumble, or he was avoiding me. I wasn't sure if I wanted to know either way.

"Mom?" I knocked on the guest room door.

She was rummaging around in there. I heard her Louis Vuitton bag zip, then her light footsteps as she walked toward the door.

She didn't open it. "Did you need something, Katherine?" I had no idea what would prompt her to use my full name, but clearly she was irritated by something I'd done.

"Cooper wants to know if there's something you'd like to do this evening." I switched to my cheery voice. I thought about suggesting bowling, which brought a badly needed smirk to my lips. I doubted my mother had ever in her life gone bowling.

She turned the lock and opened the door a crack. "Tell Cooper I would very much like to visit the little coffeehouse he mentioned at dinner." She lit up when she said his name—exactly the way I did—and I hated it. She had no right to find my boyfriend so enchanting.

"Okay. I'll tell him." I stomped down the hall into Cooper's bedroom. I was no longer on the verge of tears. I was on the verge of a temper tantrum. My new boyfriend, who I was *one*, very much in love with, and who was *two*, quite possibly a hired hit man, might just be *three*, even worse... a commitment-phobic jerk. And my mother, who spent much of her existence making mine unpleasant, was completely infatuated with him. *Fabulous.*

Who would have guessed there were worse things than having an assassin for a boyfriend?

I heard him coming down the hall, and I waited until he came in and closed the door. "Mom wants to go to the coffeehouse you told her about." I flopped onto the bed with a pout. I was sure he noticed, but I suddenly didn't care.

"You don't seem happy," he said as he climbed into the bed beside me. His grin was devilish, but I wasn't in the mood to swoon.

"You are quite observant," I crooned in my sweetest voice.

I guessed by the look on his face it came off more as sarcasm. "Wow, your mother really gets under your skin, doesn't she?"

I tried to smile. "To call that an understatement would, in and of itself, be an understatement. My mother..." I stopped when I realized I was talking way too loud and switched to a whisper. "My mother destroys my self-esteem and makes me doubt my own intelligence." I rolled away from him and curled into a tight ball.

"Katie..." He tucked himself against me so we were spooning and nuzzled my neck. "Your mother has no idea how wonderful you are. That's a terrible shame. She's missing out." His breath tickled my neck as he whispered against my skin, "I do love you, you know."

I closed my eyes. I wanted so much to believe him. I wouldn't have questioned it an hour ago. But after the whole *marriage* conversation, I wasn't so sure. "And when you've grown tired of me?" I felt my mouth move with the words, but I wasn't sure if I made any sound.

He sat up and leaned over me, wearing a look of confusion and amusement. "Do you think I'm getting tired of you?" I could tell he wanted to laugh, but he somehow knew I wasn't being funny.

"Not yet," I whispered.

He shook his head. "You are definitely in a mood tonight. I'm afraid to say anything at all for fear you'll misconstrue my meaning."

"Misconstrue?" I almost laughed. But I wasn't quite ready to let go of my irritation.

He raised his eyebrows. "You don't understand the meaning of the word?"

"Of course, I understand the meaning. I read, you know." I glowered at him. "I just wonder sometimes."

"About?"

"Your vocabulary. No one actually says *misconstrue* in a sentence, do they?"

"I do." He lightly caressed the furrow between my eyebrows with one finger. "You're going to get a wrinkle here if you don't stop making that face."

I bit down on the insides of my cheeks to keep from smiling.

He took advantage of my weakness and rolled me toward him, tucking me into his arms. "You're being very stubborn tonight. I think I may have to resort to extreme measures." He pressed his lips into the spot between my eyebrows and kissed his way down my nose to my mouth.

His lips moved quietly against mine as his breath replaced the oxygen in my lungs. I felt his warm tongue lightly tracing my bottom lip, and a jolt of heat went through me. He smiled as he realized he'd won. I would have fought back, but I no longer had the strength—or the desire—to stay angry at him.

"My mother is down the hall."

"She's not invited."

I giggled. "We should stop now, while we still can."

"Speak for yourself," he growled.

"You started it."

"You could finish it."

"I don't think I can. Not with her so close."

"Ugh. Okay. Okay. Give me a few minutes. I don't think I can get up just yet."

I kissed him as if my life depended on it.

"That isn't going to help, you know," he whispered against my lips.

"Mmmm."

"Katherine?" My mother's voice carried through the door and we both froze.

"Katherine?" he mouthed.

"I've apparently pissed her off."

He shook quietly with laughter, and I rolled my eyes at him.

I rose up a little. "I'm coming, Mom!"

He flashed that lopsided grin at me. I knew what he was thinking. I jumped up from the bed and swatted him on the thigh. After tucking my hair behind my ears, I checked myself in the mirror to be sure my clothes were straight before running to the door and slipping into the hall. I closed the door and spun around to find my mother standing outside the guest room with an irritated look on her face.

"Where were you?" she asked.

"I was talking to Cooper." Well, it was only a little lie. We did some talking.

"Are we going to the coffeehouse?"

"Yes, Mom. Are you ready?"

"I've been ready for some time now. I was waiting for you." She slipped her hands into the pockets of her long coat and pulled out a leather glove from each one. She was stunning again in a different outfit. She always looked very stylish.

I didn't. Except for lately. I was much more put together since Cooper and I had been dating. I wore my cashmere dress and dangerous boots. It amused me to see my mother wearing cashmere, too. I almost felt like I was in *US* magazine's "Who Wore it Better?" section.

"You look nice, Katie," Mom said.

I couldn't help but smile. She rarely said anything positive about my appearance.

"Cooper must be picking out your clothes for you." The excited tone was back in her voice when she said his name, and I couldn't blame her. She was right. I *was* dressing better because of Cooper.

"She always looks beautiful."

I jumped a little as he came up behind me, snaking his arms around my waist and leaning around to kiss my cheek.

"Are you ladies ready?" he asked.

"Ready when you are," Mom said with a disgustingly sweet smile.

Cooper led the way down the stairs. "Let's go then."

He could be quite devious when he wanted to be. My mother was all set to climb into the front seat when he opened the door to the back. The ride to the coffeehouse was short. I had it in my head we were going to Starbucks. I should have known better. When Cooper said *coffeehouse,* what he really meant was a little jazz club that served coffee.

Cooper held the door for both of us. A stage was directly to the right of the entryway, where a lanky middle-aged man with a scruffy salt-and-pepper goatee played guitar and sang an acoustic Les Paul cover. It was another place with a romantic atmosphere. I guessed Cooper probably knew every single one in a thirty-mile radius.

He towed me toward the back—with my mother close behind—where we took the last available table.

A young, blond waitress came over. "Cooper! I haven't seen you in weeks!"

"Hi, Izzy." He smiled back. "I've been keeping pretty busy lately, but I brought my girlfriend, Katie, and her mother, Grace. Anyone good coming up tonight?" Cooper nodded toward the stage.

"Katie?" Izzy swatted at Cooper's arm and then turned to me. "Well, it's about time he brought you here. It's nice to finally meet you. I've heard a lot about you."

"Thank you. It's nice to meet you." I felt my cheeks burn and looked at Cooper. I wondered what he'd said about me so often she knew me by name.

"I think you'll be pleased with the next act," Izzy said. "Now, what can I get you to drink?"

"Irish coffee for me." Cooper gave me a serious look. "Would you like to try Irish coffee? I think you'll like it."

"Sure." I shrugged. Coffee was coffee. "I like lots of cream."

He gave me a little grin. "It has lots of cream in it."

"I'll have one of those too. And I like mine fairly strong," Mom said.

"Okay, three Irish coffees on the strong side. Got it! Anything to eat?" Izzy asked.

"I don't think so. Thanks, Izzy." Cooper took my hand again, weaving his fingers between mine. "So, Mrs. James, how long do you plan on staying?" He kept his tone pleasant, but I knew he was fishing for information.

"I have a flight booked for Saturday afternoon."

"That's great! I know exactly what we should do tomorrow evening." He looked at me as he spoke, and I could read the devious expression in his eyes.

Mom narrowed her eyes. "What would that be?"

"Katie, tomorrow is Friday. We should invite your Mom for margaritas and señoritas." His lopsided grin wavered slightly as he watched my expression turn from shock to amusement.

I inherited my inability to hold my liquor from my mother. "That sounds like fun."

Izzy returned and set three frothing mugs down in front of us.

"Irish coffee?" I asked.

"Yes. Now, drink up," he said as he brought his mug to his lips.

Mom and I both followed suit, sipping the hot coffee carefully.

"How unusual," Mom said, licking cream from her lips. "I've never had one of these before. It has an odd flavor."

There was something familiar about the taste, but

admittedly, I wasn't a coffee connoisseur. By the time I'd finished mine, I felt much more relaxed. My mother had excused herself to "powder her nose," and it was nice to be alone with Cooper, if only for a few minutes.

"You've had a rough day," Cooper said. "Don't feel like we have to stay if you're tired."

"Mmm-hmm." I leaned into him. "It's just easier to keep her entertained."

"Do you like the music?"

I smiled. "I do."

"Would you like to dance?" He stood up and held out his hand.

"Oh, I don't know."

"Please?" He brought his face close to mine and whispered his plea straight to my heart. I couldn't say no.

I let him lead me to the makeshift dance floor. When I turned, I saw my mother watching from our table in the back. In a way, she looked happy. Maybe I was wrong about her. Maybe she was glad I'd finally found someone.

His arms wound around my back, and I put mine around his neck. We fit against each other like puzzle pieces as we swayed to the music. I'd stepped into a fairytale and wished I could stay like that forever. There was no space for worry when he held me in his arms. He let his forehead rest against mine, and I closed my eyes as his breath washed over me. Peppermint and whiskey.

Whiskey? I didn't remember him drinking any whiskey. In a strange way, it smelled kind of nice. In fact, I liked it enough to kiss him right there on the dance floor. It was a gentle, quiet kiss, just my lips moving carefully with his. But it let loose the butterflies and made my knees go weak. After an exquisite, but far too brief few minutes, he put his hands on either side of my face and pulled away. He gazed deep into my eyes until we both smiled.

"Time to go back to the table?" I murmured.

He nodded. I knew it was taking all of his concentration to control his body's responses.

"That was a bit intimate for a public place," my mother said, licking a bit of cream from her lips.

I shrugged. "Sorry." I felt the heat flooding into my face, but there was little I could do about it. "Can I get another coffee?" I asked Cooper.

"Sure." He waved Izzy over to take the order.

She was back in a flash with three more Irish coffees, and after ten minutes, those mugs were empty too.

I was feeling a little giddy, and unfortunately, I recognized the symptoms a little too late. When Mom started giggling like a schoolgirl, I knew it wasn't just me.

"Um... Cooper?" I whispered, trying not to let my mother hear.

"Hmm?"

"What's in an Irish coffee?"

"Well, coffee, of course. And heavy cream. And whiskey."

"Whiskey? A little or a lot?"

"Maybe a little. Unless you order it on the strong side."

I nodded. *Right—unless you order it on the strong side.* That was wonderful. I had drunk two already, and I was feeling the effects. If my mother's mood was any indication, so was she. One more and she would be out for the night.

"Can we get three more?" Mom shouted to the petite waitress.

Cooper raised his eyebrows and looked at me.

I felt my lips curl up in a grin. "Whatever you do, *don't* tell my mother."

BREAKFAST

I CRACKED OPEN ONE EYE AND immediately closed it again. The room was too bright. And my head was not happy at all. In fact, it was pretty much screaming obscenities at me. Despite the pounding behind my eyes, I smiled. It was worth it.

I was sure my mother wouldn't feel the same way. Her headache wouldn't have the same lovely edge to it mine did.

I peeked over at Cooper. He breathed slowly and deeply, with his face buried in a pillow. I wasn't surprised he was still sleeping. Last night had worn him out. And not just from carrying Mom up the stairs.

After tucking her into bed, we spent several hours testing the theory she was really, truly passed out. The woman was no better at holding her liquor than I was, but I was getting better. I passed out too, not from all the drinking, but out of sheer exhaustion and ecstasy.

I tried my eyes again, opening them to slits to let them adjust to the white light coming in through the windows. I had no idea what time it was. The clock was missing, and the bedding was scattered across the nightstands, except the one pillow holding Cooper's head.

I'd used Cooper as a pillow. The blankets were half off the bed, and one of the lamps was tipped over, hanging over the edge of the table. Basically, the room was wrecked.

I eased from the bed, careful not to disturb him, and tiptoed into the bathroom. I welcomed the warmth from the heated floor as I padded across the marble to the shower.

The water became hot almost immediately, and I stepped into the spray, letting the water flow over my tender skin.

I felt at home in his house. So much so it was almost worrisome. The ghost of our conversation the night before came back to me, and I desperately tried to push it away. I didn't want to think about the possibility I was nothing more than a temporary distraction for him. If my mother hadn't visited, I would never have mentioned the idea of marriage. Then he wouldn't have reacted the way he did, and I'd have no reason to be concerned. But that wasn't how it happened. It was a snowball effect.

My mother *was* here. And I *did* mention marriage. And he most *definitely* had an uncomfortable reaction to the word. Forget worrying about assassins, mysterious deposits, and men with guns... I was suddenly worried about commitment.

I felt guilty about my icy thoughts, so I let the hot water melt them away and instead concentrated on last night. The sex had been more intense than usual—almost possessive. The way he touched me... kissed me. How could I possibly doubt he loved me?

A cool blast of air hit me as Cooper stepped into the shower. Immediately, his arms wrapped around me, pulling me against him. He kissed me carefully, as if he were reading my thoughts. "You always sneak off without me," he said with an uneasy smile.

"You always look so peaceful when you sleep."

He grabbed the shampoo from the corner and squeezed some into his hands. He worked the lather into his hair before taking my hands and bringing them up to take over. His face brightened as he began to wash my hair for me. He started to hum a familiar song, the one I'd sung on my birthday.

"My mother's still here," I reminded him.

He grimaced. "So she is."

"She'll be hungry, and she doesn't cook," I warned. He

never said anything, but I was sure he was tired of having her as a houseguest.

"I would never be a bad enough host to let someone go hungry," he said, sliding his shampoo-covered hands down my body. "I think it's extremely important to satisfy one's hunger at all times, don't you?"

His hands had found their way to my weak spot, and all I could do was nod.

"I'm glad you agree. Where was I?"

"You were taking me to the bed to finish what you started."

He growled a response and rinsed his hair. Then he rinsed mine before carrying me, soaking wet, from the shower to the bed.

He tossed me down and pinned me under his hard frame. "I was so afraid I would lose you yesterday." He pressed his lips against mine in a desperate, hungry kiss, then pulled back to stare into my eyes. "I would have killed him with my bare hands if he'd hurt you," he said through gritted teeth.

My breath caught in my throat.

"I don't know if I can ever let you out of my sight again." His lips curved up in a smile. "Especially when you're all wet and slippery like this."

A second shower later, we were finally getting dressed.

I slicked my hair behind my ears with a glop of gel and pulled on my last clean outfit— form-fitting jeans and a clingy black sweater. "I've run out of clothes," I announced. "I need to do laundry... or go shopping." I started to apply my makeup.

"Hmm, no clothes, huh?" he said from the doorway where he watched me, and the lopsided grin I loved spread across his face.

"Yes, well, they do expect me to wear clothes at work. Preferably clean ones."

"Right, work." He sounded like a spoiled five-year-old as he came up behind me and tugged at the hem of my shirt. "I'm glad they gave you today off."

"Me too."

We'd definitely earned it. It wasn't every day we got held hostage.

I tried to keep my hand steady as I put on my mascara, but it was difficult when he started to kiss the back of my neck. "So do you want to go shopping again?" I asked.

"Can we leave your mother behind?"

"Probably not. She would snoop through everything you own," I teased. Or I hoped he thought I was teasing. I was actually telling the truth. I would have been afraid she had been snooping in the night, but I was fairly sure she had been in no condition to be up. Plus, the alarm would have been triggered. I almost laughed at the thought.

He stopped kissing my neck and snapped his head up. "Why would she snoop?"

"You don't have much experience with women, do you?" I asked, turning around to face him.

His eyes went wide. "You wouldn't snoop, would you?"

I did my best not to lie. "Now, why would I need to snoop? You don't hide anything from me, do you?" I tried to turn back, but he caught my chin, lifting my face to his and looked at me with an unreadable expression.

"I'd love to take you and your mother shopping," he finally said, then gave me a quick kiss and left the room.

I stood there for a minute until I heard a knock on the bedroom door.

"Katherine Grace James." My mother bristled when I opened the door. "What was in that coffee last night?" Her voice was scratchy, and although she had applied her usual layer of makeup, she had dark circles beneath her eyes.

"What do you mean, Mom? Was there something wrong with your coffee?"

She scoffed at me. "Don't play dumb with me, young lady. I was your age once, and trust me, I wrote the book on playing dumb. There was something other than coffee in my coffee last night, and you very well know it."

I struggled to keep my expression completely neutral. "That must be why I have a headache this morning." I tried to keep my voice flat, but it was really difficult. I wanted to laugh so badly. "Besides, you're the one who kept ordering more."

She glowered at me for a long minute. "It's past ten o'clock. What are we doing for breakfast?"

The coffee conversation was closed. I knew it would be reopened at a later time. I would have to warn Cooper. "Breakfast should be done in a bit. I'm going to check on it right now. Should I come get you when it's ready?"

"That's fine." She went back to her room and closed the door.

I broke out in a wide smile and would have skipped down the stairs if I wasn't sure I'd fall. Instead, I held the rail and hurried down them, then skipped into the kitchen, where Cooper was stirring something in a large red ceramic bowl.

"You look happy. Is your mother enjoying herself?"

"Nope. She's madder than a hornet and extremely hung over. She's accused us of slipping something into her coffee last night."

He looked confused. "And that makes you happy?"

"You have no idea." I leaned over the bowl and peered inside.

"Then I wish I had," he muttered.

"What?"

"Never mind... just thinking out loud." He gestured with his spatula. "I'm making crepes."

"You're kidding."

"Why would I be kidding?"

"You have *seriously* been holding out on me."

He just smiled and went back to stirring. I spied a bowl of juicy cut fruit and picked out a strawberry.

"Put that down," he snapped. "That's for the crepes."

I dropped the berry. "Sorry." I leaned against the granite counter to watch. "Where did you learn to make crepes?" I asked as he poured the batter onto a hot skillet.

"Le Cordon Bleu, of course."

My mouth fell open, and he reached over and lifted my chin to close it.

"I'm kidding." He smirked. "My mother used to make them for Sunday brunch. Well, she probably still does, but I'm not there for it."

I caught a flash of sadness in his eyes. It was evident how much he missed his family. I had no idea how anyone who valued family so much could be opposed to marriage.

"Why don't you invite your family for a visit?" I used my cheery voice and spread a wide smile across my face. "I'd love to meet them." But as soon as I said it, I regretted it. Meeting his family meant we were getting serious. And although I thought we had already gone past that point, I was afraid I was crossing that scary line again. *The line that leads directly to the altar.*

He either chose to overlook the deeper meaning, or he didn't catch it. He ignored my comment and slid the first crepe onto a white porcelain plate. "Ah hah! C'est magnifique!"

A few minutes later, I went up to the guest room to get Mom for breakfast. When we came down, the table was set with the expensive china and sterling flatware. I expected her to comment on the finery, but she seemed too distracted to notice. She picked at her food, saying more than once how good the crepes were, but as far as I could tell, she hadn't taken a bite of anything other than the fruit.

There was definitely something different about her. She wasn't fawning over Cooper the way she had the day before.

I felt a pang of guilt, realizing she seemed uncomfortable around him. I supposed I should've expected as much after the Irish coffee incident, but it somehow surprised me just the same.

Cooper made a fresh pot of coffee, and I poured her a cup. She picked it up and brought it all the way to her lips but froze before taking a sip. She stared at the cup then placed it back on the table untouched.

"It's exactly the way you like it, Mom."

She frowned at me and stole glances at Cooper.

"It's quite fresh. The beans were just ground this morning," Cooper added.

She raised her eyebrows and eyed the cup suspiciously.

"Mom, there's nothing wrong with your coffee. Please try it."

"Hmph." She went back to picking at her food, glaring at the cup every few minutes as if it was going to get up and do something. Eventually, she dipped her pinky finger into the hot coffee and then put it in her mouth.

I pressed my lips into a hard line, trying not to laugh, and glanced at Cooper. He watched Mom with a perplexed expression as if he wanted to say something, but didn't know what.

His phone vibrated in his pocket, and he pulled it out, frowning at the display. "I'm sorry. I need to take this." His features darkened further. "Will you please excuse me?" He got up from the table and made a hasty exit.

"Does he often take secretive calls?" Mom whispered, staring after Cooper.

"Don't be so nosy," I replied.

"That's my job, Katherine. If you aren't going to look out for yourself, who will?"

"Mom, please?" I tried to dismiss her words as nonsense, but I knew she wouldn't drop it.

"How serious are you about him?"

I wanted to be angry, but I was confused. "I thought you liked him."

"I do... or rather *did*. He's extremely handsome, but..."

My stomach twisted almost painfully. "But?"

"He seems to have a lot of secrets. It's not natural for a man to refuse to talk about his livelihood. I don't like that at all."

I didn't like his secrets either. But I wasn't going to tell her about my insecurities. I picked up Cooper's plate and took it to the sink. "I thought we might go shopping this afternoon. I know you love to shop, and I could use a few new things." I smiled at her, hoping she would lighten up a little.

"That sounds nice." She smiled back, but I could see she was still distracted.

"Do you need a few minutes to get ready?" I asked, watching her expression go from distracted to unnerved. "Is something wrong? Did you tell Daddy you were in a hostage situation?"

"Don't be ridiculous. You father would've had a heart attack." She leaned forward. "Is Cooper still around the corner?"

I could feel the little furrow forming between my brows. "No, I think he went upstairs. Why?"

"Oh, thank God," my mother said, dropping her fork onto her plate with a loud clank. "I thought I'd never get you alone."

"Mom, what's wrong?"

"There's something very wrong going on in this house."

My heart dropped into my stomach. "What do you mean?"

"Well, the minute I woke up this morning and discovered my drinks had been spiked last night, I realized I couldn't trust Cooper." She held up her hand when I started to protest. "Hear me out, please. No honorable man would ever slip something into a lady's drink like that. As I said, I felt I could no longer trust him, and if I couldn't trust him, it goes without saying *you* shouldn't trust him."

"Mom, it was *my* idea not to tell you about the whiskey in the coffee."

"It's noble of you to take the blame, but you must see my point here. He's not to be trusted."

I started to say, "I do trust him," but the words wouldn't come.

"While the two of you were doing whatever it was you were doing in the shower this morning—"

I blushed. "I... we—"

"Don't try to deny it, you were hardly quiet. Since you are either unable or unwilling to do it for yourself, I decided to take advantage of an opportunity to do a little investigating of my own."

"Mother! You can't just go around snooping through Cooper's things!" She had no idea how lucky she was she hadn't tripped the motion detectors on her little *expedition*.

"You might change your mind when I tell you what I found." She lowered her voice, watching for Cooper to come around the corner.

My eyes followed hers, and we both waited to see if he would reappear. He didn't.

"You need to come with me," Mom said, pushing away from the table.

I followed her up the stairs and paused outside her room. She shook her head and pointed at the door to the bedroom adjoining Cooper's office.

I shook my head. "I'm *not* going in there," I whispered.

She reached out and grabbed my sleeve. "Yes, you *are*," she hissed.

"What if he catches us?" I wasn't entirely sure where he was at that moment.

She thought up a lie, and she thought it up quick. "Then you'll tell him you were giving me the tour. Now come on."

Realizing she wouldn't let it go and feeling a healthy dose of curiosity, I allowed her to pull me into the other guest room. "So tell me what you found so we can get out of here before Cooper catches us," I said, plopping down on the bed.

My mother flashed a grim smile and nodded at the foot of the bed.

I leaned over to stare at a low cedar chest with a seat cushion. "So? It's a bench."

"It's not a bench. It's a trunk." She lifted the lid with one hand and waved me closer. "Look."

I peered into the cedar-lined trunk and felt my breakfast threatening to come back. "Are those what I think they are?" I gaped at the two long cases.

She nodded.

"Are they empty?" I asked hopefully.

"I'm afraid not." She reached into the trunk to open the top case, exposing a gleaming wooden rifle... complete with a scope.

I took a small step back. "There has to be a reasonable explanation."

"What possible reason could anyone have for possessing two rifles like these?"

I swallowed hard. "Hunting?"

Mom shook her head slowly. "Your father has hunted for years. These aren't the type of guns you use to hunt animals. They're the type you use to hunt *people*."

THE SPANISH INQUISITION

OR THE THIRD TIME IN less than two weeks, I was staring at the barrel of a gun. What were the odds?

"Katie, listen." Mom carefully closed the gun case and then the trunk. "Did you hear that?" She crept closer to the bathroom.

"No, Mom. Cooper's office is through there. He's probably still on the phone," I said, blocking her path.

"That's exactly why we're going to listen!" She shoved me out of the way to poke her head into the bathroom, then looked at me with raised eyebrows.

I blew out the breath I was holding and followed her. I could hear Cooper talking to someone, and he didn't sound happy. He sounded exasperated.

"For the last time, Vivian, I'm not doing it." *Vivian.*

I didn't have a clue who she was, but I knew her name from the checks I'd discovered.

I could hear his foot tapping against the wood floors. Then he chuckled. "No, I don't care about the big payoff."

Mom poked me hard in the side when he said *big payoff,* and I almost cried out.

"No, I don't. We're doing it my way this time." He got quiet again, but I heard his swivel chair roll on the floor. "No, you listen to me! We're not just talking about a job here. We're talking about my life." His footsteps moved around the room, and I could tell he was pacing.

I was terrified he would open the bathroom door, exposing us as the eavesdroppers we were.

"No, I don't really care what your opinion is on this." He raised his voice. "I've listened to *your* point enough times already. You're not listening to mine. Of course, I'll discuss this with the family, but leave Katie out of it."

My pulse quickened, making my knees all but buckle beneath me. *Leave Katie out of it?* What was she trying to drag Katie... I mean... *me* into?

He raised his voice to another level, yelling into the phone. "How many times do you expect me to do this, Vivian? How many times have I done it already? Can you even count at this point?" His voice dropped to a normal tone. "Listen, I'm tired. I don't want to do this anymore. No more secrets."

There was a long break in the conversation, and I assumed he'd hung up until he groaned and spoke again. "Fine. If that'll shut you up, I'll take the weekend to consider my options, not that I think you're actually giving me any."

I'd heard all I could bear and dragged Mom out of the bathroom by the arm, shutting the door gently behind us. Mom started to say something, but I shook my head.

"Not in here," I whispered, pointing toward the door, and she followed me into the hall.

"You need to help me pack," Mom urged, pulling me toward her room. "We're getting out of here. Leave that strange bracelet he bought with his blood money."

"I'm not going anywhere, Mom." I held my ground, tucking my hand behind my back. "You'll get my bracelet over my dead body." I stomped my foot like a spoiled child.

"Excuse me?" Her eyebrows shot up. "I hope it doesn't come to that."

"I'm not leaving over a little circumstantial evidence." I turned to head back to Cooper's room and paused outside his office, hearing the sound of fingers furiously clicking against a keyboard.

"Have you completely lost your mind?" Mom marched

over to where I stood and seized my arm again. "Weren't you listening? He mentioned you by name! And the family? Anyone who's seen *The Godfather* knows what that means... the mob!"

I frowned at her and knocked on Cooper's office door with my free hand, but he didn't answer.

My mother yanked my hand away before I could knock again. "Katherine Grace James, you need to have your head examined!"

"Mom, he's not a *murderer*." I wasn't about to tell her Cooper's favorite book, *The Bourne Identity*, which had an assassin for a main character.

"Just a minute!" Cooper snapped.

The hair on the back of my neck bristled. I was suddenly running all kinds of crazy scenarios through my suspicious mind. I thought I'd put all that behind me after my ill-fated snooping forays. I didn't want to be suspicious. I wanted to trust him without hesitation. But his unwillingness to share his secrets with me was always in the back of my mind. And thanks to my *mother's* snooping—and our eavesdropping—I had new worries fueling my not-so-easily forgotten ones, leaving me with a brand-new sense of insecurity. There were just too many things piling on top of each other in my head. I had to find a way to get back into his office and onto his laptop.

"Katie!" Mom shook me until I turned to look at her. "I really don't think it's a good idea to spend one more minute in this house!"

The door creaked open, and we both screamed.

"Did I scare you?" Cooper asked.

I ran his question through my head. The answer was a very complicated *yes*.

I wasn't sure what was worse—arguing with my mother or the sudden icy strain between Cooper and me. I wasn't even certain the strain was real—I may have made it up in my head—but real or manufactured, I felt it.

We all stood in the hallway, staring at each other without speaking. I had no idea what *they* were thinking about, but I was busy thinking unpleasant things. I played every frustrating discussion over again in my head until I was twisted into a state of panic. I tried to replay the conversations where he told me he loved me—but he hadn't told me he loved me all day—and he seemed distant... distracted. His thoughts were somewhere else. Somewhere I wasn't invited.

Cooper broke the silence with an uncomfortable laugh. "Did I miss something?"

My mother cleared her throat, so I jumped in first. "Mom doesn't feel up to shopping after all."

"Is there something you'd rather do?" Cooper asked.

I peeked at Mom out of the corner of my eye, and she was seething, but she kept silent.

Sometimes, I wondered if my mother wasn't really all that bad, but maybe I just interpreted her that way.

"So, Cooper, what is it that you do?" Mom asked, speaking to Cooper but staring straight at me. On second thought, she was definitely that bad.

"I do lots of things. Did you have something *specific* in mind, Mrs. James?" His smile was disarming, as usual, but it wasn't enough to sway her from her mission.

"Actually, yes I do." She turned to scrutinize him. "What *specifically* do you do for a living?"

He let out the same nervous laugh I remembered from every time I'd asked him what his occupation was. "I wouldn't want to bore you with the details."

She smiled, but it was a cunning, deliberate smile. She glanced toward the spare room where we'd discovered the guns, and I knew she was planning her attack. "Oh, go ahead. Bore me. I'm sure I've heard worse."

His jaw flexed. "As I've already told Katie, I'm a contract employee."

"And *precisely* what sort of contracts are you carrying out?"

"I try not to talk about work when I'm not working. I don't want to waste a single minute of the time I spend with Katie." As if to underscore that, he wrapped his arm around my shoulders and tugged me close to kiss my hair. Even then, I could feel the tension mounting in him.

She must have felt it too because she didn't relent. She locked her eyes on his. "That's exactly why I ask. Katie's my daughter, and I think she has a right to know who she's getting involved with."

"I think Katie knows me very well." He held his smile in place, but it obviously took great effort.

"I don't think she does, actually. For all we know, your secrecy is masking something sinister."

Cooper's body went rigid, and his hug became uncomfortable.

"Mom—" I wasn't really sure what I was going to say, but I didn't have a chance because Cooper cut me off.

"Katie understands *precisely* who she is getting herself involved with." He sounded angry.

"Does she?" Mom's voice was calm and flat, but I felt the current of severity building just below the surface. "Why don't you ask her then?"

My stomach lurched. "Stay out of it, Mom." But secretly, I was hoping she would get the truth out of him, once and for all.

"What is it you think I should be asking her?" he asked through gritted teeth.

"Ask her how she feels about all the secrets."

"Mom... really!" My voice rose an octave, and I quickly cleared my throat. "Cooper and I have already discussed this."

But that was before we found the guns and listened to his phone conversation. Although I wasn't going to say anything about that! And I did understand—in fact, his way of thinking seemed completely reasonable then—but standing in the hall outside the guest room—the one that contained guns—I wasn't sure.

"For all she knows, you could be a *murderer!*" Mom blurted.

"Mom!" My eyes went wide as I watched Cooper's expression go from irritation to fury.

Mom didn't seem to care about the effect she was having on him. "Since you've already discussed this with Katie, you shouldn't have a problem letting me know exactly what your intentions *are* with regard to my daughter."

My mouth fell open with a pop. "You have got to be kidding me!"

Cooper spoke to my mother, but he locked his eyes with mine. "Your daughter knows how I feel about her." He took my hand and brought it to his lips for a light kiss.

"You've gotten very serious in a fairly short amount of time. Don't think I haven't noticed you stayed in the same room last night." She whispered the last part as if talking about something unsavory.

I was horrified. "Mother! I'm almost thirty years old. I think it's a little late to be concerned about my virtue."

"Don't be so naïve, Katie. How could you even consider marrying a man when you don't know a thing about him?"

She'd finally done it. She'd said the M word. I was mortified. Cooper blushed, and it was painfully obvious he was horrified as well.

"That's enough," I hissed. My stomach twisted into a new knot, and I wanted the conversation over and for my mother to go home. *Immediately.*

"Katie..." Cooper looked at his watch. "I have a phone call I need to make. Will you excuse me for a minute?"

I wasn't sure if he really had a phone call or if he was just giving me an opportunity to rebuke my mother in private. Either way, he disappeared into his office, taking the only warmth in the hall with him, and I was left to face her alone.

"You were way out of line," I snapped.

She grabbed me by the arm and pulled me toward her room. "Katie, have you already forgotten the guns? Or the big payoff? You have no idea how many people he's killed!"

I wanted to scream at the top of my lungs, "He's not a murderer!" But I wasn't really sure what to believe anymore. "We have no *proof* he killed anyone."

Just a day ago, I had been convinced Cooper loved me, and it didn't matter what he did as long as that was true. In a matter of twenty-four hours, not only was I worried that I was just a fling and he was getting bored with me, but more pieces of the puzzle were coming together, and they looked suspiciously like dead bodies. All of this because my stupid mother couldn't keep her nose in her own business.

Hot tears built up behind my eyes. The floodgates were opening, and I was powerless to close them again. I turned my back on her to wipe away the first few tears with the back of my hand.

She interrupted my meltdown. "Who walks away from a conversation like this?"

"Anyone talking to you, that's who!" My voice cracked, but either she didn't notice or didn't care.

She just scoffed and walked away. I wiped furiously at a new barrage of tears and wished for a box of Kleenex. I made a beeline for Cooper's bathroom and locked myself in the CRWAT.

How unbelievably pathetic of me. I tried to muffle the gasping sounds coming from my throat but knew it was a feeble attempt. My body shook as sob after sob ripped through me. A new storm of tears came with it.

My cell phone vibrated in my pocket, and after a brief struggle, I dug it out and flipped it open. A text.

Cooper: Where are you?

I didn't feel like lying to him. Right then and there, I officially swore off lying for good, and I quickly texted him back through a blur of more tears.

Katie: Crying in the bathroom... where are you?
Cooper: Hiding in my office... where's your mother?
Katie: With any luck she's jumped out the window.

He didn't text me back, and if I were honest with myself, I didn't expect it. I wouldn't have known what to say to me if I were him. He must have finally realized I was too emotional.

"Katie?" He was right outside the door.

I hesitated for a second then squeaked, "I'm in here."

"Please let me in. I don't want to have this conversation through the bathroom door."

I almost laughed at that image, but instead I turned the lock, letting the door swing ajar.

"Please don't cry." He pulled me against him in a crushing embrace. "I can't bear to see you so upset."

I sobbed. "You must think I'm a wretched mess."

"You're a beautiful mess," he whispered.

"But still a mess."

"I'll take you however I can get you."

I shuddered. "How can you stand to be around me? My mother is ruining everything."

"Your mother is definitely challenging my patience today. I won't lie to you about that. But ruining everything? I think you're overreacting just a little."

"She's putting you through the Spanish Inquisition. How can you say I'm overreacting?"

He leaned down and kissed me gently. "Well, she's right about a few things. You and I need to sit down and have a long talk. But not today."

That didn't sound good at all. My mother had said some pretty awful things, and I didn't want to imagine even one of those being true. I certainly didn't want to have a talk of any length about them. What if he was going to tell me he *was* a murderer? Or worse, that he wanted to break up?

"I love you, Cooper," I whispered against his neck.

"And I'm a very lucky man to have you love me."

But he didn't say he loved me back.

MARGARITAS AND SENORITAS

Y CELL VIBRATED, AND I checked the caller ID. *Silvia.*
"Margaritas, señorita?" she asked with a Spanish accent.

I peered up at Cooper. "Is everyone still going?"

"Well, of course everyone is going," she replied. "We're not about to let a little hostage situation spoil our Friday night. If we're lucky, we'll get free drinks, since we were on TV. The world loves celebrities."

"Well, all righty then. Mom's still here. Is that going to be a problem?"

She laughed. "Nah, bring the old bitch. A few margaritas ought to do her good."

"Oooo-kay," I said, drawing out the word. "So we'll see you at seven?"

"Make it eight. Phil wants to sing tonight, and they don't start karaoke until eight thirty."

"Gotcha. Eight. Sounds like a plan."

At eight o'clock on the dot, I hugged Silvia a little tighter than I had intended.

She furrowed her brow. "Whoa there, sweetie. Are you okay?"

"I'm fine." So much for swearing off lying.

She looked at Cooper and something entirely wordless passed between them.

His thumb rubbed circles in my shoulder. "Katie's had a rough day."

And if there was ever an understatement... *that* was it.

"Well, we'll fix that right up," Silvia promised, pouring a frozen green concoction into a salt rimmed glass for me.

I grimaced. "Oh, no. You know I don't do margaritas."

"Tonight you do," she insisted.

Cooper slid into the large corner booth and tugged on my hand until I scooched in beside him. Silvia climbed in after me, sandwiching me between the two of them, thankfully, protecting me on both sides from my mother, who sat across from us.

I sucked a mouthful through the straw and swallowed, shivering from the cold.

"Be careful with those. They're deceptively strong," Cooper warned as he filled his glass.

Phil strode across the room a minute later. "James! I'm so glad you're still alive." He slid into the other side of the booth to sit next to Mom and immediately waved for the waitress. "I'll have a pitcher of whatever you have on draft." Phil then turned back to me. "No inappropriately sexy outfits tonight?" He laughed, checking out my fairly staid choice of clothes.

Silvia sighed. "We're all lucky to be alive."

"Some are luckier than others, I dare say." Mom raised her eyebrows at Cooper.

"I guess you can never really be sure you know someone," Silvia added, and although I knew she was referring to Dean, I glanced at Cooper.

Cooper bristled beside me at the mention of our ordeal, and I actually found some comfort in his *discomfort*. In some backward way, it made me feel like he still cared. I knew I shouldn't need constant proof, but I was a little desperate, especially with my mother's words still swirling around in my muddled brain.

June plopped into the booth. "Hi, everyone!"

"Hi!" we all chimed in unison.

"Katie, you look like shit," Vicky said with a playful edge as she slid into the booth as well.

"She looks beautiful as usual," Cooper corrected with a frown, tucking a stray hair behind my ear.

Vicky rolled her eyes at him and poured herself a margarita. We had reached capacity in the corner booth, but a man I didn't quite recognize managed to squeeze in next to Vicky anyway.

"Has everyone met my husband?" Vicky said with what I could only interpret as a blush.

"No, I haven't. I'm Cooper Maxwell. It's nice to meet you." Cooper stood as much as he could in the tight space and shook the man's hand.

"Jim Dixon. Nice to meet you, Cooper."

Vicky's comment about me being his first-round draft pick flashed back to me, and my stomach twisted uncomfortably. I had only met her husband once. He looked younger dressed in jeans and a polo.

"Jim wouldn't let Vicky out without an escort tonight," Silvia said with a giggle. "He seems to think her flirting might be on the dangerous side these days."

We all paused for an awkward moment, then the laughter spread through the table. Even my mother laughed, though she probably didn't get the joke.

"Who's singing tonight?" Phil asked, waving the song list above his head. The waitress had brought his beer, and he drank it straight from the pitcher like a giant mug.

"Katie will," Cooper volunteered with a grin.

I didn't mind. I liked that he wanted me to sing. I told Phil what song I wanted, and he wrote it on a slip of paper then jogged over to the DJ to put in our requests.

"Hey, Katie." June leaned across the table so I could hear her over the noise. "Do you have the next book in the *Immoral Blood* series you let me borrow? I want to catch up before the movie comes out."

"You mean the '*Immortal*' *Blood* series? Sure. I'll bring the rest on Monday. I've already read them all. You can keep them if you want," I said, and everyone at the table— even Cooper—looked at me with mild shock.

"Giving up books, Katie?" Silvia smirked. "I'll believe *that* when I see it."

I giggled. "Who has time to read?"

I barely caught the glance she gave Cooper, but when I turned to look at him, he was sucking in his cheeks to hide the smile on his face.

"But, no. I'm not giving up *reading.* I'm just not going to let reading keep me from living anymore. Besides, it's time for a few *new* books, don't you think?"

Silvia flashed a smug smile as she clinked her glass against mine. It was just like old times. Old times being a week ago. And I relaxed for the first time all day. Despite my aversion to margaritas, the drinks weren't bad either. I was working on my second one when the DJ called my name.

I made my way to the stage with excitement instead of fear and belted out my favorite song with enthusiasm. Cooper stood up next to the booth, cheering wildly.

I'm having so much fun! I, Katie James, boring banker and romance novel fanatic, was finally having fun. Hanging out with the gang, cuddling up with my boyfriend... no one—myself included—would have believed it if there hadn't been witnesses.

My mom kept to her word and didn't drink a single drop of alcohol. She was definitely *not* having fun, which made mine that much sweeter. It was time I did things without worrying about how it would affect her. I was officially smoothing out the crimp she'd put in my weekend.

After I'd belted out the lyrics to Celine Dion's "Because You Loved Me," I swooped off the stage and ran straight into Cooper's waiting arms. He spun me around and kissed me before sliding us back into the booth.

Silvia smiled at me. "You're getting good at this. It's hard to believe you had to be dragged up there just a few weeks ago."

"Are you talking about the singing or the kissing?" Vicky tossed in.

"Both," they said at the same time, and everyone laughed.

Unfortunately, Cooper's iPhone rang at that very moment, and after checking the caller ID, he looked at me and said, "I'm sorry. I need to take this." We all scooted to let him out of the booth as he answered the call. "Vivian? Hang on. It's really loud in here. I can't hear you."

I watched him walk through the bar to the back door, and he disappeared outside. My stomach plummeted as all the hummingbirds that fluttered around in there took a synchronized nose-dive. *Vivian.*

Of course, my mother chose that exact moment to rejoin the conversation. "Who is that woman? He's been talking to her all day."

"I'm fairly certain that's none of your business," I snapped.

She flashed that know-it-all smirk of hers. "I see. So you have no idea then."

I exhaled sharply and turned away from her to watch Phil on stage singing about someone's lyin' eyes. I shivered, and not just because he wasn't keeping up with the melody of the Eagles' song he'd chosen.

My mother announced, "I'm very concerned about all these secrets he's keeping from you, Katherine. It's dangerous to be so deeply involved with someone you barely know."

Silvia chimed in. "She may have only met him a year ago, but *I've* known him a lot longer than that."

I spun around to face her. "How long have you—"

"Several years. Before you started with the bank, he was *my* client."

"Oh." There was nothing secretive or unusual about that fact. Obviously, someone had been his banker before I got there. I'd just never bothered to think about it.

"Well, I find his behavior very suspicious," my mother muttered.

"I'm not surprised *you* would," Silvia said.

Mom's mouth fell open. "What exactly do you mean by that?"

Silvia gave a dismissive wave. "Nothing at all."

Mom excused herself to go to the restroom, and Silvia took the opportunity to pounce on me before Cooper came back to the table.

"You listen to me, Katie James." She wagged a finger mere inches from my nose. "You have been telling me *forever* about how your mother gets into your business and how much you can't stand it. From what I understand, she's interfered in almost every aspect of your life, which is why you moved so far away from her to begin with. So do not—I repeat, do *not*—allow her to get between you and Cooper. I can see the wheels turning in that pretty little head of yours as you toss around the seeds of doubt she's planted, and I am not pleased by what I'm seeing."

"He's keeping secrets, Silvia. What am I supposed to think?"

"We *all* have secrets." She stared into her drink, then back at me. "Just promise me you'll let your heart steer you from here on out, not your mother's mean-spirited implications."

I was still mulling that over when Cooper came back inside a few minutes later. He stopped beside the bar and motioned for me with his index finger. I looked at Silvia for moral support. She gave me a steely look I took to be a warning, and I slid out of the booth.

"Hey." I flicked the straw wrapper I was playing with toward an empty table.

He stuffed his hands into the pockets of his jeans. "Hey," he said with just a hint of the smile I needed to see.

I pulled my eyebrows together and felt the little crease he'd warned me about. "What's wrong?"

"I missed you." He bent down to place a careful kiss on the little O formed by my surprised lips.

"You weren't gone that long."

He sighed. "It's always too long if I'm away from you."

His melancholy mood worried me. "Cooper, you're scaring me a little. Is something wrong?"

He pulled one hand from his pocket and shoved it into his hair, making it stick up on one side. I would have laughed, but the look on his face was pained.

"I have to go out of town," he said.

Relief spread through me. I could handle a day or two away from him. "Oh, good. I was afraid you were going to say something horrible." As soon as I said it, I got a bad feeling in my stomach. "Oh, wait. It's nothing with your family, is it? Is everyone okay?"

He shook his head, giving me a faint smile. "It's nothing like that. Everything's fine, really. It's just work-related."

"Oh, um... New York again?"

"California." He grimaced. "I need to take care of a few contracts."

"Oh. When do you have to leave?"

"I *should* leave tomorrow, but I told them it would have to wait until Sunday. So Sunday morning. That should give me enough time to prepare for my meeting Monday."

"And when will you be back?"

He tucked a lock of my hair behind my ear, and my skin tingled where he touched me.

"I'm hoping I'll be home by Tuesday night. It's still a little up in the air." He bent down and rested his forehead against mine so he could whisper, "I'd love to take you with me. But I can't. Not this time."

"That's okay. I understand." The hummingbirds in my stomach woke up when he said he'd love to take me with him. I didn't care so much that I couldn't go. It was good just knowing he wanted me to. "At least we still have Saturday."

"Well..." He shifted his weight, pulling his face back from mine slightly. "Actually, I'm going to have to work on a few things. I'll be home, but I won't be much fun to be around."

"I see." I forced a smile. "Do we need to leave now?"

"I don't see why we should. I'll just have to get started bright and early tomorrow."

My head bobbed a few times. It wouldn't matter if we stayed or left—my night was ruined. I tried not to think of it that way. I didn't want to be unfair, but I was disappointed.

"Well, let's have all the fun we can tonight," I said in my cheery voice.

Cooper pressed his lips to mine then took my hand and led me back to our table. "Back in you go." He grabbed me around the waist and tugged me into the booth with him.

I laughed despite my new mood.

Silvia's eyes darted between Cooper and me. "Everything okay?"

"Peachy," I said. "Can I get another one of those margaritas?"

HERE WE GO AGAIN

I TIPPED MY GLASS UPSIDE DOWN above my mouth and stuck my tongue inside, trying to scoop the last drops of the frozen drink from the glass. I did a quick sweep of the sides and tried to touch the tip of my tongue to the bottom. I gave the glass a quick shake, hoping to dislodge the remaining slush, and what was left came rushing at me with a splash against my nose. I stared at the glass and frowned.

"Sweetie, wouldn't you rather just pour some more?" Silvia said.

"Sure, Sil. Pour for me?" I slammed my glass down on the table a little rougher than I intended and cringed. "Whoops." I giggled.

Cooper was away from the table again on his third phone call from Vivian. He apologized each time, and I said I understood—but I did *not* understand. I recognized the emotion I was feeling, but I wasn't going to give it power by saying it out loud. *Jealousy.*

I shook my head as Silvia stuck a new straw into my fresh margarita, and I sucked a long swallow of the frozen drink down my throat until I was cross-eyed and my head felt like it might explode. *Brain freeze!*

"You'd better slow down. Do you remember the last time you were here?" Silvia said.

I most definitely remembered. That was the night I fell in love with Cooper. But last time was completely different. First of all, I had been drinking shots, and secondly, after far too many of those, I added champagne to seal my fate. Besides, the margaritas were little more than spiked slushies.

"Are you getting drunk, Katherine?"

I shook my finger at her. "Listen, Mom. I'm a big girl, and I can get drunk if I want to."

"That's right. Listen to her. She can get drunk if she wants to," Vicky imitated with a laugh. She was on her best behavior with her husband sitting practically in her lap. She hadn't uttered a single sexual innuendo all evening, and I had to admit, she wasn't nearly as entertaining with a leash.

I burst into hysterical laughter. I was still laughing when Cooper came back to the table.

"Did I miss a good joke?" he asked.

"I think the joke's on Katie, actually." Vicky smirked, oblivious to what had sent me into hysterics.

"Are you okay?" Cooper leaned in and touched his lips to mine, but I couldn't really feel it. I couldn't taste his peppermint breath either. The only things I tasted were salty lime, tequila, and resentment, but I thought that was all me.

"James, you're up," Phil said as he walked up to the table, empty beer pitcher in hand.

"What am I singing?" I asked.

"Don't ask me. I don't even know what I was singing." He laughed.

That made two of us. But I only knew what Phil was singing half the time, anyway. Cooper reluctantly released me to slide out of the booth and even more reluctantly let me leave his side to make my way to the stage.

I didn't know why everyone was acting so weird around me. I was fine. *Really.* I knew my limits. I had run right up to them on a few occasions and peered over the edge. I knew what it was like to tumble over, and I wasn't even close. I'd only had three margaritas. Or was it four? Either way, they were small.

I snatched the microphone from the DJ's hand and winked at him. The music started and I froze. That was *not* the song I'd picked. Someone must have switched them, and I could take two guesses as to who it might have been. I knew "Foolish Games," by Jewel. It was a great song, but the lyrics were *exactly* what I *didn't* need in my current emotional state.

The words rolled up on the screen, and I felt the first wave of tears pricking my eyes. I tried to hold it back, but once I got into the chorus, I was doomed. My voice cracked, and I looked away from the audience while I failed miserably at pulling myself together. Somehow, I got through the song. But when it was over, I was a basket case. I managed to stumble my way off the platform without falling. I tried to sneak around the side of the stage so I could duck into the ladies' room. I tripped on something and did a full on belly flop onto the floor in front of the bar, and the air in my lungs was forced out with a sudden *whoosh*.

Stunned, I lay on the hard floor, my face just inches away from a crushed cigarette and an empty peanut shell. I couldn't move. I was staggered by how much it hurt. I might have been knocked unconscious if I hadn't put my arms out in front of me; my head had smacked into my forearms rather than the cement floor. The rest of me was not as lucky.

If the impact hadn't knocked the wind out of me, I might have yelled for help. But I was unable to pull enough oxygen into my lungs to make a sound. I rolled onto my back into a puddle of what I hoped was only beer... and waited.

Cooper was clearly distracted and hadn't seen me fall. My heart sank. He was never too distracted to pick me up when I fell. A girl could get used to that. A nice man reached down and roughly yanked me back to my feet.

I was about to say thank you when he yelled, "Stay out of the aisle," as if I were actually *trying* to be a road hazard.

I tried to zip around the corner to the ladies' room but ran head on into the wall of Cooper's chest.

"Where are you going?" His eyes scanned my body with an uneasy look.

I glanced down at the front of me. My shirt was sticky and dirty. "I was trying to escape to the ladies' room, but I must have done something to create bad karma because I've had nothing but trouble getting there."

He laughed, but it wasn't a funny laugh. It was a *you are in big trouble* laugh. He hooked his arm with mine and tugged me toward the group. "Come on, you little lush. Let's go back to the table."

I raised both eyebrows. "What about the restroom?"

"We can stop there first. Are you okay to go by yourself?" he asked without a hint of humor.

"If I can't manage to use the bathroom on my own, I am in serious trouble."

Cooper frowned. "Without a doubt."

He dropped me off at the door, and I wobbled my way into the last stall. Okay, I was officially in serious trouble.

I dropped to my knees on the unspeakably vile tile floor, gripping both sides of the nasty public toilet with my hands, and violently threw up. Waves of heat rolled over me as my head spun. The horrible smells permeating the stall made me more nauseous than I already was. I desperately wanted to lay my cheek against the cold faux marble, but no matter how sick I was—and I was *sick*—there was no way my face was going anywhere near that bacterial buffet.

I had no idea how long I was in there or if Cooper was still outside the door waiting. None of that was even remotely important while I revisited every single thing I'd eaten all day. Thankfully, I hadn't eaten much. More than once, I thought I was finished and I stood up, washed my hands, rinsed my mouth, and started for the door, just to turn around and fall to my knees for another wave of vomiting.

Margaritas. They seemed so innocent—the cute little

frozen concoctions in fancy glasses—but they were pure evil, and I needed to perform an exorcism.

My cell phone vibrated in my pocket, but I didn't have the strength to fish it out. I leaned my elbows against the cracked plastic seat and cradled my head in my hands, my face hovered over the bowl, just in case.

I had no idea how I was going to get out of the restroom, but I desperately wanted to figure a way to get all the way home unnoticed. If I could just sneak out the door and hail a cab. I didn't care that my mom thought cabs were petri dishes; nothing could be as bad as where I was. Then I remembered my purse, my keys—and all my money—still in the booth. I was stuck.

A few people had come and gone in the time I was hunched over the toilet—I could hear them doing their thing in the other stalls—but no one bothered to speak to me. I wouldn't have spoken to me either. I couldn't even see what I looked like, and I really didn't want to know.

As I prayed for someone to come looking for me—since escape was highly improbable given my current condition— the door opened again. *I should have been more specific.*

"Katie?" She didn't sound angry, but I knew better than to assume anything with her.

I lifted my head up so my voice wouldn't echo in the bowl and cleared my throat. "Yes?"

"What are you doing in here?"

I let my head drop back into my hands. I wanted desperately to say something witty, but nothing came to mind. "I'm sick." My voice cracked, and I felt the tears in my eyes again.

"I knew you were drinking too much." She didn't say it in a mean way. It was almost compassionate, at least, for my mother.

She pushed open the door to my stall. "Katie, you look like shit."

I snapped my head up and spun around to look at her.

My mom said *shit*. She *never* swore. But moving my head so quickly had been a mistake. My stomach lurched again, and a fresh wave rippled up from the depths of my body. I leaned back over the bowl just in time.

Barfing wasn't what I had in mind when I set out for Margaritaville. I had no idea where it was all coming from. Certainly, I couldn't have drunk *that* much.

"I'm getting Cooper. Let him deal with you. I have no words."

Mom left, and a few minutes later, Cooper poked his head into the ladies' room. "Katie?"

A quiet groan was the only answer I could muster.

"Oh, Katie."

"Just let me die," I muttered, head in my hands.

"Sorry. Can't do that. You're going to have to suffer through this, sweetheart." He crouched behind me, rubbing circles on my back. "For someone who doesn't drink, you spend an awful lot of time drunk. I do believe this is the third weekend in a row you'll spend nursing a hangover."

Fabulous. I whimpered. "It's not my fault."

"Who should we blame this time?"

I held back a sob, determined not to cry again. "You're mad at me."

"I'm not mad. I am disappointed." He combed his fingers through my hair. "I have to leave on Sunday, and you'll be sick long after I'm gone."

"I'm sorry."

"I just don't understand what got into you tonight." He never stopped rubbing my back, even as he scolded me.

I knew what had gotten into me—jealousy. Suspicion. And *Grace James*. And none of those things should *ever* be mixed with tequila. "You've just been so distracted tonight..."

"I do have responsibilities I can't ignore."

I opened my mouth, and the words just flew out. "Who's Vivian?"

He stopped rubbing my back for a minute. "She works for me."

"That's all? She works for you? Nothing more?" I was actually thankful I was still facing the ghastly toilet so I didn't have to look him in the eyes.

He hesitated for a very long time, then exhaled sharply. "Are you jealous?"

I kept my voice low and even, masking the building panic. "Wh-what if I said yes?"

"If you said yes, I would tell you you're being ridiculous." His hands resumed caressing my back, but not quite as gently. "Katie, I told you, I haven't thought of another woman since we met."

I shifted my weight, turning until I was sitting flat on the dirty floor, facing him. My eyes brimmed with tears, but I blinked them back. *Pathetic.* "I hate this. I hate the secrets. I hate the guilt. I hate knowing *Vivian* gets to know where you work and I don't. And I hate that you're talking to *her* when you're supposed to be spending time with *me!*" I slapped my hands over my mouth to stop the flow of verbal diarrhea.

His eyes studied me for a moment, then they hardened. "What the hell, Katie? I thought we talked about this. You know I just need a little time."

"No, Cooper, *we* didn't talk about this. You said you needed time, and I'm giving you time, but that doesn't mean I have to like it."

"I don't know whether to kiss you or strangle you sometimes." He pushed my hair from my face, tucking it behind my ears. "Listen, we'll work everything out, okay? But right now, I really think we need to get you home and cleaned up, because, sweetheart, you look like total shit."

Again with the looking like shit? I stood carefully, and try as I might, I couldn't avert my eyes from the mirror fast enough. I really did look like I could be an extra on *The Walking Dead*. I put my hands against my head and groaned.

"Are you okay?" Cooper wrapped his arm around my waist, holding me up.

"I caught a glimpse of myself in the mirror."

He winced. "Ouch."

"Yeah, you're right. I look pretty awful."

"It's a temporary condition."

I coughed out a laugh. "Which one? My appearance or the insanity that caused me to drink too much?"

He frowned. "Hopefully both." He shook his head. "What am I going to do with you?"

"Probably nothing tonight."

He laughed. "Probably not."

YOU CAN DEFINITELY DIE
OF A HANGOVER

I CRAWLED INTO BED FEELING LIKE someone had beaten the crap out of me. I drifted in and out of sleep, restless from the lingering effects of the alcohol but also from the burning in my throat from the violent retching and the bumps and bruises from falling. I'd set a new record for humiliation—impressive even for me. If my antics at the bar weren't bad enough, I'd managed to embarrass myself further on the ride home. I had now ruined the carpet in both Cooper's bedroom *and* his BMW.

I buried my face in the pillow, breathing in his scent and taking what solace I could from that small part of him—the only part I would have for the rest of the night.

Cooper didn't say anything, but I was certain he was still upset with me. I couldn't really blame him. I would have been furious with me if I were him. I knew better than to drink so much. He'd made me swallow two aspirin, then put me into bed with a cool, damp cloth resting on my forehead. He climbed in beside me, tucking me into the crook of his arm.

"I don't know how much longer I can be patient," I murmured.

As I drifted off to sleep, I heard him reply, "I know."

I woke up in the middle of the night, and he was gone. I was vaguely aware of his phone having vibrated and him sneaking out of the bed, but I didn't know when that was.

I lay staring at the dark ceiling, not really seeing anything, just running the memories from the past few days through my head and trying to find the exact moment when things had spun so out of control.

I traced it back to Thursday morning; everything had been perfect Wednesday night. I'd locked all of my worries and suspicions into a dark place in my head and refused to let them out. Then my mother came to town and, like Pandora, unlocked the box and freed all my worst fears.

Silvia was right about my mother. The woman screwed with my head. The good news was that she was leaving in a few short hours.

I slipped into unconsciousness again and didn't wake until the sun was cresting over the horizon. Cooper still wasn't in bed with me and must have been gone all night long. I'd dreaded the morning as fervently as I'd looked forward to it. I knew Mom was packed—her flight was less than four hours away—and I was more than ready to see her go.

I pulled myself out of bed and dragged my naked body to the bathroom. I didn't want to think about what had happened to my clothes. I'd managed to wipe the floor with every inch of me last night. I was mortified by my behavior and decided to officially swear off drinking. I only hoped that would be easier than swearing off lying.

As I passed his office, I faintly heard Cooper's voice. He sounded angry. I desperately wanted to knock on the door and force him to pay attention to me, but I knew I couldn't do that. He was engrossed in something that wasn't me, and maybe that was the thing that had me most jealous of all.

I poked around his kitchen, trying to find something that would appeal to my misplaced hunger, and settled on a few slices of cheese and an apple. It figured that as soon as I found a man who liked my curves, I'd lost my appetite.

Despite my unpleasant reaction to the smell, I scrambled

eggs for Mom, but of course, she didn't eat them, nor did she drink the coffee I made. Her loss. I scraped the eggs into the trash and drank the coffee myself.

Mom left her bags by the door for me, like I was her personal valet, and I loaded them into my Prius. I started the engine and backed slowly out of the driveway onto the main road, with Mom sitting quietly beside me. I was a little miffed at Cooper. He hadn't even poked his head out of the office to say goodbye. We hadn't talked about it, but I was sure the plan had been for us to take Mom to the airport together. As it got closer to time, I just decided to take her myself.

"I'm telling you, Katie, there is something very wrong with Cooper. You need to be careful."

I scoffed at her, but truthfully, I was worried. Things were definitely different, and I didn't need to be paranoid or suspicious to sense that.

"Are you sure you don't want to come stay with your father and me for a while?"

I gasped. "No!" It took every ounce of self-control to keep my eyes on the road with her spouting off crazy ideas like that.

We got stuck in traffic. It was as if my bad luck was on a winning streak. Mom nagged at me the whole way there, panicking she was going to miss her flight. I was deathly afraid of the same thing, for a different reason. I didn't want to spend a single extra minute in her presence.

Once we reached the airport, I gave her our usual ultra-polite air kiss and hug, and she hurried off to check her bags and dash through security.

I expected to find silence in the car after I dropped her off, but I was wrong. My head was screaming at me... in Spanish. I didn't speak Spanish, but I picked out the words *tequila* and *margarita* more than once, and I knew I deserved it. Cooper was right. For a girl who never drank, I'd definitely been drunk a whole lot lately. All I wanted was to sleep off the hangover, so I headed back to Cooper's.

I fell asleep almost immediately after I slid between the magnificent sheets. I slept like the dead, and when I later awoke, Cooper's arms were wrapped around me, and I was nestled into his chest. I nuzzled my nose into his neck.

"You were gone," he murmured into my hair.

"I had to take Mom to the airport."

"Oh, I'm sorry. I completely forgot. I was supposed to go with you." He sounded apologetic, which was almost enough for me.

I curled my hand into his hair and snuggled closer. "Yeah. She's gone now." I ran my lips along his jaw.

"Mmm."

"So you didn't miss me?" I whispered.

"Of course I did."

"How much?"

"This much." He took my face in his hands and kissed me until I was dizzy.

"Cooper..." I muttered when I could breathe again.

"Hmm?"

"I love you." My voice was barely a whisper, but I knew he heard me.

He pulled back to gaze into my eyes. "I love you, Katie. More than you can imagine." For a man professing his love, he looked awfully grim.

We made love for most of the rest of the afternoon, stopping only once to eat. Even then, it was a picnic in bed. He ran down to the kitchen and filled his arms with whatever he could find—fruit, cheese, bread—and he fed me until I was hungry for nothing but him.

When I started to drift back to sleep, he vanished again. I heard his heated voice coming from the other room. I was pretty sure I knew who he was yelling at, but it made me uncomfortable. And it flavored my dreams.

Dreams that had me prowling in the shadows. Dark shapes danced across the white walls as I walked the hall at night, pausing outside each door to knock and getting no answer. I wore a white gossamer dress that reflected the sliver of light coming from the moon. I knew he would be pleased when he saw me.

I heard his voice, but I couldn't find him. The hallway stretched out further in front of me, and suddenly there were dozens of doors. Doors that didn't open for me. I think I knew it was a dream, but I couldn't bring myself to wake up. Instead, I continued to knock until I stopped in front of what I knew must be Cooper's office.

The heavy door was taller and more ornate than I remembered. I paused to listen to the muted voices on the other side, recognizing Cooper's but not the other voice—a woman's. I slowly turned the knob, opening the door a crack, and peeked inside. The room was dark except for the blue glow of the laptop sending eerie shadows across his stony face. He stared at the screen with furious determination.

I whispered, "Cooper," but he didn't look up. His fingers continued to dart across the keys. I flinched as someone moved behind him. The shape of a woman stepped to the edge of the shadows, never fully coming into the light.

"You know what you have to do," she hissed.

"I won't." He spoke with resolve, but his lips never moved. His eyes stayed focused on the blue glow of the screen.

"You have to kill her," she demanded.

"I don't want to kill this one, Vivian," he responded in a low, angry voice, almost too soft to hear.

A shadowy hand snaked its way across his shoulders, long white fingers tangling into his hair. Her face was still completely in the dark, but I knew her lips were just a breath away from his ear. I struggled to see her, but every time I thought I could almost make out her face, it vanished again.

I instinctively knew she was shouting, but the sound was barely a whisper. "You know you have to kill her. That's what you do. They won't be satisfied until she's dead. You need to kill her before anyone finds out you planned to let her live."

"I don't want it to end that way, not this time."

"This isn't about what you want, Cooper. Your career will be over if she lives." Her voice turned sweet, almost adoring. "You don't want your career to be over, do you?"

"No, I don't." He spoke with such sadness. I could feel his resolve slipping, and I knew he had acquiesced to her demands.

"That's my Cooper," she purred.

I froze in the doorway, too paralyzed to move. The shadowy figure of Vivian faded back into the dark recesses of the office and vanished. Cooper lifted his eyes to me and smiled, but it wasn't the smile I loved. His lips twisted, revealing two razor sharp fangs that dripped with blood.

My eyes flew open, and I sat bolt upright in Cooper's bed. I immediately ordered my heart to return to a normal pattern, but it refused. *It was just a dream, a nightmare— nothing more.* It was my ridiculous subconscious playing tricks on me, but I could still see the malignant smile on Cooper's face and still hear the words Vivian had spoken.

I willed my heart to slow, but the dream hadn't quite cut me loose. Worse than that, it was after midnight, and Cooper wasn't in bed. His absence made it easier to believe the things my subconscious was shouting at me. Only it wasn't my subconscious anymore. I could hear his voice carrying into the hall.

Pulling the blanket with me, I slipped a leg over the side of the bed and crept toward the door.

"Goddamn it, Vivian. How many times do I have to spell it out for you? How many ways can I say *no* before you understand?" He was yelling so loud, his voice echoed off the walls as if he were standing right in front of me.

Her voice didn't carry as far as his, but as I reached the door, I could hear it just as clearly. "Then you may as well lay down your sword right here and give up. There's absolutely nothing I can do for you if you walk away from this. It's not just the money. It's not just the notoriety or your reputation; it's the whole shooting match. You'll be dead in the water, and I don't want to see that happen. Cooper, you know I love you. I always have. I only have your best interests at heart." He must have had her on speaker.

So it wasn't just a dream, after all. I'd been listening to their entire conversation. I pressed my ear to the door.

"Listen, I can't spell it out any clearer than this. Either she dies, or you do," Vivian said as calmly as if she was ordering lunch.

"Stop being melodramatic, Viv. I don't accept that option."

"Well, you'd better. You knew when you signed your contract you were going to have to kill her. You can't back out now, not when we're this close to the end."

I heard a thud that sounded as though he'd picked up an entire ream of paper and thrown it across the room. "You want me to kill her? Fine, you'll get your way. You always get your way. But this is absolutely the last one. Do you hear me? After this, I'm done," he said, his voice strained.

I recoiled from the door, my legs barely supporting me.

Vivian laughed as if she could see my reaction. "You know you can't just walk away from this..."

She went on, but I'd stopped listening. I registered the sound of their voices, but not a single word sank in. I'd heard all I needed to hear. *Cooper was going to kill me.*

My feet wouldn't work. My brain sent the signal to run, but my heart must have intercepted the message. It was racing so fast I was afraid it would leap straight from my chest from the sheer force of it. But my damn, traitorous feet were frozen in place.

It took me several seconds to realize I was hyperventilating. My lips had gone numb, and I couldn't feel my fingers. The blanket slipped to the floor, and the cold chill hit my skin, bringing me out of my daze.

Once I'd committed to moving, it was as if I'd been set on fire. Lava coursed through my veins, followed closely by liquid ice, and before I knew it, I was in his room, pulling my clothes on and stuffing my things into a bag. I had to get out of his house before he discovered I knew... or worse, before he set his own plan in motion. With my bag and purse slung over my shoulder, my shoes in hand, and my cell phone in my pocket, I crept into the hall again to listen, terrified he would step out of his office at any moment and catch me sneaking out.

The voices had quieted, but I heard Cooper's fingers furiously clacking against the keys on his laptop—sending her messages, no doubt. I had never hated anyone with the same fury I hated Vivian at that moment. Somehow, I still believed it was all her doing, that Cooper would have never... but it didn't matter.

With slow, deliberate steps, I made my way down the dark hallway to the stairs, too afraid to switch on a light or even to risk the glow from my cell phone to light my way. I slid forward one step at a time, searching for the edge of the stairs with my bare feet.

As my toes slipped over the top step, I gripped the handrail and got my bearings. I was scared I would fall in the dark. Any sound would pull Cooper from his office. I couldn't risk that happening. My shattered heart lurched in my chest as I took each step. Once I reached the bottom, I carefully pulled on my shoes and hurried to the kitchen to grab my keys.

I felt along the top of the island where I knew where they should be, but they weren't there. I was still too terrified to switch on a light, so I opened the refrigerator as I had the first night I'd fumbled around Cooper's kitchen snooping for clues in what seemed like another lifetime.

Finally, I found them hanging on one of the hooks inside the pantry door. I snatched them up and made my way to the mudroom and the garage beyond, where my Prius waited like a life raft. I rushed to pile my bags into the backseat as I dug into my front pocket for my phone to dial 9-1-1. Before I could catch it, my cell slipped from my trembling fingers and tumbled to the concrete floor.

"Oh no!" I squealed, and then slammed my hand over my mouth to stop the sound as I crouched down to collect the pieces. There was no salvaging it. All the times I'd lied to my mother, telling her I'd broken my phone, had suddenly caught up to me. *Karma is a bitch, and her name is Grace James.*

There was no avoiding the sound of the garage door opening, so I smashed the button and scrambled into the driver's seat. I pushed the button to start the car and slammed it into reverse.

I'd barely made it out of the garage when two cars pulled up behind me, and two uniformed men approached. I was momentarily blinded by a light shining in my eyes.

"You need to step out of the car, ma'am."

"How did you know?" I asked, thinking of my failed attempt to dial 9-1-1.

"Step out of the car," he repeated. "What are you doing here?"

As I scurried out of the driver's seat, I recognized the uniform. I realized I'd forgotten to disable the security system before going downstairs. "Thank God you're here! My boyfriend is going to kill me!"

NOTHING IS WHAT IT SEEMS TO BE

I F ANYONE HAD TOLD ME I would be relieved to see Le Guarde's security team—the same guys who had pointed guns at my head not two weeks ago—I would have said they were crazy. But I was elated, so thrilled in fact, I'd practically jumped into the burly man's arms and kissed him.

"... and guns," I continued my rant. "My mother found guns. Not hunting guns, mind you... sniper guns. Upstairs in his guest room. And he got this huge wire transfer two weeks ago, and Phil—he's my boss—he said someone would have paid at least that much money to kill a judge and a politician and even this guy in New York." I took a huge breath. "And then I heard him on the phone saying he would kill *me* like he killed the *others*. That's when I got the hell out of there."

The tall guy with the crew cut turned to his partner. "Did you call it in?"

The second guy nodded. They didn't exactly have a warm bedside manner, but they had some pretty big weapons of their own. The sound of sirens got closer, and I could see the flashing blue lights in the distance telling me the cavalry was on its way. I was caught up in watching the cars rush down the road when I heard his voice behind me.

"Katie, what's going on?" Cooper asked.

I spun around and screamed. "That's him!" I jumped back, bumping into the wall of someone's chest, and pointed at Cooper. "He's the one planning to kill me."

Cooper took a step toward me with his hands outstretched, and I flinched. Crew Cut stepped forward.

"Katie?" Cooper said my name as if I were a stranger. "Sweetheart, what are you talking about?"

"You want to kill me!" I shrieked. "I heard you tell Vivian you would. I found your guns, and I know you killed the others." I tucked myself behind Crew Cut and peered around him at Cooper's face.

His eyes were as wide as saucers. He was caught!

"Guns? What are you...? Jesus, Katie." He groaned, forcing both hands into his hair. "You need to calm down and listen to me."

"I've listened enough. You can't talk your way out of it this time."

The police cars had pulled in and parked. A sheriff's deputy walked over to where we stood. "Can someone please tell me what's going on here?"

"This lady—" Crew Cut nodded toward me. "—says the gentleman has threatened to kill her. She has apparently seen multiple weapons on the premises and overheard the gentleman telling someone he was planning to kill her."

"No... no... no." Cooper's fingers knotted in his dark waves, yanking it until it stood up. "Officer, there's been a terrible mistake. My name is Cooper Maxwell. This is my house."

"We show this house as being owned by the former British Consul-General and his wife."

"That's my parents. They left me the house when they went back to England.

"My girlfriend overheard a phone conversation I was having with an employee and obviously misunderstood the context."

"What are you talking about?" I gaped at Cooper's deer-in-headlights expression. "Your parents are farmers! And I didn't misunderstand anything." I turned to the cop and pointed at Cooper. "He has guns, and I heard him very clearly tell someone on the phone he would kill me like he did the others." I launched into the whole story again.

Another uniformed officer came up behind Cooper and shoved him onto the hood of my car, where he frisked him.

"Katie, please..." Cooper said as he was handcuffed. "I thought we agreed this whole *assassin* theory of yours was ridiculous before your mother got here."

"That was before Mom found the guns in the cedar chest," I declared triumphantly. I felt as if I were playing Clue. *It was Cooper in the guest room with a wooden rifle.*

"Please, just let me explain. I know you heard me talking to Vivian, but it's not what you think. I wasn't talking about you." His voice was strained.

My lips fell open. "Then, who are you going to kill?"

Cooper sighed. "Nobody. It's complicated."

"Mr. Maxwell, would you mind explaining the situation? Do you know what the young lady is referring to?" the sheriff asked.

Cooper groaned. "Unfortunately... yes. I do have two antique rifles in a chest upstairs. They don't even work. They were a gift from my father. I almost forgot I had them. As far as the phone call..." Cooper drew his eyes away from the sheriff to glance at me. "You heard me speaking to Vivian Allen. She's my publicist." He turned back to the officer. "We were arguing over a character she wanted me to kill off in my next book."

"A character in a book?" I choked out. "Really? That's the best you can do? I think I'd know if you were a writer. I would have seen your name in a bookstore or when I *Googled* you. There's no author I've ever heard of named Cooper Maxwell."

He nodded, his face fallen. "You're right. You would have to Google my pen name. Elizabeth Jayne."

Elizabeth Jayne? "That's not possible," I said. "You're lying..." I turned from Cooper to the sheriff and swallowed hard. "He *must* be lying. He saw her books in my house."

I reached for any explanation I could think of. I couldn't believe what I was hearing. "He knows she's my favorite author. I saw him flipping through one of my books just a week ago."

"No, Katie. I may have kept things from you, and I'm so sorry for that, but I would never lie to you. I love you." His impassioned plea cracked my resolve just a little. "Sweetheart, do you remember the first time you had dinner with me? Do you remember asking me if I'd gotten the idea from a book? You were pretty sure I had. Well, I did, and I know you remember the scene from *Blood Everlasting*."

My eyes filled with tears as I turned to the sheriff to say something, but I was at a loss for words.

The sheriff nodded to two other officers. "I think we need to go ahead and take them in to get this sorted out. Damnedest thing I've heard in a long time," he said as he walked off, shaking his head.

The first officer led Cooper, still in handcuffs, to the back of a cruiser, and roughly shoved him inside the vehicle. The second one led me to another car, where he opened the door and politely ushered me into the backseat.

I sucked in a jagged breath as I watched the vehicle carrying Cooper Maxwell pull out of the driveway, and I knew he'd been telling the truth. I did remember that dinner... all too well. I always knew there was something about Cooper that defied reason. He was different from other men... more romantic. But I could never put my finger on it.

His revelation explained why. And in the dark recesses of my mind, I was certain I'd crossed that imaginary line, forever changing the dynamics of our relationship.

WELL, I CERTAINLY DIDN'T EXPECT THAT

NO ONE WAS AT THE bank when I arrived on Monday morning. For the first time ever, I'd beaten them all. In another lifetime, I would have been proud of that accomplishment. But as it stood, I simply felt pathetic. I hadn't rushed to work out of love for my job, but because work was the only place that felt like home anymore.

I'd spent all day Sunday curled up by the fire, crying. And burning every book in my house that reminded me of Cooper. One. By. One. And the Elizabeth Jayne books were the first to go. Once I'd realized what a fool I'd been, I couldn't stand to look at the name in bold red print across the cover, let alone ever read them again. Not only had the first man I'd ever really loved broken my heart, but I'd lost my fictional boyfriend, too.

I wondered how many times Cooper had tried to call me, or if he had at all, and then I stamped those thoughts back down where they belonged. I didn't need to know, didn't want to know. I was glad my cell phone was broken.

I hadn't spoken to anyone since Saturday, and I was a jumble of nerves waiting for Silvia to come in to work. I'd considered showing up on her doorstep Sunday with a box of Kleenex and a bottle of really bad chardonnay, but I didn't want to admit what I'd done... to her of all people.

I heard a key in the lock and ran to the front.

"James?" Phil asked. "What are you doing here so early?"

"Couldn't sleep," I said. It was just easier to lie. I resolved to wait for Silvia in her office and turned to head in that direction.

"Well, go get some coffee," Phil barked as I crossed the lobby. "It's going to be a busy day! I expect we'll have news crews storming the gates before it's time to open."

I stopped dead in my tracks and spun back around to stare at Phil. "What? Why?" An immediate wave of hot fear cut through me. *Cooper?*

"Don't you ever watch the news?" He scrunched up his face. "Dean... he's all over the news. That son of a bitch was the one knocking off politicians and judges in Atlanta. I heard he even killed some big shot in New York. They're calling him the Singing Assassin."

"*Dean*? He's the killer?" A bubble of hysterical laughter burst out of me. If only I'd had that little bit of information a few days ago.

"I know." He shook his head. "Unbelievable, right? He was right under our noses the whole time."

The whole time. "Have you spoken to Silvia?" I asked. "Does she know?"

"I'm sure she does. It's on the news." He smiled, shaking his head at me again as he pushed the power button on the TV remote. "CNN, James... all news, all day."

I didn't need to see the news. I'd lived it. Leaving Phil to his morning routine, I wandered into Silvia's office and plopped down in her chair with a sigh. I followed the sweet smell to the vase filled with roses on her desk. They had all but withered and died, but the fragrance hadn't faded a bit. So much for feeling like home.

I rocked back in Silvia's chair to stare at the ceiling. Everywhere else I looked reminded me of Cooper: Silvia's roses, my orchids, even the chair across from my desk. Just looking at them caused me physical pain. I was trying to stay in the present, but it was next to impossible when my broken heart kept drifting to the past.

I let my eyes wander around her office. A familiar swirl of red caught my attention on top of her cabinet, and I jumped up to grab the crisp new book tucked between two regulatory manuals. *A Lust for Blood*, by Elizabeth Jayne.

I choked out a strangled laugh. "This one isn't even out yet."

"I was going to give that to you today." Silvia's voice came from behind me, and I jumped at the sound, spinning around to face her. She looked pale.

I gasped. "Where did you get this?"

Silvia gave me a weak smile. "Oh, you know me. I have my ways." She stepped into the office and took the book from my trembling hands. "It's even autographed." She flipped open the cover to reveal the author's name scrawled in familiar handwriting.

"Were you ever going to tell me?"

She sighed, closing the book. "It wasn't my secret to tell."

I pushed my hair behind my ears. "How long have you known?"

A sad smile played on her lips as her eyes darkened. "I've always known. That sort of thing had to be disclosed when he opened his accounts. He was my client first, remember?"

I nodded, about to fall over as I stared blankly at her, almost afraid to let the reality sink in. "And you knew about his family?"

Her expression told me all I needed to know. *Silvia knew everything... all along.*

"I also knew fairly soon after you started working here he was falling for you," she said. "That's when I decided to assign his accounts to you. I mean, it was obvious... to me, anyway. I think he was as blind as you were for a long time, but I knew you were falling for him."

I frowned and played with a loose button on my jacket, tugging at the thread until the button came off in my fingers.

Silvia put her hand on my shoulder, squeezing gently. "Katie, take a deep breath and sit down before you fall over."

"I'm not sure I want to sit down." I tormented another button on my jacket until it too hung by just a few threads.

"Just sit," Silvia ordered.

I sat, arms crossed in front of me.

She stared at me for a moment. "It became even more important to him that you not find out what he did for a living. I don't really understand why. He was embarrassed, of course, and we can't forget the gag order from his family, but more than that—"

"Gag order? What are you talking about? What gag order?"

"Oh, Katie. You don't know, do you?" She shook her head. "Cooper's father was the Consul-General of Atlanta. Even after that, he spent years in high profile diplomatic service. Apparently, Cooper's parents had a huge problem with their son writing racy romance novels using the family name. They were adamant he keep it a complete secret. He even had it written into his publishing contract. So he couldn't tell. But I'm pretty sure he was more afraid *you* would be embarrassed... especially after you went on and on about reading his books."

I went back to playing with the button on my jacket. It came off as well, and I tucked it into a pocket, shoving my hands in to keep from dislodging a third.

Silvia flashed an unconvincing smile. "You know you were never subtle about how obsessed you were with that vampire."

"So you just let me look like a fool?"

She fell into her chair. "Like I said, it wasn't my secret to tell. I made him promise *he* would tell you, and I think he was just about to but never had the chance."

I shook my head. "When I think of how many times he's heard me, or one of you, say I was obsessed with those damn books. Or that I felt like the writer was peeking into my fantasies. Oh, my god, Silvia! I feel so stupid." I pulled my hands from my pockets with such force the loose buttons clattered to the floor. I sank my fingers into my hair, pushing it back from my face.

"I'm so sorry, honey. But at least now you know he's not trying to kill you."

"You don't think so? I may die of embarrassment." I paced in the small space, trying to decide what to feel. Embarrassment was short-lived as anger replaced it. "How could you let me make a fool of myself like that?"

"Oh, Katie, nobody thinks you're a fool. I know he made a terrible mistake, but can't you see how much he loves you?"

"How much he loves me? You think he loves me? Why didn't he love me enough to be honest with me? Do you have any idea how many times I put myself in danger trying to discover his secrets? I almost got shot by his security people!"

She covered her mouth to suppress a laugh.

"Yeah, funny. Did you know *why* I almost got shot?" I didn't wait for her to respond. "I'll tell you why. I was snooping around his house—practically naked, by the way—trying to find evidence of him being a murderer. Go ahead. Laugh at that. It's really *funny*."

I could see the amusement in her eyes as she started to say something.

I cut her off. "Then, if that wasn't bad enough, my mother snooped through his house and found *guns*. Did I tell you that? Guns! She even convinced me to eavesdrop on his phone conversations, and believe me when I say, those were some doozies." I cringed. "I don't think the average person has an opportunity to talk about killing someone in normal conversation. Then, to make matters worse, I practically accused him of cheating on me with Vivian. So after he had his laugh about being a murderer and a cheater, I gave him something even funnier to write about. I thought he was trying to kill *me*. And you'll love this... this is the real cake topper. I had him arrested."

The color drained from her face. "I had no idea," she whispered. "He said you were angry when you found out, but he didn't elaborate."

"This just gets funnier and funnier, doesn't it, Silvia? It's not bad enough I manage to embarrass myself *without* help." I was so angry I couldn't see straight. Flashes of white light and black spots swam in front of my eyes. "And throughout all of this, you—my only real friend—just watched me getting deeper and deeper into my own personal humiliation while you said nothing—not *one single thing*—to let me know what was going on!" I stopped for a minute to let it all sink in. I was on the verge of tears. Again. "You were supposed to be my friend."

"Oh, Katie, I am your friend."

"No, you aren't. You're more like my mother all the time." I pushed past her to escape her office but changed my mind and spun back around. "You know the craziest part about this whole thing? In the end, my *mother* was the only person who actually had my back. You have no idea how difficult that is for me to process."

She recoiled as if I had slapped her. I didn't care. I went straight to my office to type out my letter of resignation. I needed to get out of there. Fast. Before I changed my mind.

Without bothering to check for grammar or spelling errors, I printed the letter. Then after scribbling my signature across the bottom, I placed it on Phil's desk, then headed to the vault. I didn't want to leave anything behind that would make me have to return. I knew I was running and might even regret it later, but at that moment, I didn't see any other way.

After opening my safe deposit box, I sat down on the floor with the contents, tucking each item roughly into a bank duffel bag. The numbness I felt Sunday was back with a vengeance. It may have been worse because I was certain I knew the whole truth, and the truth was excruciating.

"Katie," Cooper whispered.

I swiped at my eyes before turning to look at him. My traitorous stomach flipped. "Oh, lookie here. *Henry*, the Earl of Devonshire. Namer of imaginary cats. Author by day, drinker of blood by night. What are you doing here? Aren't you supposed to be in California with Vivian doing *book* things?"

He stared at his shoes. "I... um... missed my flight."

I raised my eyebrows.

"I spent the night in jail?"

"Right... jail. I forgot." I stuffed a folder into my bag. "Did Silvia call you?"

"Please don't blame her. She feels horrible."

"Good," I snapped.

"I begged her not to tell you. She wanted to... so many times. *I* wanted to. I was *going* to. I just wasn't ready."

"Well, it's too late now. I already know everything. Or are there more secrets you haven't told me?"

He reached out to touch my hair, but I slapped his hand away. "No." He sighed. "No more secrets. Katie, please." He slid down the wall to sit on the floor beside me with a dull thud.

I couldn't stand to hear the sound of my name on his lips. I wiped at the tears spilling from my eyes. "Stop calling me that." I held one hand out in front of me like a blockade. "I revoke your permission to call me Katie."

"Please be reasonable."

I glowered at him. "I'm not the one in trouble here. I'm not the one who lied."

"I never lied to you. Not even once. I was very careful about that. I just—"

I cut him off. "No, you're right. You didn't. You're a writer. You *edited*. Badly."

"I wasn't ready."

"What does that mean? You didn't love me enough to trust me with your career, or you'd rather I thought you were a murderer?"

Something flashed in his eyes. "How could you for even *one minute* think that of me? What have I *ever* done that would lead you down that path?"

"I'm sorry about that, but in the absence of the truth, I was left with nothing but my overactive imagination and a collection of damning pieces to an incomplete puzzle. The simple fact is you didn't love me enough to trust me with the truth."

He opened his mouth and hesitated before taking a deep breath. "It's not like that. I do love you... so much it hurts."

I flinched. "Don't even go there." I felt more tears coming and blinked them back. "I have to get out of here." I stood and grabbed my bag.

"Don't go." He scrambled to his feet. "Please give me a chance to explain."

"You had your chance. You wasted it." I turned to leave, but the door seemed to be moving. Then I was sure it was moving; it was closing. "Stop!" I shrieked.

Too late. The door shut with a bang. I dropped my bag and threw myself against the thick steel. It didn't budge.

"Silvia! Let me out!" The first wave of panic hit me like a bucket of icy water, and I shivered.

"Silvia, this isn't funny!" Cooper yelled.

"Do you see what you've done?" I screamed at him, backing away. "This is all your fault." Hot tears fell down my face, running over my lips and down my chin.

"Katie—"

"I told you not to call me that!"

"I promise I didn't ask anyone to lock us in."

"You wouldn't have to ask them." My voice bordered on hysteria. "They'd do it anyway. They all like you better."

"They don't like me better."

"They do!"

"They just know I love you."

"You don't."

"I do," he said firmly. "I always have. That's why I was so reluctant to tell you."

"You thought so little of me that you believed I would

be ashamed of your job? Or maybe you were ashamed to tell your family about me."

"It's not like that." He pulled his eyebrows together in a tight furrow. "You made me want to be better. I want to be able to tell the whole world what I do. Because of you."

"What's wrong with being a romance writer?" I cringed from the sarcasm in my own voice.

"Nothing." He let out a nervous laugh. "It pays the bills. But my parents insisted my contract stipulate—"

"I don't want to hear about your stupid contract."

"It's not about the contract. Until very recently, I was required to keep it a secret because my parents were diplomats. They didn't want it coming out that their son wrote unseemly escapist fiction."

"I know. I heard all about it from Silvia. And now?"

"And now, my parents live on a farm and couldn't care less. I had to wait for them to give me the okay, and then I wanted to disentangle myself from my contract and all that entails before telling you. Sweetheart, I had no idea how to be in a relationship with you while I was hiding behind someone else. There would always be three of us. I swear I was going to tell you."

"Silvia knew."

"Yes." He lowered his eyes, staring at some spot on the floor.

"Then why didn't you tell me?"

"I wanted you to be proud of me. I wanted to be *me* when I was with you... not Elizabeth Jayne."

"You didn't trust me."

"It was never about trusting *you*."

I shook my head. "We rushed into this. We didn't know each other well enough."

His hands were in his hair again, twisting it into a tangle. "We've known each other for a long time. The biggest mistake we made was not trusting the intensity of our love for each other. All I know is I want a future with you. I want forever."

I flinched away from the word *forever*. "After everything that's happened, I don't know what's real anymore."

"This is real. We're real." He stepped forward and tipped my chin. "I don't want to be away from you, Katie. Ever."

I let the tears spill freely down my cheeks. "Too many things have gone wrong."

"Nothing was ever really wrong. It was all an illusion." He wiped the wetness from my face with his fingers.

"It *was* all an illusion," I echoed. "All the good things, too." I closed my eyes to block out the realization.

He leaned in and kissed me. "You know you love me," he murmured against my still lips.

"It doesn't change anything," I whispered, pulling my face from his.

The vault door eased open, and Phil poked his head in. "Everyone okay in here?"

Cooper's face twisted with anguish. "Can we have another minute?"

"We don't need another minute. We're done here." I kept my gaze on Cooper, and I was sure he understood what I was saying. *We were done.* As in over... as in goodbye.

I faced Phil and pulled in a shaky breath. "I left my resignation on your desk."

Phil nodded and walked out. That pretty much said it all.

I turned around to look at Cooper one last time.

"I'm so sorry, Katie," he whispered, his eyes filled with unshed tears.

I started to hyperventilate, and I knew the shaking wouldn't be far behind. If could just make it to my car, I might get home before the sobs ripped out of me.

It wasn't likely I'd get that far, but I had to try.

MY LIFE IS AN OPEN BOOK

A LMOST EXACTLY A YEAR TO the day later, I sat frozen in front of the television screen and waited. In a few minutes, Cooper Maxwell would be sitting in a chair beside the most popular daytime TV talk show host, Marcy Michaels, promoting his new book, and I was tied up in knots with nervous anticipation. I'd known about the appearance for quite a while, but it didn't ease the butterflies in my stomach one bit. I wasn't looking forward to the things he would say. It was bound to be embarrassing. *For me.*

His new book was on shelves, and that was bad enough, but to imagine him telling the entire world the intimate details taken directly from my life was just too much to bear. I actually winced when Marcy announced his name, and he stepped onto the stage to shake her hand.

Once the applause died down, Marcy bounced to her chair with perfect comedic timing, making her short blond hair flop into her eyes. She pushed it back, tucking it behind both ears before turning her attention to Cooper. As usual, he looked amazing, making my stomach flip the same way it always had.

"So, Cooper, tell us about your new book. It's quite a departure from what made you famous, isn't it?" Marcy didn't give him a chance to answer before she launched into a new thought. "You know, maybe you should go back a bit further and tell us about your other books first. You wrote vampire romance novels. Did you have to do a lot of research for that? I'll bet you had to bite a lot of people."

Cooper shifted in his seat. "Yes, I wrote vampire romance novels. But no, there was no biting involved."

"Are you sure? I've had vampires on the show before." Marcy leaned in, exposing her neck. "Go ahead. Take a little. I've got plenty."

"Tempting." Cooper laughed. "But no, thank you. I've already eaten today."

"Too bad." Marcy sat straight again. "So... romance... really? But you're a man. How different was that?"

"Well, it was a little odd, I suppose." Cooper smiled. "That's why I didn't write under my own name."

"Of course. You wrote your tragic vampire series under the name of Elizabeth Jayne. Why vampires?"

"Well, Marcy, there's something very romantic about vampires, isn't there? An underlying thread of violence wrapped up in sexual tension."

"Okay, so who is Elizabeth Jayne?"

"Elizabeth Jayne is my mother's name. I wrote under that for several years. My publishers felt the books would be more successful if written by a woman."

"Elizabeth Jayne Maxwell... and your father's a former British diplomat?"

"Yes, that's right. He retired from diplomatic service just over a year ago."

"So the son of a British diplomat, writing romance novels under an assumed name, gets arrested for attempted murder. That's an interesting bio."

Cooper laughed. "I suppose it is."

"Did you dress up as a woman while you were writing? You know, a cute little dress, a pair of nice pumps, some pearls?"

"Well..." He chuckled. "I suppose that might have been a good idea, but sadly, no. My publisher hired a very nice lady to pose as Elizabeth Jayne for promotional purposes."

Marcy was obviously having fun teasing Cooper. "After making buckets of money writing under your mother's name, how much of a cut did Mom get? She probably deserves something, don't you think?"

He smiled. "I've tried to give her money, but she won't take it."

"Oh. Well, you could send it to me. I'm sure I could find something to do with that much money." Marcy grinned. "But buckets of money aside, you decided you wanted to be yourself for a change, right?"

Cooper got serious. "I decided I wanted to do something a little different, and yes, I wanted to write under my own name."

"So what did your publishers think about that? They were about to say goodbye to the cash cow... cash bull." Marcy crossed her blue eyes in a comic expression.

Cooper nodded. "They were intent on having the series continue indefinitely. It was a very successful run."

"And now they've made the first book into a movie, right?"

"Yes. *Blood Everlasting* will be in theaters later this month, and I'm quite proud of that. But it was time to put the book series to rest. I was adamant we end the story with *An Immortal Heart*. Unfortunately, that set events in motion that caused a little trouble in my life."

Marcy smiled. "More than a little."

"Yes, actually." He chuckled again. "It caused a lot of trouble."

"So what happened?"

I cringed. I wanted to turn away, but I forced myself to watch.

"I was constantly at odds with the direction I'd decided to go with the last book. I wanted to tie up the story by allowing the vampire to find his forever love... his mate."

"And that was because you'd fallen in love with your banker, Katie?"

Cooper nodded.

Marcy said, "Don't tell anyone, but I fell in love with my banker once. It didn't work out. She was only interested in my money." Marcy paused while the audience laughed. "Okay, so back to your story. Exactly *how* were you planning to kill Katie? Poison? Strangulation? A good hard knock on the head?"

Cooper shifted in his seat. "I wasn't actually planning on killing her. In my mind, everything was perfect. We were in love, and it was wonderful."

"Oh, come on. You can tell me. I won't turn you in."

Cooper let out a nervous laugh. "Well, she certainly *thought* I was planning on killing her. I was oblivious to the turmoil she was going through. She was imagining all sorts of crazy scenarios."

"So it was all in her imagination then?"

"A scary place, her imagination." He laughed. "She was constantly worried the bottom was about to fall out."

I frowned as I stared at the television. I wanted to scream at the screen that it wasn't *all* in my mind. There was a good little bit of circumstantial evidence almost *any* woman would have mistaken for truth.

"But you didn't know what she was thinking, what she was worried about?" Marcy asked.

Cooper shook his head. "I had no idea."

"You don't pay very close attention, do you?" Marcy deadpanned.

"It would seem not."

"But you did finally figure it out. Was it that last day at the bank?"

"Yes, well... it was actually a few nights before that day."

"Was that the night you were going to kill her?" Marcy was clearly amused with the direction the conversation was going.

"Yes... I mean, no. I wasn't going to kill her."

"If you say so," Marcy said, looking straight at the camera.

"It was the night she *thought* I was going to kill her."

"You're smiling. What's so funny about killing your girlfriend? That's not funny at all."

Cooper leaned back and looked Marcy dead in the eye with a familiar smirk. "You know, you're right. There's nothing funny about killing your girlfriend. Didn't Bill Pullman try to kill you in a movie once?" He was obviously pleased with his own wit.

"Oh, nice. You've done your research." Marcy then pulled her expression into a serious one. "No, Bill Pullman didn't try to kill me. He's actually a pretty nice guy. It was his character. You surprise me. We don't talk about that movie. I'm surprised you know about that. I thought I'd personally burned every copy in existence."

Everyone laughed, and then Cooper went back to his original train of thought. "Even now, it seems ridiculous to imagine she could think for one second I would hurt her."

"Because you loved her?"

Cooper blushed. "Immeasurably."

Marcy led the crowd in a chorus of *awwws*, and I knew how they felt. There was something in his eyes and his voice when he spoke of how he felt about me. I blinked back the urge to cry.

"Okay, so that brings us to the new book, *To Katie With Love*. Oh, and we've given everyone in the audience a signed copy." Marcy held up a copy of the book to the cheers of the audience. "The story is obviously near and dear to your heart."

"Absolutely. It's the story of falling for and losing the love of your life."

"So you were really in love with Katie? Even though you were trying to kill her?"

Cooper smiled. "Amazingly so. Katie is permanently a part of me."

I got goose bumps when he said my name. My stomach rippled with that familiar fluttering.

"You know I've read the book. There are a lot of funny moments in there."

Cooper chuckled. "Yes, I think even Katie would admit

to being a little on the clumsy side. She managed to get herself into a few unusual situations. I think she can laugh about it now. At least, I hope so." He turned and looked at the camera, and I knew he was talking directly to me. I wasn't sure if I could laugh at anything at that moment, let alone myself.

"And the other characters? All real... or made up?"

"Oh, they're all real. Of course, I had to change the names to protect the not-so-innocent." He flashed a crooked grin, and I knew he was thinking of Vicky. "But for the most part, it all happened the way I wrote it."

"There really was an assassin? And you really got locked in a vault? What about the girl with the piercing?" Marcy looked down at her lap, and the crowd roared with laughter.

"Even that."

"Did anyone get fired for locking you in the vault?"

He laughed. "No, everyone was forgiven."

"And what about Katie? Did you forgive her for getting you arrested?"

"Well, we worked it out before I was put on the chain gang, so... yes."

"So no mug shot? I was hoping to see a mug shot," Marcy said with a serious face.

"No." Cooper laughed. "Sorry to disappoint you. No mug shot."

"It's a year later. Any regrets?"

Cooper's expression quickly changed from sunny to serious. "I regret the secrets."

Marcy nodded. "I heard you married your publicist recently." She paused and looked out into the audience. "Wasn't Vivian Allen your publicist?"

The audience sighed collectively, and I held my breath. I was too aware they would be getting to the part where Cooper's wife would walk out onto the stage to join him. I wasn't ready for that yet. I wasn't sure I ever would be.

"Yes, six months ago. We're still on our honeymoon,

if you will." He hesitated for a minute before flashing his grin again. "But no, Vivian isn't my publicist anymore."

"She's not?"

"No, I hired a new one."

"A lot of changes then?" Marcy asked with a smile.

"Yes. A lot of changes in my life over the course of the past year."

"But what about Katie? Is she still your banker?"

"No, she found another job."

"That's too bad. She was a good banker, wasn't she?"

My palms were sweating, and I felt a little sick to my stomach. I was having flashbacks of everything that had happened during the past year.

"She was a great banker," Cooper said.

"But—" Marcy grinned. "—she's a better wife, isn't she?"

Cooper's face broke into a triumphant smile. "She's a wonderful wife... and publicist."

The pride in his voice was evident. The audience let out a collective cheer.

"Shall we bring her out to meet everyone?"

That was my cue, and someone from behind me called my name, dragging my attention from the monitor to the doorway.

I was led carefully to the stage by a tall, gray-haired man who didn't seem to grasp the fact that I was less than steady on the stupid three-inch pumps I wore with Cooper's favorite dress. I was nervous I would fall, and the universe would see my scanty underwear as I sprawled out on the floor on national TV.

"Katie?" Marcy called.

I stepped out in front of the audience, which had begun chanting my name. It was the most surreal moment of my entire life. Caught in the hot lights on the stage, I carefully put one foot in front of the other, concentrating on not falling. I took Marcy's hand with a shaky grip and proceeded to trip as I approached the chairs. Luckily,

Cooper was close at hand, and he righted me before my panties became the next YouTube sensation.

Everyone, most of America I imagined, laughed, and I was certain my former bank colleagues were watching from home and laughing, too.

Cooper leaned in to give me a quick kiss. "Mmm... peppermint," he said.

I smiled. I had my own peppermint breath, but I had been sworn to secrecy.

When the crowd calmed, Marcy directed a question to me. "Katie, everyone is dying to know. How long did it take you to forgive Cooper for trying to kill you?"

I laughed despite my nerves. "Do you mean how long before I forgave him for keeping secrets from me?" I wrinkled my nose at Cooper, trying to mentally calculate the equation.

"Less than five minutes after we made our daring escape," he said with a grin.

Marcy looked surprised. "Five minutes?"

"Five minutes after my manager let us out of the vault, I ran out of the bank, thinking I'd never see him again, but I never made it out of the parking lot," I admitted with some embarrassment. "As soon as I climbed into my car, I knew I couldn't do it."

Cooper took my hand in his, and we shared a quick moment staring into each other's eyes, remembering that day.

I turned to look at Marcy again, blinking back the threat of tears. "Cooper came rushing out the door and ran straight to me. He just about yanked me from my seat for one of those curl-your-toes kind of kisses."

She clucked her tongue, fanning herself with her hand. "Well... oh my."

I nodded. "Very."

"So did he propose right then?"

Cooper squeezed my hand and answered, "We're saving that story for the sequel."

"So how do you feel now, with all of this attention?" She gestured to the stage, the audience, and to the image of Cooper's book—*my book*—on the big screen behind us.

"Well..." I bit my lip. "It has taken some getting used to."

"And what does your mother think about the book... and the marriage?"

Cooper and I both laughed.

"Mom's still convinced Cooper is one of the Goodfellas."

"Really?" She raised her eyebrows. "Well, you know, mothers do know best."

"It's actually quite convenient. She doesn't visit often," I added in an aside.

Everyone laughed. I was pretty sure Mom was somewhere watching... and she would not be laughing.

"What about you?" Marcy asked. "You don't mind sacrificing your honeymoon for the press junket?"

"Well, we've been on our honeymoon for six months, so I don't feel I'm giving up anything there. I do always feel like I'm about to trip over something and embarrass my husband."

Cooper leaned over to whisper, "I would never be embarrassed by you."

"What did he say?" Marcy asked.

"He said he would never be embarrassed, but I think he's forgetting the few times I was drunk. I find it hard to believe he *wasn't* embarrassed, at least for me."

"But you've given up liquor and lying, right?" Marcy quoted a line from the book, and laughter rang out through the studio.

I beamed. "The liquor anyway."

"Just the liquor?" Cooper asked with a curious grin.

Marcy raised her eyebrows, flashing me a knowing smile. "I thought there were no more secrets?"

"Well, just one more." I bit my lip, and my stomach flipped because I knew I was going to spill it right there on national TV.

Cooper looked truly perplexed.

I shifted to whisper, "I have a secret I've been keeping from you."

His eyes widened. "Are you going to tell me?"

I leaned in closer, until my mouth was almost touching his ear. As the words spilled from my lips, he sucked in a harsh breath. Then I pulled myself back slightly before he grabbed both sides of my face for a very public kiss, followed by the second most profound *I love you* I'd ever heard him utter.

"That must have been some secret," Marcy said.

Cooper was bursting at the seams with excitement. "Can I say it?" he asked me, and I nodded. "We're having a baby!"

Marcy turned to the audience. "Now that's what I call a sequel!"

ACKNOWLEDGEMENTS

Thank you to those who each, in some small way, helped to bring this book to life. To my parents, for always believing in me and giving me the courage and freedom to color outside the lines. To my husband and children, for allowing me to listen to songs on repeat for hours on end, often into the wee hours of the morning, while I wrote.

To my amazing beta readers and friends; Kelly, for forcing me to cut words I didn't want to cut in order to craft a better story, Mercy and Raine, for sharing their two cents during the beta process. And especially to Laura, for volleying ideas with me like a fast and furious game of imaginary ping pong. Without your help, I would've never gotten through the weeds of words to find the magic hidden within, and I never would've had the courage to submit the final product to a publisher.

To Lynn and the staff at Red Adept Publishing, for taking a chance on an unproven author. To Michelle, the very best content editor a girl could ever ask for. You got me. You got my characters. And you managed to pull things from my brain I would've never guessed were possible. And Lynn, thank you for making the hard decisions when I couldn't. I may have lost a battle or two, but together, we won the war.

And a special thanks to my former crew from the Pine Mountain branch—Melissa, Alicia, Donald, Gail and Bette—for inspiring some of the quirky characters in this book.

I thank you all, from the bottom of my heart.

ABOUT THE AUTHOR

After walking away from her career as a business banker to pursue writing full-time, Erica Lucke Dean moved from the hustle and bustle of the big city to a small tourist town in the North Georgia Mountains, where she lives in a 90-year-old haunted farmhouse with her workaholic husband, her 180 lb lap dog, and at least one ghost.

When she's not writing or tending to her collection of crazy chickens and diabolical ducks, she's either reading bad fan fiction or singing karaoke in the local pub. Much like the main character in her newest book, *To Katie With Love*, Erica is a magnet for disaster and has been known to trip on air while walking across flat surfaces.

How she's managed to survive this long is one of life's great mysteries.